SEVENTH NIGHT

BY
ISCAH

AMOEBA INK

To Troop #983
Try to leave the world better than you found it.

ACKNOWLEDGEMENTS

I want to thank my dad, Paul, and my Girl Scout troop for being my early guinea pigs; my excellent betas P.J. Lockabey, Jordan Ross, Sam Beckett, Janine K. Spendlove, James "Sithspit" LeMaire, for their support and helpful suggestions; all the internet denizens who voted for bookcover designs and followed my Blitzkrieg and serials for their valuable feedback; and my lovely editor Megan Hines for helping me squeeze out the remaining flaws that everyone else missed or was too polite to mention.

Crystal Inn City

Cylene

Lo

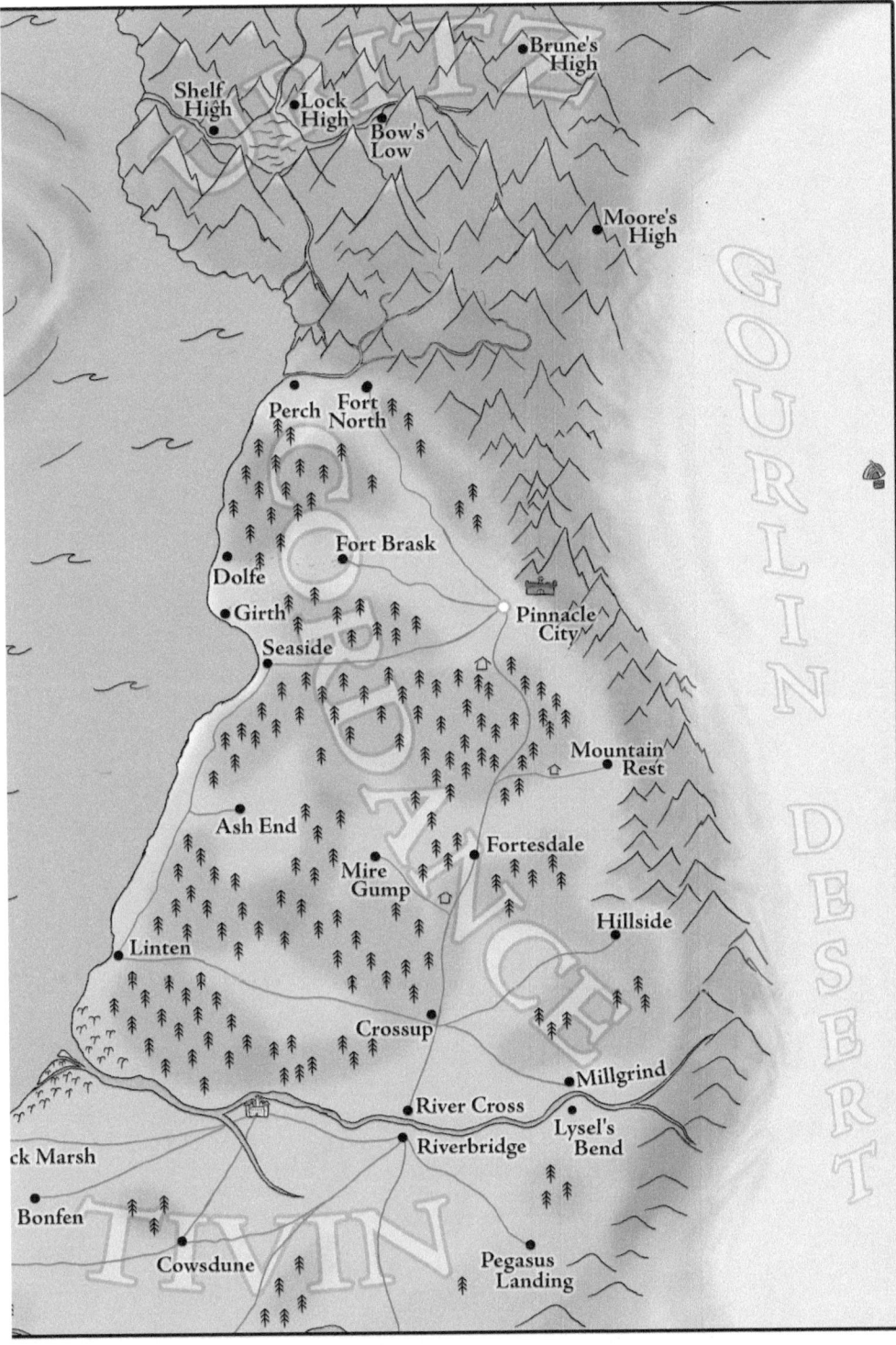

TABLE OF CONTENTS

ACT I:
THE FAIRYTALE

CHAPTER I:
THE WINGED UNICORN..................1

CHAPTER II:
AN IMPORTANT DELIVERY..................7

CHAPTER III:
THE PRINCE'S PROBLEM..................16

CHAPTER IV:
A DARK AND DANGEROUS DESERT...25

CHAPTER V:
THE MONARCHY..................33

CHAPTER VI:
INSIDE THE HUT OF BARK AND BONE...39

CHAPTER VII:
A CLEAR NIGHT..................51

CHAPTER VIII:
A HAPPY ENDING..................62

ACT II:
MONSTERS & MAGIC

CHAPTER IX:
WHAT THEY LEAVE OUT IN FAIRYTALES..67

CHAPTER X:
COURTSHIP...76

CHAPTER XI:
CARRIED AWAY..85

CHAPTER XII:
A VERY LONG TIME AGO....................91

CHAPTER XIII:
AND VERY FAR AWAY............................97

CHAPTER XIV:
HIDDEN THINGS....................................105

CHAPTER XV:
IMPOSSIBLE THINGS............................115

CHAPTER XVI:
THE CYCLOPS..120

CHAPTER XVII:
THE PRIDE OF CORDANCE................124

CHAPTER XVIII:
THE CRYSTAL INN CITY TAVERN.....130

CHAPTER XIX:
MYTHS ABOUT MERMAIDS................135

CHAPTER XX:
MOTHER VYN.....................................142

CHAPTER XXI:
THE GUARDIAN...................................152

ACT III:
BREAKING THE SPELL

CHAPTER XXII:
THE PRINCESS'S NEW POSITION.....167

CHAPTER XXIII:
THE HAWK'S FLIGHT..........................172

CHAPTER XXIV:
THE RELUCTANT REBELLION............178

CHAPTER XXV:
THE ELUSIVE GIRL NEXT DOOR......191

CHAPTER XXVI:
BIG, DARK CLOUDS............................197

CHAPTER XXVII:
IN AND OUT...............................207

CHAPTER XXVIII:
THE WIZARD KING..........................214

CHAPTER XXIX:
A DUAL....................................221

CHAPTER XXX:
THE SLEEPING PRINCESS.................229

CHAPTER XXXI:
LOVE'S KISS..............................235

CHAPTER XXXII:
THE FORGOTTEN SOLDIER...............239

CHAPTER XXXIII:
WEDLOCK..................................246

ACT I
THE FAIRYTALE

CHAPTER I

THE WINGED UNICORN

Fortesdale was not a large village, nor was it terribly small. It was not well-known, nor unheard-of. It was not extremely wealthy, nor was it wretchedly poor. The village was not considerably important to the kingdom of Cordance, nor was it useless. In simple terms, it was average.

So when an unknown cloaked figure tore through the town square on a white winged unicorn, many people stared and gossiped, it being the great pastime of the day, and some did not, for there are always those who will resist great pastimes. However the gossips worked quickly and by the next day the whole village had heard of it, regardless of whether they chose to repeat.

A regular unicorn would have soon been forgotten, for reckless soldiers occasionally traveled the trade routes connecting Fortesdale to Pinnacle City. At times a well-to-do merchant would prance about the streets on a pegasus, which was about all they could do. As a result of crossbreeding with regular horses, most pegasus' wings were too weak for flight. Winged unicorns were far more difficult to breed and raise to maturity. However, the grown result was spectacular. Therefore, only wealthy noblemen and royalty rode the distinguished beasts or sent trusted messengers with important messages on them.

If the townspeople had been able to see under the rider's hood, they would have considered this brief moment something to tell their grandchildren. As rare as winged unicorns were, it was rarer still, if not unheard-of, for one to have a female rider.

The rider galloped through the village without a "how-do-you-do?" or slowing. Eventually she rode out of sight of the excited children that had followed her to the edge of town. She did, however, slow several miles later at the extensive farms belonging to Lord Harold of Fortesdale.

The rider lifted her hood for a better look around, revealing her pretty, young features and raven hair tied back in a practical braid. Her riding clothes were simple and brown. Her eyes were a strong blue, and her skin fair. Her lower lip was slightly larger than the upper, fixing her with a small but permanent pout. She wore no decoration other than a gold clip to secure the braid and a large crest ring on her finger.

She spotted a farmhand lounging next to a covered, stone well. A tug on the reins and a tap with her boot on its hindquarters urged the unicorn in the proper direction.

At a closer look, the hired hand was not much older than herself. He had shaggy, dirty-blond hair and baggy work clothes. He did not see, or simply ignored, her as she approached.

"Boy, do you work here?" she asked from her mount.

He raised his head, eyes lingering on the unicorn's silver horn. He had a clean-cut, boyish face, though he was old enough to take aversion to the term. "Last time I checked," he finally acknowledged her. "And the name's Phillip."

The rider shrugged to show how little that meant to her. "Fetch my horse some water," she told him as she dismounted.

"Why?" he asked.

The girl paused with one foot still in the stirrup. She saw he had not budged from his spot. "She's thirsty," she replied patiently, pointing out the obvious.

"So?" he asked, making a show of yawning and stretching.

"There's a well there," she said, feeling like she had lost control of the situation. It was not a good feeling, but she was determined not to show how it frustrated her. "Fetch some water from it for her."

He shook his head. "No," he said, still not moving from his spot. He made a mockingly sympathetic face. "What's wrong? Are you too weak to get it yourself?"

For a moment she just stared at him. Her winged unicorn and royal crest ring should have insured cooperation or at least respect from any peasant. Lacking that, she expected the courtesy due her gender. She could easily have gotten him in trouble with his employers, but she was in a hurry. Besides, he had challenged her.

"Fine," she said with her head held high. She stepped beside the well, pulling her unicorn behind her. As she lowered the bucket, the farmhand at last felt obliged to stand. The small sign of respect encouraged her.

Raising the bucket proved to be more difficult than she had thought. The rope bit into her uncalloused fingers, and the weight challenged her untrained muscles. She almost asked for help, but she would not give him the pleasure of seeing her falter. When the bucket finally reached the top, Phillip set it on the edge for her without ceremony or vexing. The act surprised the girl, and she forgot to thank him.

"Where are you headed?" he asked as if they had just had a pleasant conservation instead of a battle of wills.

"Pinnacle City," she said reflexively, wondering at the sudden change of attitude.

"If you wait 'til tomorrow noon, I'll travel with you," he said. He continued when he saw her skeptical expression, "I'm starting an apprenticeship to a magician that works in the castle."

The girl seemed to find this funny. "You believe in magic?"

"I'm not sure whether or not I do," he admitted. "But I believe in learning, and I should at least learn some good tricks. So is it a deal?"

"I'm afraid I'm in a bit of a hurry," she explained, while the unicorn drank. "I can't wait 'til morrow."

"You shouldn't travel alone," he warned. "There's a group of bandits on the route to Pinnacle that attacks lone merchants."

The girl patted her unicorn. "We'll be fine. Won't we, Toshk?" she said, confident in the unicorn's swiftness and wingspan. Phillip looked over the beast and its master and did not seem quite so certain.

The unicorn snorted and nudged the girl. She broke her gaze with the odd farmhand and remounted. "It was nice meeting you, Magician," she said. Phillip nodded in response, and she started off toward the road. After the unicorn had trod a few steps, she turned back. "My destination is the king's palace as well. Perhaps I shall see you again," she called to him.

"Perhaps," he smiled. With that, the winged unicorn galloped away.

She traveled the rest of the day and most of the night while the road was clear, stopping only to let the unicorn feed near a stream. Such a trip would have completely exhausted a common horse. But unicorns were known for their strength, and by outstretching its wings the beast could add a glide to its run, easing the burden on its legs. Full flights were tiring for a winged unicorn with a burden and a dangerous business for the rider, so she kept close to the ground. But the sort of road ruts, muddy patches, and fallen branches that would delay the normal equine were jumped over easily with the aid of wings.

Just before morning the girl led the unicorn into the forest so they could get a little rest. When she awoke, the sun was already in the west. She scolded herself for oversleeping and quickly roused Toshk. After a brief meal, they headed back to the main road.

A few miles later she met a merchant caravan heading the other way. "Hold there," she called to the head wagon driver. "Can you tell me how far it is to Pinnacle City?"

The old man gave her a crooked smile. It might have been her outfit that amused him. For even though women did wear loose leggings for long trips on horseback, it was not common, nor was it otherwise considered to be decent.

"We came from Pinnacle and've been travlin' a'most two days," he said in a friendly manner, a far cry from how the arrogant farmboy had spoken to her. She thanked the man and rode on. It was not as bad as she had feared. She was only one without wares and would travel faster than the caravan. Since she had been pushing Toshk hard, she allowed the unicorn to slow to a trot.

When the sun was halfway west, she thought she heard the beating of hooves behind her. She recalled the thieves the farmboy had warned her of and hastened the unicorn to a run, but when she looked back, there was no one. After a while, she slackened its pace.

By the time the sun had dropped to the brink of the horizon, the girl found herself incredibly bored by the endless forest. She hummed an old nursery tune to keep herself awake and watched the sunset colors form in the heavens. She let her thoughts drift to what had been and what was to come. So lost in thought was she, that she did not see the shadowed figures up the road slip out from the trees.

She would not have noticed them until they were upon her if Toshk had not taken a dislike to the men and reared up. The girl snapped out of her fantasies and guessed what was wrong. She jerked the unicorn around in an attempt to outrun the thieves, as Toshk needed a bit of a run before she could fly over them. But three other bandits blocked the road back, and several more were seeping out from between the trees and behind rocks.

The girl's mind might have been clear enough to react. The same could not be said of the unicorn. Toshk reared and bucked wildly as the men pressed closer. It was all the girl could do to hold on and stay in her saddle. The bandits threw lassos around Toshk's neck and ropes across her wings in an attempt to overcome the startled animal with brute force.

When the bucking stopped enough for the girl to free one arm, she tried to cut the unicorn's bonds with her dagger. She sliced two of them before a rope caught her wrist. Struggle as she might, the bandits eventually overcame Toshk. Several pairs of arms snatched the girl from the saddle. She screamed and put up a struggle to equal the unicorn's.

Despite her effort, the bandits lost no time relieving her of her dagger, purse, and gold hair clip. They were in the process of removing her cloak when the pounding of a new set of hooves was heard above the thieves' hollering.

"Hold there!" a man's voice shouted above the ruckus.

The group became quiet; their harsh breathing and the horses' snorting were the only sounds to be heard. They turned to face the newcomer, and the girl struggled for a better look. A large, black winged unicorn with a golden horn stomped its hooves on the path. Its eyes shone like fire in the night. From her position she could not see the rider's face.

The thieves stood tense and traded uneasy glances. Superstitious people believed black horses, especially unicorns, to be sure signs of evil or at least bad luck. At last a few of the braver ones took a step forward. "You just made a big mistake, stranger," one of them said menacingly. In one mass the bandits started for him.

The black unicorn reared back, spreading its wings. "Wait! I'm a friend," the rider said quickly, sounding a bit jostled by the unicorn's jerk. The girl's eyes widened. It was the farmboy's voice. "Pac-a-shen-tall," he called. The thieves halted again and exchanged glances.

Finally one of the largest men stepped forward. "Sprat?" he yelled in a booming voice. "Dat you?"

SEVENTH NIGHT

CHAPTER II

AN IMPORTANT DELIVERY

P hillip let go a sigh of relief. "Yeah, Jonhan, it's me," he called back. A wave of ease seemed to sweep over the crowd; some chuckled.

The large man laughed. "Hey, it's Sprat," he called to anyone in the crowd who might not have heard. Jonhan turned back to Phillip. "Got yourself a pretty pony too, I see. Where ya goin?"

"The girl's with me," he called from the unicorn's back. "We're headed to Pinnacle.

Got myself an apprenticeship to a magician."

The bandits found this hilarious. They broke out in a chorus of belly laughs. The ones holding the girl released her, but she was too stunned to run.

"You dine with us tonight," Jonhan more commanded than asked. "I want to hear 'bout where you've been the last few years."

The girl silently pleaded with the farmboy. There was no telling how long dinner would take, and time was very important.

"I'd love nothing more." Phillip bowed as much as the saddle would allow. "But the lady's in a rush." He saw the displeasure on Jonhan's face and quickly continued. "Besides there's nothing to tell. Been working at Lord Harold's farm and taking what I could get on the side. Won the horse in a bet. Nothing more to tell.

"I'll stop by next time I'm this way and give you every detail if you wish," Phillip promised. He held his breath to see if that would please the thief.

"Promise us a concert an' it's a deal." Jonhan's proposition was followed by a round of cheers from the thieves.

Phillip smiled. "My pleasure," he agreed.

Jonhan signaled to the thieves. The girl found her possessions being roughly thrown at her, except for the dagger, which the thieves had the courtesy to hand her. She refastened her hair clip and returned her purse and dagger to her belt.

"Sprat," Jonhan said seriously. "We went to a lot of trouble, an' she cut two good ropes. Don't we get some compentation?"

Phillip frowned. "What do you want?"

Jonhan nodded to Toshk. "We keep 'er white pony; nobody'd want your demon one."

Phillip shrugged. "It's yours," he said. The girl's blue eyes widened. He had no right. She began to object, took another look at the rugged, burly bandits, and thought better of it. She took a last longing look at Toshk and realized it could have been much worse.

The thieves parted to make room for Phillip to pass. It was not that they had the greatest respect for him, but they were a superstitious lot and did not wish to be too close to a black unicorn. One of the thieves helped the girl climb up behind Phillip.

When they came to the edge of the group, Phillip turned and shouted a hearty farewell to the thieves and promised to return as soon as possible. He then whispered to the girl, "Hold on tight. I want to put some distance between us before they have a chance to change their minds." Without further warning, the unicorn kicked up a cloud of dust and was soon out of the thieves' sight.

A while later when the forest had thinned into farmland, Phillip allowed the unicorn to slow to a walk. The girl eased her grip as much as she could. Phillip did not mind riding in silence, but they would have to talk sooner or later. He figured there was no sense in wasting time.

"You haven't told me your name," he reminded her.

"Seventh Night," she said.

Phillip chuckled, "What kind of name is that?"

Seventh Night made a face at him. "A perfectly good one," she retorted. "I was born the seventh night of the harvest festival, and my mother named me accordingly." She watched stars appear over the field, so she would not have to look at the back of his head. "You have to be the most impudent person I've ever met."

"Then you should remember me...at least until someone worse comes along." He looked up to the stars as well. "Do you have any money?"

"About sixty deriks," Seventh Night answered, then scowled. "Why?"

"The tavern owner won't give us food and lodging otherwise," he said simply.

"But we can't stop tonight," she pleaded. "It's important. I have to get to the palace by noon morrow."

"I'm afraid you don't have much of a choice, Seven," Phillip told her, irritation finally seeping into his voice. "Thunder has flown most of the day and run with two people on his back the rest. If you are above sleeping, then great, but I'm not and neither is the best of unicorns. Are you, Thunder?"

The ebony beast snorted.

"See," Phillip said. "While I'm at it, I might note that you have not thanked me once for saving you."

"I'm sorry, thank you," she said softly. "Do you think we'll make it to the palace on time?"

SEVENTH NIGHT

"If we get up early," he answered. "You're not from 'round here are you?"

"No," she said, slightly confused by the question. "Why do you ask?"

Phillip shrugged. "No reason, you just talk funny."

"What's wrong with the way I talk?" she shot at him.

"First, 'round here someone would have said 'how I talk,' instead of 'the way'," he explained. "Second, you say palace instead of castle. Third, when you apologized you said sorry. 'Round here we say 'offer apology'. And you said I was impudent. Here we say saucy or brash."

Seventh Night laughed. "Then I offer apology for how I talked before on the road to the castle, even if you were saucy and brash."

Thunder shook his head.

Phillip grinned. "Does sound funny when you say it. Stick with *the way* you talk, Seven." He noticed a light ahead, which he had earlier mistaken for a star. "I think I see the tavern."

Tivin's week-long Harvest Festival had

drawn most of the traveling merchants down south, leaving the large tavern with several vacancies. It was therefore quite simple to obtain two rooms and a stall for the unicorn. Dinner was better than expected, broiled pheasant with steamed maize and seasoned greens.

Phillip picked at the maize, wondering how the tavern owner had arranged to get his share before the merchants returned. There were local farms, but maize usually came from the southern countries. He noticed his companion had nearly finished. "Why are you in such a hurry anyway?" he asked her.

She swallowed her mouthful. "I'm afraid I can't tell you until we reach the palace."

"Not even a clue?" Phillip was eager to solve this girl's mystery.

Seventh Night smirked. "All I can tell you is that it's a matter of great importance."

"So you're a messenger from...Tivin?" he guessed, referring to the country on Cordance's southern border.

"Why do you think that?" she asked.

"Well, royalty always rides with an escort. I don't think you belong to any of the noble families 'round here, and they'd probably give you an escort as well. Which only leaves a royal messenger. Besides," he said. "You talk like a Tivan. So I'm guessing you're a messenger from Tivin."

Seventh Night gave him an odd grin. "That's right," she said and took another bite of maize.

"In that case," he observed. "You're wearing your ring on the wrong hand."

Seventh Night almost choked on maize. "What do you mean?" she asked sharply.

"Messengers always wear the emblem on their left hand," he pointed out. "You wear it on your right like that, and someone might think you're trying to join the royal family."

Seventh Night laughed and swapped the ring from her right hand to the left. "Wouldn't want that." She pushed her plate away. "I think I'll get some sleep. Good night, Magician."

As Phillip watched her leave, he got the funny feeling she had been laughing at him.

The next morning Seventh Night woke early, as Phillip had said they need do. She settled the debt with the tavern owner and made sure Thunder was saddled, fed, and ready for the day's trip. As the sun peeked over the eastern horizon, she noticed Phillip had not yet come down.

She knocked on the door of his room. When there was no response, she slowly opened the heavy wooden door and slipped inside. The lazy farmboy was still asleep.

"Wake up," she hissed at him. He did not stir. Seventh Night shook him. "Wake up."

"Huh," he mumbled. She shook him again, and Phillip shot straight up in bed. "What happened?" He looked at Seventh Night and his surroundings and groaned. "For goodness sake, Seven, the sun's not even up yet."

Seventh Night was unsympathetic. "Yes it is. Your window just faces west. Now get dressed. We've got to get to the palace before noon," she reminded him. Phillip yawned and nodded and motioned for her to leave.

Once they got on the road, the rest of the trip to Pinnacle City went without incident. Thunder was swift and took to flight in a few short bursts. It was Seventh Night's first experience with full flight, but she was too anxious about the time to spare much thought to the height. Phillip was practiced enough at it to fly smoothly, and she felt safe with him. They reached the king's castle with time to spare before the sun hit its zenith.

The castle was built on a high bluff overlooking Pinnacle City. Long ago a wide winding road had been carved into the bluff leading to the castle. The king's castle was grand, but it was dwarfed by the high mountain that wrapped around it. Some rumors said part of the castle was actually built into the rock. Whether or not that was true, there were tunnels leading to lookout posts hidden throughout the mountains.

Pinnacle City itself was nestled at the foot of the mountain. Some said Pinnacle got its name for being the capital city. Others said it received its name from the castle, for only the highest tower could be seen over the fortress walls surrounding the citadel.

As they approached the huge main gate of the fortress, Phillip let out a whistle. Thunder's nostrils flared as he breathed hard, exhausted from the long climb. Unfortunately the path was too narrow for him to easily fly up and land. A difficulty no doubt intended by the designers. "Hang on, fellow. It'll be over soon," Phillip assured him. "See, Seven, told you we'd get here on time."

Seventh Night pulled back her hood and let out a sigh of relief. "I will feel better once we get inside."

"I'll feel better when you tell me what—" Phillip stopped short when a pair of guards crossed spears in front of their path. Thunder snorted at the guards and stretched his wings. "Easy, fellow," Phillip soothed. "Is there a problem, soldiers?"

"King's orders," one of the guards said stiffly. He had a rusty red, oversized mustache that almost completely covered his mouth. "No one's admitted into the castle until the Princess and King have arrived from Tivin."

"You don't understand," Phillip started. "We're—"

"Shut up, Magician," Seventh Night hissed from behind him. "The prince is expecting us," she told the guard, then leaned forward to show him the ring on her right hand.

The guards clicked their heels in attention and hurried to open the gate. The senior guard shouted something to a nearby soldier that sent the man running. Phillip shook his head in disbelief and wondered again what kind of message Seven was carrying.

They were barely inside the gate when they were flanked by four squads of soldiers and the honor guard. Thunder enjoyed all the attention and strutted on proudly until Phillip pulled on his reins. Thunder shook his mane and snorted to show his displeasure at being stopped. A few of the steadfast soldiers flinched, and Phillip smirked.

Prince Neithan stood atop the stairs of the main entrance, looking over the proceedings and talking with one of the soldiers. Phillip had never seen the prince in person, but he recognized him by dress and reputation. Neithan was young, handsome, and of a tall, muscular build with a thick mane of chestnut hair. If rumors could be believed, he was a great swordsman, great hunter, charming, witty, strong, gentlemanly, and well-favored by both the men and women of the court. As the king's only son, he was the country's darling, which had always made Phillip do his best to ignore any news about him.

SEVENTH NIGHT

The prince descended the stairs, keeping his eyes on the black unicorn. He crossed the courtyard with a set expression. For a moment Phillip thought Neithan would rebuke Seven, perhaps harshly, for being late. The look in his eyes was not kind.

Phillip mentally prepared to defend her in that event. He would tell the prince about how the robbers took her horse and almost her life. If that did not work, he would risk telling the prince it was his fault for making her stay at the tavern. As the prince approached, he took a deep breath.

But instead of rebuking her, Neithan helped Seventh Night off the unicorn's back. Phillip had expected the prince to strike or yell at her. He did not expect Neithan to spin her around and kiss her, or that the dark look in his eyes could be replaced so quickly.

"I was afraid you wouldn't make it," Neithan said in an excited voice.

"Almost did not," Seventh Night told him. "You would not believe all that has happened."

"Where's your father?" he asked.

Seventh Night gave him a wry smile. "He'll be along in a few days. We had planned on coming early, but the carriage wheel broke before we got out the gate. The first wheel the blacksmith made was too small, and it would take too long to make another one. So I came on alone, incognito."

Phillip stared at the two with his mouth hanging open.

Neithan finally noticed him. "Who's he?"

"A farmboy who's becoming an apprentice to a magician here in the palace," she explained. "Neithan, he saved me from some bandits on the road from Fortesdale."

"In that case I owe you thanks," Neithan said while putting an arm around Seventh Night, who was beaming. He glanced at the unicorn. "You have a fine animal there. Are you apprentice to Magician Gadolin?"

Phillip pulled himself out of his stupor. "Ah—yes. Gadolin."

A shadow of something ran across the prince's face. "Then we will meet again." He smiled at Seventh Night. "Come on, Princess, let's go inside and get you a dress." He guided her around the unicorn's wing and up the castle stairs.

The soldiers dismissed, returning to their

duties.

"Princess?" Phillip said.

One of the king's stableboys timidly edged his way toward the unicorn. "Sir, I'm to lead you to the stables."

Phillip did not hear him. "Princess?" he repeated.

"She is the Princess Seventh Night of Tivin," the lad said impatiently. "Please, sir, I have other duties to attend to." Feeling much the fool, Phillip followed him to the stables.

CHAPTER III

THE PRINCE'S PROBLEM

That evening in the banquet hall Phillip stood behind his new master at the end of the king's table. To his surprise, Gadolin had turned out to be exactly what he expected. The magician was a tall, elderly man with a long, white beard. He had a gaunt face with dark eyes and wore an oversized, midnight blue cloak.

Phillip was supposed to be attending to the magician's needs, but his attention kept drifting to the girl sitting beside the queen. Seventh Night looked more the part of a princess dressed in her elegant pale blue gown with her raven hair spilling over her shoulders instead of knotted in a braid. She seemed quite content in her natural habitat, smiling radiantly and laughing at the king's jokes. Phillip still had a hard time believing he had been so easily fooled.

The king's table stretched across a slightly raised platform, facing the other tables in the banquet hall much the way the castle faced Pinnacle City. The monarchs sat at the center of the table in grand, meticulously carved oak chairs. The chamber buzzed with merry conversation, but when the king stood and raised his goblet, the hush that fell was absolute.

"My friends, honored guests, and subjects," the king proclaimed in his deep voice. His hair was still dark, though streaks of grey were slipping from under his crown and into his short beard. Physically he was not as large as his son, but the king had a presence that made him seem like a giant. "I would like to drink a toast to my son and his future bride. May their union be a long and happy one. May they rule with strength and wisdom and the blessing of their subjects."

SEVENTH NIGHT

A cheer of agreement rang through the banquet hall, followed by the lifting of goblets. With a grimace, Phillip recalled his first sip of beer and wondered how the courtiers could down so much.

"Boy, I need a fresh cup," the ancient magician commanded him. Phillip reached for Gadolin's goblet. He did not mind being ordered around by his new employer. An apprentice was to expect such treatment, but he took issue with the idea that anyone with wealth was entitled to order about anyone without it. Still, he had thought Seven was closer to his own station when he had rebuked her. Lord Harold had suggested he guard his tongue more closely at the castle, and he had already managed to slip up in that regard.

"Neithan!" Seventh Night yelped. The goblet forgotten, Phillip jerked his head up to see what the commotion was about. Prince Neithan had slumped lifelessly over in his chair like a rag doll.

"The prince is dead," one of the stunned servers thought out loud. This started an uproar from noblemen and servants alike.

"Come with me, boy!" Gadolin shouted over

the ruckus. The old man made his way to the prince's side. He felt Neithan's forehead and neck. "He is not dead," Gadolin announced loudly, then murmured, "but close enough."

He motioned with bony fingers to two guards. "Take the prince to his chamber," he ordered. He pointed to his apprentice. "You take the prince's food and drink to my laboratory." With a last glance at Seventh Night, Phillip did as told.

Phillip was awake most of the night assisting the magician in his tests and running errands. Gadolin proved much more than an illusionist, but his lab was more worthy of a chemist than a magician.

By midnight, the tireless old man had finished his tests on the food and drink and abandoned the underground lab for the high tower to doctor the prince. They fell into a rut that lasted until dawn. Gadolin would meet Phillip at the prince's door and give him another task, something else to fetch. The latest of these was to help bring down Neithan's fever.

With weary legs Phillip climbed the stairs

to the prince's chamber while attempting to balance a large bowl of cool water from an underground stream. From the hall outside Neithan's chamber, he could hear the magician speaking to the king and his councilmen.

"The prince's wine was poisoned," Gadolin said gravely. "But I do not recognize the type. Nor do I believe I can cure him."

"Can you not try the cures for the poisons you do know?" Sir Charles suggested, his tone carrying a hint of accusation.

Phillip managed to edge open the door without drawing attention.

"I have attempted every remedy that wouldn't kill Neithan if it failed to cure him," the magician snapped back.

The water sloshed a little as Phillip set it on the pedestal beside the prince's bed. For the first time he noticed Seventh Night, sitting in a scissor chair at the bedside. She was listening intently to the men's conversation. Her tired eyes were stained with tears, and she was wearing the same blue dress that she wore the evening before. Realizing she had been there all night, he placed a hand on her shoulder. Seventh Night turned to him. "Oh, Magician," she whispered piteously and buried her face in his shirt. Quietly, Phillip tried to comfort her.

"Your Highness," Lord Tauch addressed the king. "I would bet my life Gourlin spies poisoned Prince Neithan to stop the alliance between Cordance and Tivin. We should interrogate the kitchen staff and the servers."

"If the poison was from Gourlin, that might explain why I do not recognize it," Gadolin admitted.

"Interrogate the servers if you must," Sir Afphan cut in. "Any spies would have already fled. Besides if the Gourlins could poison the prince so easily, why didn't they also poison—pardon, Sire—His Highness or use a more fatal poison."

"To our knowledge this poison is fatal," Gadolin reminded him. "The prince is in good physical condition, but this may only slow the inevitable."

"Excuse me," Phillip spoke up and was completely ignored.

"Why weren't the servers gathered last night?"

"No one knew there was poison involved last night. Besides, they are all accounted for. I checked this morning."

"And the kitchen staff?"

"They're being searched and counted now. Would you like me to count the courtiers as well?"

"I think that's exactly what you should do."

"Excuse me," Phillip tried again and was again ignored.

"I don't think we should jump to any conclusions."

"Gourlin knew if they killed the king we'd attack."

"There is no proof who is responsible."

"I agree with Sir Afphan. We don't know who's responsible."

"Certain parties even in our midst have objections to the alliance."

"Or Tivin itself decided to weaken us instead—"

"Excuse me!"

The squabble cut off; every head in the room turned to the magician's apprentice. Phillip withered slightly under their glares. He cleared his throat and threw in his two bits. "I know of a sorceress that lives in the Gourlin desert. She was said to be a great healer and may know the cure for this poison."

"I've never heard of this sorceress," Gadolin said. The skin around his old eyes tightened as if he were looking through Phillip.

"She's a sort of hermit," Phillip managed. "I heard of her while I was in Gourlin." He noticed a few nasty looks from the council at the mention of Cordance's enemy nation.

The king found his voice. "Take what provisions you need and find her," he said simply but finally. Phillip bowed in acceptance of the task. With that the king left, followed closely by his council.

The muscles in his legs burned. Phillip silently swore that this was the last time he would walk up these stairs and questioned Prince Neithan's sanity for having his room in the highest tower, despite the view.

Seventh Night and Gadolin held a vigil at the prince's bedside. They acknowledged Phillip as he entered. "I got my supplies together," he told them. "I'm leaving tonight to find the sorceress. Is there any change?"

Gadolin shook his head. "How long will you be gone?" he asked him.

Phillip shrugged. "If I'm lucky, not over a week." The magician's expression became grimmer, but he said nothing.

"Will you stay here 'til it is time for you to leave?" Seventh Night asked. Phillip walked across the polished stone floor to her.

"No," he said simply. "I'm goin' to get some sleep, and so are you." Seventh Night moaned something like a protest but accepted Phillip's offered hand. He gave her a sympathetic smile. "Can't do him any good if you pass out," he told the princess as he helped her to her feet.

"Promise to wake me before you go," she said. Phillip nodded. A soft rapping at the door interrupted. Seventh Night sighed, "I'll answer it." Her skirt swished as she hurried across the stone.

With every new visitor a hope would spring in her heart that they could wake the prince.

Six years ago her father had brought her to Cordance to meet Neithan. At the time she had been almost resentful of the prearranged marriage. Everyone had been telling her how handsome the prince was, how kind and gentlemanly he was, how intelligent he was, how happy she would be, and how good the marriage would be for the country. They were so insistent it was all true that Seventh Night came to the conclusion the prince was an ugly, scabby simpleton, she would be miserable, and the country was doomed.

When she finally met Neithan, she was surprised to find he was everything they had told her he would be except more so. From the first moment of their acquaintance, they were on good terms. In less than two weeks, he confessed he loved her. It had left her suspicious at first, but her regard for him had grown until she lost all doubt. She was barely thirteen at the time, Neithan eighteen, but she had never been more certain of anything else. She had stayed nearly a month before returning to Tivin and left thoroughly satisfied with the arrangement.

But Neithan might be gone soon. Seventh Night took a long look at her prince and opened the door.

She froze with shock. The familiar face and stance was not hidden in the common garb. Convinced she was seeing her love's ghost,

Seventh Night fainted. The apparition caught her before she hit the floor.

"Seven. Seven, wake up."

Seventh Night squinted against the sudden light. She was lying on something soft but stiff like bench cushions. "Magician?" she asked.

"I'm here," Phillip assured her. "Are you all right?"

"I'm not sure," she answered rubbing her temples. "I thought I saw—" For the first time she noticed the second concerned face. "Neithan?!" she shrieked.

"Shhh," Phillip hissed and covered her mouth with his hand.

Neithan smiled as if she had just told a joke. "Yes, I'm Neithan," he said. Seventh Night gave Phillip a look with a clear meaning, and he removed his hand.

"B-but how?" she stuttered. "You're, you're..." She glanced through the gap between Phillip and Neithan to see the unconscious figure on the bed twitch. The sheets rose and fell as the sleeping prince filled his large form with a deep breath.

Only, the prince was standing over her, looking

slightly sheepish.

"I best explain," a third voice cut in. Phillip and Neithan moved aside so the princess could see Gadolin. The old man gave her a half-apologetic look. "I assure you we had planned to tell you at a more convenient time."

"Tell me what?" Seventh Night asked.

Gadolin cleared his throat. "I'll start at the beginning. When Prince Neithan was born, I was the doctor who delivered him and a surprise. Prince Neithan had a twin brother, Kaleb; not only a twin but identical. The midwife had already taken Neithan away to bathe him, so only the king, the queen, and I were present for the birth.

"At the time Cordance had even worse relations with the adjoining countries than it does now. The king got it in his mind to hide the younger brother. His majesty told me his reasons were so if one of the children was kidnapped or killed the other could take his place without the subjects' knowledge of the change. Nor did he want bad counsel to try to turn the brothers against each other.

"As they grew older Neithan and Kaleb changed places regularly. They have completely fooled the courtiers...and their parents when they feel the need. They've made such a science of it, even I at times need to ask to tell one from the other." Gadolin paused to see if this was sinking in.

Seventh Night was normally quick, but this took a while to fully absorb. Her gaze went from Gadolin to the Prince to Phillip and back again. New information usually raises a few questions; this raised several. Seventh Night tried to choose hers carefully. "Which are you?" she asked the prince.

"I'm Neithan," he said. A hint of sadness entered his eyes. "Kaleb received the poison."

"But, which one of you—?" Seventh Night stopped, not sure how to finish the question.

"You only knew Kaleb before," Neithan answered. "We've never met." Seventh Night only nodded. She had lost her love and found him only to lose him again. It was not a fair sentiment, but she was a little angry with Neithan for letting Kaleb be poisoned. "You're a bit late if you did not want anyone to notice a change," she pointed out.

Phillip smirked, "That's what I said."

"Things are always more complex in practice

than in theory," Gadolin explained. "If Kaleb's poisoning had not been so public, a transition would have been possible."

"So why couldn't the Prince have a remarkable recovery?" Seventh Night asked, her voice betraying some of her agitation. Phillip tried to cover another chuckle. She guessed he had already said that too.

"For Kaleb's sake," Neithan answered. "It'd be impossible to move him. The tunnels are too narrow and uneven to safely sneak him out, and the guards would see him otherwise. He is my brother. As long as he's alive, I can't give up on him. I will travel with Phillip to find the sorceress."

"You will?" Phillip asked. He had not heard about this.

"What tunnels?" Seventh Night interrupted.

"The castle has a network of hidden tunnels and chambers," Gadolin explained. "One of the boys would hide there while his brother played the role of the prince."

Seventh Night pushed herself out from between Phillip and Neithan and to her feet. She took a few paces across the floor and turned back. "I'm going too," she said.

Phillip was first to catch her meaning. "No, Seven," he said. He gestured to Neithan. "It's bad enough he's going. But there's two of him; you'd be missed. I don't even know if this sorceress is friendly. I doubt she lives in the desert 'cause she likes the climate." Seventh Night kept a stubborn look on her face. "Please," Phillip pleaded. "For Kaleb."

Her expression softened. "Very well," she sighed. "For Kaleb's sake."

Satisfied, Phillip stood. "We leave at twilight," he told Neithan and headed for the door.

"Where are you going?" Gadolin asked him.

Phillip sighed and turned back around. "To catch a nap."

CHAPTER IV

A DARK AND DANGEROUS DESERT

Dusk was setting in when Phillip reached the end of the tunnel. He found himself on the other side of the mountain facing the Gourlin desert. He had chosen to ride at night for the desert was a burning wasteland by day, and it was much easier to warm up than cool down. The promise of clear sky and a full moon made the night time trek possible.

Prince Neithan was securing the last of their supplies to a grey unicorn. He was dressed in common traveling clothes with a hooded cloak and a thin scarf covering the lower portion of his face. His stature and bearing still shouted prince to Phillip, but it should be enough to fool any sentries who might spot them from their lookout posts far up on the mountainside.

Thunder was restless, snorting and stomping around as much as the rope allowed. The lone soldier accompanying them was in the process of mounting his ivory unicorn. Phillip walked over to the prince and asked him if he was ready.

"Ready as I can be," Neithan answered from under his hood. "Shall we begin?"

Phillip nodded and mounted Thunder. "This might be faster if I flew on alone," he tried one last time.

Neithan did not bother giving him so much as a glance in response, and Phillip knew he was right. He had traveled enough to know a small group was more likely to return than a lone adventurer. Winged unicorns might be faster, but the king of Cordance only had two. Their disappearance would raise too many questions and light loads were preferable for flight. Between food, water, and tents, they needed the fourth unicorn just to act as a pack horse.

Phillip was glad for the company, even glad

for the soldier, since it did not leave all the responsibility for Neithan's return on him. He noticed the soldier was rather slight. Probably a young recruit, one less likely to recognize the prince. He asked the lad if his affairs were in order. The soldier, whose nose and mouth was covered to keep out the sand, nodded under his hood in response. In a moment they were under way.

After a few miles of travel, boredom got the better of Phillip. Neithan did not turn out to be much of a talker. Phillip rode up beside the soldier in hopes of striking up a conversation. "What's your name, soldier?" he asked.

The lad pushed back his hood and pulled down his mask; only it was not a lad but a lady. Seventh Night smiled at him. "You've forgotten me already?" she said, mock upset. "I'm hurt."

Phillip jerked Thunder to a stop. "Seven, march yourself back right now," he commanded her, pointing to the mountain, smaller but still quite visible behind them.

Seven sniffed. "That's no way to talk to a princess," she chided him.

"I'm not talking to a princess," he countered. "I'm talking to an empty-headed girl who should have learned to listen to my warnings from the last time."

Seven was unmoved. "The trouble last time was that I went on without you, so I've learned to go with you. *I am* going with you. I was not doing Kaleb any good sitting around worrying over him."

"Neithan?" Phillip pleaded. "She'll listen to you."

Neithan chuckled. It occurred to Phillip that he had been in on this all along. "I couldn't send her back alone," he said. "What if something happened to her?"

"There could be bandits," Seventh Night said with an innocent lift of her eyebrows.

"They're going to notice you're missing," Phillip reminded her.

"It's taken care of," she assured him. "Only the king, the queen, Gadolin, and I are allowed in the prince's chamber, where I will be keeping watch over my fiancé most of the time. Otherwise I'll be asleep in my room."

"The king and queen are just going to play along?"

"The poisoner has not been caught," Neithan said soberly.

SEVENTH NIGHT

"Neithan and Gadolin think I may be safer if I'm not easily found for the next few days."

Outnumbered, outthought, and mostly out-ranked Phillip threw up his hands. "I give up," he said. "It's your head; it's on your hands." He patted Thunder's mane. The unicorn was restless with the pause. "You still owe me an explanation for why you were in such a hurry before."

"What? When?"

"On the road to Pinnacle."

Seventh Night shook her head in amusement. "You have the uncanny ability to jump from one subject to another without a moment's pause."

Phillip smiled as if she had complimented him. "Thank you, Seven." He urged Thunder to resume his pace. "Transitions take too long," he went on. "By the time you finish getting off the last subject you forget what you want to say in the first place. So, why were you in such a hurry?"

Seventh Night shrugged. "The arrangement had a time limit. If I didn't make it to the palace by noon of the first day of the tenth month the engagement would be called off."

"What arrangement?" Phillip asked.

Neithan made a sound somewhere between a snort and a chuckle.

"It's not funny," Seventh Night said.

"It's absurd," Neithan said as much to himself as the princess.

"Perhaps a little," Seventh Night admitted. "But it was Cordance's absurdity."

"What was?" Phillip tried again.

"The time limit on the arrangement, the treaty. They did not trust us," Seventh Night said, glancing at Neithan. "Some of them still do not. The Cordance nobles insisted on a time limit on the grounds that, if we could not arrive on time, we could not be trusted to keep the treaty. The time for arrival was set at the first day of the tenth month at noon, as you know. The wedding was set for the eighth day of the tenth month right after I turn nineteen. With the current circumstances though, even the nobles agreed to postpone 'til the prince is recovered."

"What would happen if you were late?"

"Renegotiations at best," Seventh Night said. "War at worst."

"I guess that explains the hurry. Still, it seems a bit of an overkill just for being late to a wedding," Phillip said. "Even a royal wedding."

SEVENTH NIGHT

"It's not just a wedding," Neithan said. Phillip was looking at Seventh Night when he said it and thought Neithan was trying to be romantic. But when he turned, he saw nothing remotely sentimental in Neithan's expression.

"We are joining the countries," Seventh Night explained, and Phillip returned his attention to her. "Not right away. The wedding is supposed to encourage better trade and interaction. But after there is securely an heir, my father will abdicate the throne of Tivin to me and my husband. And Cordance's crown will naturally pass down to Neithan."

"But to have war over a wedding?" Phillip said. "That hardly seems fair. I thought Tivin and Cordance got along alright."

"We're not worried about Tivin," Neithan interjected again.

"Then what are you worried about?"

"Gourlin," Neithan said, looking uncomfortable. "There's been no war in my lifetime, but my grandfather's time was different. My father settled the border disputes with Uritz and Tivin, but Gourlin remains a threat. When the Gourlins started taking over their neighboring lands, the nobles became uncertain that the desert was enough of a buffer zone. They thought taking over Tivin would help solve our problems, make Cordance bigger, stronger."

Phillip glanced at Seventh Night. She was listening, trying not to look too intent. The princess was biting her tongue, perhaps literally, but Phillip could tell there were words waiting just inside her closed mouth.

Neithan looked ready to end there, but the other two watched him expectantly. "There was debate. My father didn't want to upset a hard won peace with an invasion. Of course the king's word is law, but the nobles' private guards make up half the army. To put them at ease and avoid bloodshed, my father and Tivin's king arranged the wedding."

"In other words, you two are marrying so Tivin and Cordance don't destroy each other trying to save themselves from Gourlin," Phillip said.

Neithan nodded.

The moon was out by this time, full and bright. Moonlight reflected off the pale sand, giving it a snowy appearance. Phillip glanced back to see whether the grey unicorn was still attached to the rope anchored to Neithan's saddle. The grey beast trod along, his head drooping just a bit. The cart of water barrels, pile of food sacks, and tent poles wrapped with tent cloth strapped to his back looked like an awkward burden, but the unicorn stepped steadily as he carried it. He had steered himself between the hoof paths left by Thunder and Neithan's unicorn to make his own round holes in the sand.

There were small dunes and a few clusters of stone, but overall the landscape was open and empty. A few scraggly plants had taken root, but they did not look appetizing enough to tempt the unicorns.

"So the countries join," Phillip said out loud. His mouth could not stay closed long. Seventh Night pulled out of her own reverie to look at him, and he returned the gaze. "But what's in it for you, Seven?"

"Tivin will benefit," she replied. "Hopefully trade will increase, the size of the country will double at least, and..." she hesitated a little. "... we need an army." Phillip lifted his eyebrows questioningly. "We have one of course, just not a large one."

Neithan smiled. "Your wonderful tax policy?" he offered.

At that, Seventh Night did something quite unbecoming for a princess and stuck out her tongue at him. "Yes, our marvelous tax policy."

"I didn't think Tivin used taxes." Phillip said.

Seven sighed. "That's why we do not have an army. When Tivin joins with Cordance we'll adopt their taxes and have the protection of their army."

"Okay, Seven, but I meant what's in it for you personally?"

Seventh Night looked out across the shadowed dunes. "I'm getting married," she said crisply.

Phillip frowned. "You seemed a little more enthusiastic about it yesterday."

She did not answer him directly but turned to the prince. "Neithan? I am not clear. Who was I to marry, you or Kaleb?"

"Kaleb would've gone through the ceremony with you," Neithan said simply. "You would have been married to him legally and in the eyes of God. Only in the minds of the people would you be married to me."

Seventh Night returned her attention to Phillip. "I shall be quite happy, Magician. Kaleb and I are very much in love." She tapped her heels, making the unicorn run ahead.

Phillip shrugged and gave Neithan a sympathetic smile. "Sounds like you're getting the short end of the stick. Not only do you miss out on Her *High Stubbornness* over there," he raised his voice just enough for Seven to hear. "But you won't be able to take a wife of your own. Doesn't that bother you the least bit?"

"To be honest, no," Neithan said. "I never really cared for that sort of thing." That was not the answer Phillip had expected from a man of Prince Neithan's reputation. "Kaleb likes to flirt, but I never got much out of it." Phillip nodded his lack of understanding and tried to imagine what other peculiarities the twin princes' arrangement produced.

Seventh Night whimpered as she lowered herself to the ground. If Phillip had not been so close, she might have given in to louder complaint. The horses' tent was a clever assemblage which stood at full height to accommodate the animals while they slept. For the humans, they had brought three very small tents, just big enough to shade a single sleeper. She crawled on her elbows through the flap and collapsed on the relatively soft blankets covering the ground. It was too warm to pull one over her.

She had ignored the former stableboy's suggestion to take turns riding the horse and walking beside it. She had ridden Toshk for longer periods of time without becoming saddle sore. She had not realized regular unicorns were rougher on riders than winged ones.

Muttering several ill wishes on Phillip's head, she turned onto her back and winced in pain. Eventually, she fell asleep.

Seventh Night did not know what woke her, but when she opened her eyes, she found she was not alone in her tent. A golden snake hovered over her, tensed to strike. Frozen with fear, Seventh Night dared not take her eyes off the creature. "Neithan!" she squeaked out as loud as she dared.

After a seeming eternity, light entered as Neithan and Phillip drew back the fabric at the opening. Phillip's eyes widened. "Don't move, Seven," he whispered. "This kind of snake shouldn't strike as long as you keep its gaze locked." Seventh Night was too shaken to bring the sarcastic remark in her mind to her lips.

Neithan unsheathed his sword. He motioned Phillip back, and with one clean swipe of his blade, he took off the serpent's head. A skillful twist of the blade knocked the head away, but the decapitated stump fell on Seventh Night's robe. At this point she screamed, though more from disgust than fright. Neithan removed the unpleasant carcass with a grimace.

Phillip uncovered his ears. "You'd think it bit you," he told Seventh Night.

"Shut up, Magician," Seventh Night said in a warning voice as she sat up. Neithan wiped his sword and sheathed it. "Thank you, Neithan." She gave him a quick kiss on the cheek.

Neithan blushed. He murmured a "You're welcome" and quickly stood.

Phillip raised his eyebrows expectantly. Seventh Night rolled her eyes. "You can kiss the snake."

SEVENTH NIGHT

Chapter V

The Monarchy

None of them slept well that first day, except perhaps the unicorns, who had not been troubled by any snake. Snakes as a rule do not like the smell of unicorns. Neithan's extra long frame barely fit inside his extra long tent. He kept his sword close and thought about poisons. Phillip walked around the camp a few times looking for further signs of serpents, which proved fruitless and left him with a mild sunburn. Seventh Night tried to sleep, but every time her eyes began to close, she peeked them open again to make sure she was alone in her tent.

Despite the poor sleep, or perhaps because of it, they were all eager to rise when night came. Seventh Night rode between the two men and kept all her focus on staying upright on her saddle until the cool evening air had revived her. Neithan kept his eyes fixed ahead as though he could see a road through the featureless sand. Phillip talked.

At first he talked about the weather and other things that required no response: what they should do if it rained, what they should do if water ran short, how they should take care in doling it out. When he tired of this, he asked Seventh Night about Tivin, which he wanted to see someday, and she was homesick enough to be drawn into the conversation. The moon had traveled a quarter of its journey across the sky, when the topic twisted into a philosophical debate about the monarchy.

"Oppressive!?" Seventh Night echoed indignantly. The lack of sleep made her more inclined to be argumentative. "Neithan's father has removed torture as punishment for all but the most extreme cases, and my grandfather is remembered as a very progressive and fair minded king. How can you dare to call the monarchy oppressive?!"

"I'm not talking about specific rulers," Phillip replied evenly. "I'm sure, as kings go, your fathers are decent enough. But the entire idea of monarchy, or nobility for that matter, to pass on leadership by the accident of birth rather than personal merit is an oppressive system."

"You presume birth is an accident," Seventh Night retorted. "That God is careless who He passes a crown to."

Phillip shrugged. "Not every cobbler's son likes cobbling. A seamstress may have a daughter with clumsy fingers. Is it so strange to think royalty and nobility might also have children unsuited to their parent's profession? I've listened to nobles who visit Lord Harold complain about how poorly another manages their holdings."

"A lack of dedication to one's position in life does not necessarily mean there is no raw talent for it," the princess replied more easily. "I think in most of those cases the failing is in education rather than ability. Usually when a noble's son goes wrong, it's because he was spoiled and given privileges without being trained in the duties that accompany them. A well-trained king is slave to the welfare of his country. The ones who neglect or abuse their subjects invite uprising. By far the majority of sons, even among the peasantry, follow in their father's trade. Why should the noble class be different?"

Phillip considered her with a grin, and the princess frowned at him. "What?" she demanded.

"It's a good answer," he said. "Most girls just giggle or tell me I talk too much."

"You do talk a lot," Seventh Night agreed with a waning smile. The princess glanced at Prince Neithan who had said nothing since they had left camp, though Seventh Night believed he had been listening. "What do you think, Neithan?"

The prince shrugged, and the princess bit back her disappointment. Kaleb had been well-spoken, though far less inclined to debate than the magician's apprentice. Phillip was proving a worthy debate partner, but she had been hoping to get a better sense of her beloved's brother.

"The problem," Phillip continued, when it

was clear Neithan was not going to speak, "is that a king is far too removed from the life of the average person to know the effect his decisions have on them or what the needs of his own countrymen are. Even if the people are starving, the royalty will be fed."

"Is the kingdom starving?" Seventh Night asked with a note of concern.

"Well, no, but that's not the point," Phillip said, scratching his neck. "If the king falls sick, he will have a doctor or two and servants to care for him and no reason to worry how his family will be fed. If a peasant falls sick, a doctor is hard to come by and paying for one might take food from the mouth of his family. You have people to cook for you and wash your clothes and scrub your floors, and no idea how hard most common people work simply to live each day."

"The nobility, royalty in particular, works as much with their mind as a peasant does with their body," Seventh Night returned. "I'm not ignorant that physical labors are more difficult for the peasantry, but the fact so much of their time is devoted to the basics of life is exactly why the noble class is necessary. Someone must have the time to pursue education and look at the issues that afflict a town or a country from a broader perspective than their own household. It's like a father and mother must guide the conduct of their children, for children are ignorant of the greater world."

"You think fathers never oppress their children?" Phillip asked.

"Protection may feel like oppression when one lacks perspective," the princess said pointedly.

Phillip looked away and guided Thunder around a pile of stone. Nighttime allowed for more comfortable travel but not a fast pace. The moon gave enough light for steady progress, but a gallop would have been foolish due to the more limited visibility. Daylight had different difficulties, better visibility, but a hard ride under the desert sun had proved too much for many a steed.

"A good father doesn't stop his children's growth or education," Phillip said at last. "Protecting a child without training them to make their own way is poor parenting. So if a King is like a father, then he should take steps to prepare his children to follow in his trade, to become leaders themselves."

"A country of leaders without followers would lead to disorder," Seventh Night said, pulling her unicorn to a stop and swinging her leg over to dismount. Neithan saw what she was doing and quickly jumped down from his own unicorn to offer his hand.

Phillip decided to take the opportunity to stretch his legs as well, ducking under Thunder's wing to lead the unicorn. "I'm not suggesting every peasant would make a good leader, but I think there should be more room for change in station. At the very least, men should be allowed to fill positions based on their own merit rather than their parents' and pick their partners based on mutual attraction rather than wealth or politics."

"Neithan?" Seventh Night tried again as they walked on, leading their mounts behind them. "Surely you have some thoughts on this."

The prince would have preferred to hold his tongue. The other two spoke too quickly for him, but as they waited for him to speak, he felt an obligation to say something, if for no other reason than to assure them he had not been offended by their conversation.

SEVENTH NIGHT

"I think we have to take the world as it is and do our best in it."

"Farsong?" the princess said, identifying the originator of the quote.

After a few steps to search his memory, Neithan nodded.

"Where is this sorceress supposed to be anyway?" she asked. She knew the men had consulted a map before leaving, and she had been trusting to their guidance. But there were no roads to follow in the desert, and she was beginning to wonder if there was any aim to their wandering.

"The traveler told me she was dead center between Gourlin and Cordance," Phillip said. "Just south of Paradox, which should be just north of Pinnacle."

"How reliable is this traveler?" the princess asked.

It was Phillip's turn to shrug. "It was nearly ten years ago, but I heard about her from more than one person."

"Ten years?" Seventh Night repeated. "She could be dead or relocated."

"Or a myth," Phillip added. "I offered to look for her because it was the only thing I could offer, and I'd always wanted to see if it was true. When the King agreed, I thought he was just willing to risk a servant's life and a few provisions. If I'd realized he wanted you two spirited away, I would have made other suggestions."

Neithan was checking the sky, and the princess remembered reading how many travelers took their bearings from the stars. "This was not the king's idea," she explained for both of them, since Neithan's focus was else-where. "We're not children. Neithan thought it would take too long to get his blessing. We charged Gadolin with telling him."

Phillip tried to laugh, but it came out as more of a squeak. "Perfect. I've kidnapped you."

"Don't be melodramatic. The king will know we have gone willingly. Gadolin will vouch for your ignorance in the matter. Besides, Neithan's a hunter. He's good at tracking things."

Phillip sighed. "I'm glad for his help, and your company. But the fact you two made this decision without me demonstrates my earlier point. It's my neck if something happens to either of you, but the peasant gets no say in the matter."

SEVENTH NIGHT

"I—" Seventh Night began but faltered short of an apology. The world as it was gave Neithan the right to command and Phillip no right to criticize her for it. "I've had enough walking," she finished and remounted before Neithan could help her.

The second day they all slept very well.

CHAPTER VI

INSIDE THE HUT OF BARK AND BONE

As dawn broke at the end of the third night, the prince, the princess, and the apprentice spotted the little structure in the distance. Forgoing sleep, they rode on even as the sun rose to bake the desert. Before noon, they reached it. The hut was a collection of dark dead wood, bark, and large animal bones. In front of the hut was an uncovered well so deep the bottom could not be seen from the top.

Phillip dismounted and gestured for the others

to follow. He found the door, a large piece of hinged bark, and knocked softly. No answer. "Maybe she's not home," he suggested.

"She probably could not hear you. Knock again," Seventh Night commanded him. Phillip knocked again, this time louder. They waited. Still no answer. Neithan stepped past him and rapped on the door hard enough that Phillip worried he might knock it down. Again, no answer.

"I guess no one's home."

"Magician, should we look inside?" Seventh Night asked.

Phillip spun around with a look of mild terror on his face. "No, Seven. Three reasons. One, the sorceress might just be waiting for us to go away, but eventually she'll have to come out for water. We can talk to her then. Two, this might not be the sorceress's hut at all, and I would not feel right going through some poor hermit's home. Three, even if this is the sorceress's hut, the last thing I want is to have a sorceress mad at me because we poked 'round her things."

Seventh Night knitted her brow and looked at him askance. "A simple 'no' would suffice." She kicked her toe in the dirt. "We just wait, then." Phillip nodded. Seventh Night glanced at the well. "Should we replenish our water supply?"

"Seven!" Phillip shouted so loud she jerked back. The outburst got rid of some of his tension, so when he spoke again his voice was much calmer. "Water is a rather precious commodity in the desert. Besides, we have enough. I really doubt she'd want to help us if her well went dry. You want her to help Kaleb, don't you?"

"Yes," she answered softly.

The sun had sunk far enough in the sky that the hut cast a thin shadow. Neithan and Seventh Night rested in the meager shade, exhausted from setting up the horse tent in the heat but afraid to sleep and risk missing the sorceress. Phillip tended to the horses' needs, making sure they had enough water and were properly protected from the sun.

Seventh Night took a sip of water and offered the flask to Neithan. He gestured that he did not want any. Instead, Neithan pulled his sword from his sheath and flashed it in the sun, admiring the fine craftsmanship of the blade. Phillip approached, and Neithan returned his sword to his side. They had been waiting for through a long, hot midday, and all were ready to move on. But no one said the words, for perhaps the sorceress would return before nightfall.

Seventh Night watched the wind blow the sand, then realized there was no wind and the moving sand was a lizard. If she had been in the palace or the courtyard, she might have given a squeal of disgust or fright. In the desert however, it was simply something to keep her mind off the monotony. Something alive, somehow surviving the wasteland. The lizard stared back at her for a moment, then dashed off.

Neithan and Seven stayed in what cool the shadow offered, but Phillip ventured over to the well. He tried to determine how deep it was, how far down to the water, did it have an underground source, or did it simply catch what little rain that fell. Not that he really had a way to test any of these things, but it kept his mind busy.

None of them noticed the old woman come up until she spoke. "Please, kind sirs, please," she called in a rickety old voice. Phillip jumped. Neithan and Seven were too tired to jump and simply turned their heads toward the old hag. She was a hag at that. Her hair was grayish-white; her skin wrinkled, worn, and blotched with age spots; her eyes hollow and pink; and the hump of her bent back only allowed her to shuffle from place to place. "A drink o' water, please."

"Is this your house, ma'am?" Phillip asked.

"No, boy, no," she cracked. "Can ye spare a drop from yer well?"

"I guess," said Seventh Night, knocking some sand from her trouser leg.

"Seven!" Phillip rebuked her. "I offer apology, ma'am, but you won't want this water."

The old woman's eyes seemed to grow a bit wearier. "Is it bad water?"

"I don't know, ma'am," Phillip answered. "It may be a sorceress's well, and she may not like it if you take her water."

"If ye don't wish to get the water just say the words," the hag said. "I'll be dead of thirst anyway. What for should I fear a sorceress who might be only?" The old hag groped behind the well and found a bucket with a long rope attached to the handle. She banged the sand off it against the stone and moved to lower the bucket into the well.

Phillip stood tense and distressed. "Wait a moment," he told the ancient woman. He ran to the horses' tent, undid his water flask from the saddle, ran back to the well, and stretched out the flask to the old woman. "Here," Phillip panted. "I know that's good."

The old woman snatched the flask and drank greedily. When she had finished, she handed it back to Phillip. "Thank you, boy," she said. Some of the roughness had left her voice. With a sniff and scratch, she started for the front door of the hut.

"Where are you going?" Phillip asked her and at the same time began wondering at her sanity.

"I live here," the old woman said.

"But you said this wasn't your house," Phillip protested.

"This?" The old hag made a sweeping gesture with her hand. "This bunch of bark and bones is not what I call a house."

"Are you the sorceress, then?" Seventh Night asked.

"Oh, what a bright girl," the hag cackled. "Indeed, ask yerself who else would be crazy enough to be out in this wretched heat?" She stopped in her open door and looked at the three carefully. "I guess ye are. What does ye want?"

"My brother was poisoned," Neithan answered. "We need to find a cure for him."

"Poisoned, eh," she repeated. "Why should I help yeh? What can ye offer me?"

"We brought money to pay you for your effort," Neithan offered.

"That's all?" she said. "Think. What need have I for gold out here?"

"It is a very wretched world we live in, if favors are returned only for favors," Phillip quoted. Seventh Night had heard or read that before, but he made it sound original. The sorceress looked impressed anyway.

"How true, how true," she said with a bobbing of her head. "Tell me what can I do for you, boy?"

"Please," he said. "Call me Phillip. Not boy, or magician, or farmhand, or apprentice, or sprat, or Philleep, or Philup, just Phil-lip, please."

Seventh Night half expected the sorceress to be angered at his outburst. Instead the hag laughed, or more accurately cackled, with amusement.

She smiled at Neithan and Seventh Night and pointed at Phillip. "I like him," she said. "Come in. I'll see what I can do."

Phillip, Neithan, and Seventh Night squeezed into the small dwelling. The walls of the sorceress's hut were lined with shelves stacked with vials, dusty books, assorted jars, and unrecognizable mixtures. A crude little stone fireplace took up one corner. In the center of the room was a simple square table with clear containers resting on top. A large black cauldron sat beside it on the floor. On the other side of the table was just enough room to unroll a small mat.

The sorceress began searching through the shelves and finally pulled out a small cloth pouch. The old woman laid the pouch on the table and began searching the shelves again. "Do ye know the poison type?" she asked.

"No ma'am," Phillip answered. "But I've brung a sample of the poisoned wine."

"Yes, yes, very good," the sorceress nodded. Phillip was not sure if she was referring to his bringing the wine or the large book she had just found. She set the book on the table with a thud and a billow of dust. With bony fingers she turned the pages until she found the one that suited her. "Here it be," she said.

The sorceress read for several minutes. Seven began to get impatient and tapped her fingers together behind her back. At last the witch gave an "mm-hm". She dipped a ladle into the cauldron, which was apparently filled with water for the top shimmered when the ladle broke the surface. She poured the clear water into the glass container and then sprinkled in some powder from the bag. The mixture fizzed and popped and turned a milky white. The sorceress gestured to Phillip. "Give me the wine," she told Phillip. He handed her the small vial. The old sorceress poured the wine into the mixture, leaving a spot of dark pink where the drink hit the surface. With a thin glass rod, she stirred, and the mixture turned pale pink. "Tell me some of his symptoms," the sorceress said as she continued to stir.

"He's asleep. We haven't been able to wake him up," Phillip related what he knew. "The poison worked quick. It knocked him out almost immediately." As he spoke the mixture turned from pale pink to a faint red.

"It's been four days. His hands are cold,"

Seventh Night said. "And his brow is hot. At least it was when we left." The sorceress simply nodded to show she heard. Phillip noticed she was chanting something softly.

"Gadolin, our magician, tried all the cures he knew that weren't cure-or-kill," Neithan added.

Phillip listened carefully to make out her words. "*Werbia een opaycus, opaycus een seigno.*" The sorceress muttered these words over and over. The liquid continued to deepen in shade, until it was a blood red.

The sorceress stopped chanting and formed a satisfied smile. She turned a page in the book. "What does that mean?" Phillip asked her.

"What does what mean?" she asked.

"The words," Phillip said. "What do they mean?"

The old sorceress turned back the page. "Words into color, color into meaning." She gave no further explanation and continued examining the writing.

Seventh Night looked at the dark blood red liquid. Color into meaning? She had heard of cures for certain sicknesses that used leeches. Perhaps that was the case here. She shuddered at the thought of one of those slimy creatures on Kaleb. She did not allow herself to even consider the possibility the color could signal his death.

"Ahhh," the sorceress waved her hand in a satisfied gesture.

"Did you find the cure?" Neithan and Seventh Night asked simultaneously.

"Yes," the sorceress said thoughtfully. "I have."

"Tell me," Seventh Night demanded. "What is it?"

"On one condition," the witch said.

"Anything," Seventh Night vowed.

"Anything," Neithan repeated.

"Can we hear the condition first?" Phillip chimed at the cost of a dirty look from Seventh Night.

The sorceress smirked at Phillip's remark but then turned serious. "When you return to your homeland," she said, "you must take me along."

It was an odd request, but Seventh Night and Neithan nodded their consent eagerly. Phillip began to wonder who would have to give up their mount. "In that case," the sorceress said with a thin smile, "the answer is quite simple."

SEVENTH NIGHT

She read, *"Faymeena cum ama een cor earay oscoolum illum."*

Neithan and Seven just stared at the impossible hag. Phillip tried to contain his grin. "What does that mean?" he asked.

"Oops," the sorceress apologized. "Sorry about that. He can be healed only by the kiss of a woman with love in her heart."

"What?!" Seventh Night exclaimed. "That is the most ludicrous thing I've ever heard!" She glared at Phillip. "What kind of fraud have you brought us to see?"

This upset the sorceress. "Fraud! Indeed. The amateurs kept in the castles? The charlatans that wander about with their trick shows? And you call me a fraud? I'm probably the only one who knows real magic for several hundred miles. In all directions!

"You are a very brash, disrespectful child. Have you no manners?" The sorceress glared at Seventh Night for a moment, and some of the rage subdued. "You're a noble's child, ain't ye? Maybe a royal, for which I could care less. I need no magic for that. I can tell by your haughty airs." Seventh Night had back stepped behind Neithan for fear the hag had lost all sanity.

But the hag calmed herself. "I suppose I can forgive you then. Nobles and royals alike, you're taught only to respect yer own kind. Perhaps ye ain't so much sassy as stupid in common manners." Seventh Night bristled internally at the insult. She was not stupid. In Tivin, royalty had to act a certain way to establish their position. Her pride and manner were carefully taught skills. She started to object, but Phillip sent her a warning glance.

"Stupid girl," the sorceress repeated as more of a jest than an insult. "Few things are what they first seem. Take me for instance. Think I'm an old hag, don't ye?"

"The thought never crossed my mind, ma'am," Phillip lied politely.

"Yes, it did," she retorted almost defensively. The trio moved aside, which was not easy in the small quarters, as she hobbled around the table. She turned and faced them with an odd smile. "Things are rarely what they seem," she repeated.

As Seventh Night watched through the gap between the men's arms, something disturbing happened to the sorceress. Her straggly grey hair constricted into tight coppery-red curls. The age spots on her skin shrank and disappeared; her skin itself turned a livelier, more desirable color. Lines and wrinkles melted away. Her hollow, pink rimmed eyes turned a piercing shade of emerald. The curve of her back straightened, and her rag dress fit better.

Neithan's eyes grew round with shock as the hunched old witch turned into a tall enchantress. "You look like that?" he blurted.

The sorceress shrugged her shoulders. "Actually, I don't know what I look like," she admitted, her voice now clear and fluid. "I'm a shifter. This is the form I choose."

"How did you do that?" Neithan asked, fascinated. "What's a shifter?"

The sorceress crossed her arms. "I'll answer the first question by answering the second," she said thoughtfully. "It's a bit like a birth deformation. Such as having six fingers on one hand. Except shifters only come from parents who dabble in magic, real magicians.

"I can change into any form I choose. Usually I have to copy something, but this, as I am, is an original creation of my own." She smiled proudly at her creativity.

"What do you mean you don't know what

you look like?" Neithan clearly found the existence of real magic captivating. He had asked more in the last two minutes than the last two days. Phillip smiled but was able to practice more reserve.

The sorceress shrugged and gave him a pity-me look. "Being a shifter is not as glamorous as it may sound. I couldn't control it as an infant. Sometimes I would change shape for thinking of something too hard. I spent half a week as a sack of flour once. I've changed form so many times I forgot what I looked like in the first place."

"Is there a time limit?" Seventh Night asked.

The sorceress frowned. "To what?"

"Kaleb," she reminded her. "Curing Kaleb."

"Oh. I don't think so," the sorceress replied. "As long as he's still alive that is. I think it's a very potent sleeping potion, but things do go wrong. Who is this for again?"

"The prince," Seventh Night said.

"My brother," Neithan said at the same time.

"His identical twin brother," Phillip added.

The sorceress lifted her eyebrows. "You

mean there's two of him?" she asked, gesturing to Neithan. Phillip nodded. The sorceress laughed. "Interesting."

"Are you sure?" Seventh Night asked.

The sorceress gave her an odd look. "You're not following the conversation are you?" she asked Seven.

Seven looked at her as though she had just noticed the sorceress' presence. "No. But, are you sure about the cure? A kiss is rather hard to swallow."

"You'd be surprised," the sorceress said. "A kiss is the cure for many ills and seventeen types of poison."

Seventh Night shook her head in disbelief. "It sounds like something out of a storybook."

The sorceress put her hands on her hips. "Where do you think the storybooks got it?" Her eyes flickered around the small dwelling and settled on the three. "There isn't anything else to discuss we can't go over later," she said. "Shall we go?"

"Yes," Phillip agreed. "We should."

"You two and Her Highness there get the water we'll need from the well. It's drinkable. I'll pack." The sorceress shooed them out the door. After they left, she cleaned off her shelves and carefully stacked one item after another on the table. The three returned as she was placing the last book on top of the others.

"Have you decided what to take?" Phillip asked her.

She blew the dust off a book cover and coughed. "I'm taking everything," she said. Phillip looked at the pile in despair. They could not carry everything unless the sorceress could conjure up a wagon. "Don't worry," the sorceress assured Phillip. "I'll take care of it."

She took one of the powder sacks, sprinkled its contents over her belongings, and began to chant, "*Magna ina parwa, parwa ina minerat.*" The books quivered a little, then shrank quickly and almost violently.

Phillip knelt near the table for a better look at the miniature belongings. Even the large black cauldron was small enough to hold in one hand. The sorceress carefully collected her belongings in a small bag. Beside the door a cloak hung on a peg. The sorceress placed the cloak around her. Beneath where the cloak had hung, a bow and quiver of arrows lay against the wall. She slid these over her shoulder. "Shouldn't we get moving?" the sorceress said and headed outside.

As they followed her, Phillip whispered to Seventh Night, "Now, I believe in magic."

The problem arose, while they were preparing to leave, of how to manage the riding arrangement. There were four horses, but one was a packhorse and could not manage a rider with its load. This left three riding horses. Seventh Night wondered who would walk and when.

Neithan had an idea, but Phillip was quicker. "My lady," Phillip said to the sorceress, "I would be honored if you would ride with me."

The sorceress smiled. "I accept, my lord," she said with a comic curtsey. Phillip helped her mount Thunder; the unicorn was strong and had already proved it could handle two riders. The sorceress had no leggings so she was obliged to ride sidesaddle. Phillip climbed up behind her, and Neithan and Seventh Night mounted their unicorns.

Seventh Night glared at the magician's apprentice and her future fake-husband-brother-in-law and shook her head at how ridiculous men made themselves over an attractive woman. She had no clear words for her indignation and soon settled into distracting thoughts of her own prince.

"You haven't told us your name," Neithan prompted the sorceress.

"To be honest, I don't have one," the sorceress said.

"How's that?" Phillip asked, brushing her copper curls out of his face.

The sorceress pulled her hair in front and tied it so it would not bother him. "My mother abandoned me when I was very young," she said. "My father died before I was born. He was a real magician.

"I probably had a name, but I don't remember it. I've been called several names: witch, urchin, and a few I'd rather not repeat in present company." The sorceress rattled this list off in a matter-of-fact way as if she was telling what happened to her on the way to the marketplace. There were no tears, bitterness, or traces of embellishment.

"Why do you live out here?" Neithan asked.

The sorceress shrugged. "The people in my home town were afraid of me and banished me when I was twelve. They would have done it before, but this nice old man stopped them. He called me 'Little', but I don't think that's my proper name, and I don't suggest any of you try calling me that. Then he died. I'm a bit of a jinx aren't I? Anyway, they didn't want me anywhere else in Gourlin so I came here."

"You come from Gourlin?" Neithan asked in surprise.

The sorceress gave him an odd look. "Yes, I just said that."

Neithan's brow creased in confusion, and Phillip explained, "There's a deep dislike of anything or anyone from Gourlin in Cordance. Sworn enemies."

"Do you think I'm your enemy, Neithan?" asked the sorceress, sounding more curious than offended.

The prince shook his head, slowly, as though working something out. He flushed again under the sorceress's gaze. "I've been raised to trust nothing from Gourlin."

"Your brother's life may hang on your trust of me," said the sorceress.

"My brother teases me for the simplicity of my thinking," said Neithan.

"That's not very kind of him," said the sorceress.

Neithan shrugged. "I like being simple. I tease him for being too complicated."

"If it comforts you," said Phillip, "she was banished from Gourlin."

"It does," Neithan admitted.

Phillip changed the topic by asking the sorceress how she had eked out a life in the desert. This supplied several miles of conversation between the two while Neithan listened and Seventh Night chewed quietly on her thoughts.

CHAPTER VII

A CLEAR NIGHT

Tired but restless, Seventh Night and Neithan sat near the opening of the horses' tent. The sorceress had spread her cloak out on the sand and laid back to watch the stars with her arms folded under her head. Meanwhile, Phillip paced. It was still the cool night; though they had traveled through most of it. There was a small campfire burning, making the last of the darkness comfortable. The moon was waning, and the light from the flames cast odd shadows. In the distance the mountain could be seen over the sand dunes.

They were less than a day away from the mountain tunnel entrance. They might have gone further, but the sorceress insisted she needed darkness to fall asleep. The group had finished setting up camp sooner than expected and was attempting to find something to pass the time.

Phillip stopped pacing and removed a pack from Thunder's saddle. He sat down on the sand and rummaged through it.

Seventh Night watched him curiously. "What is that?" she asked.

"This?" Phillip said as he pulled a long wooden box from the sack. "This is my necessary pack. I can live off what's in it."

"Oh..." she said. Seventh Night wanted to make him think she did not care, but curiosity tugged at her like a noose. "What's in it?"

"A few coins, an extra cloak..." He opened the wooden box and showed her the flute it contained. Gingerly he lifted the flute and held it. "...my flute, and a special powder."

Seventh Night jumped at the chance to challenge him. "How in the world is a flute a necessity?"

Phillip looked hurt. "I can make a living from it."

Seventh Night looked as closely at the flute as possible from a distance. "Can you play?" she asked.

"Well enough," he said. "But I prefer another method." He pulled a leather bag from his sack. The bag was just small enough he could hold it with one hand. Phillip opened the bag and sprinkled some powder from it onto the flute.

The princess's brow creased. "What are you doing?"

"Seven, I'm going to tell you a story," Phillip said. Seventh Night began to tell him she did not want to hear it, but he would most likely tell it anyway. She sighed and settled in to listen. "This is Potkope powder," he began.

Suddenly, the sorceress became interested. "Potkope?" she repeated, rolling up to a sitting position. "Where'd you get it?"

"A small shop in Linten," Phillip said, eager to continue. "The owner had somehow obtained a load of the stuff and was trying to sell it to the townspeople. I was passing through and stopped to watch the demonstration. The shopkeeper had five instruments playing at once. All the skeptics were trying to figure out the trick or find strings attached. I thought it would be good fun to watch and try to figure it out for myself."

"Wait," Seventh Night interrupted. "What are you talking about? What is Popkok?"

"It's Potkope," Phillip corrected her. He wanted to savor her ignorance and rub it in slowly, but the sorceress could not wait for that.

"It's this amazing magic powder made from the ground seeds of the Potkop flower that grows only on a small floating island northwest of Cordance; the island floats around so it's almost never in quite the same place and practically impossible to find." Neithan almost applauded after the sorceress finished for she had not taken a single breath. "Potkope can make an inanimate object do a single task on its own," the sorceress continued. "But the catch is the person has to have the right spirit." Seventh Night knitted her brow, trying to make sense of what the sorceress said.

"May I continue?" Phillip asked. The sorceress nodded. "The townspeople were not convinced, or if they were, they did not see the use in owning any of it. So, the shopkeeper got one of the farmers to run get his plow. The man brought the plow, and the shopkeeper sprinkled it with the Potkope. The shopkeeper then had one of the hardest working farmers tell the plow to plow. Immediately, the plow started to move. The townspeople were convinced, and all the powder was sold before I had a chance to buy any.

"I was a little short on deriks anyway, so I asked the shopkeeper if he had any work for me. He did. I had been working a week when the first disappointed customer came to demand his money back for the powder. The shopkeeper insisted the man was simply using the powder incorrectly and showed him again. After the man was satisfied, he left. But the next day another customer complained and another and another. The shopkeeper did not have enough to return their money, and the townspeople were getting hostile. I sympathized with him and offered to buy some of the powder back from the townspeople. He would buy the rest out of his pocket, and I would work it off."

Seventh Night tried not to laugh, but she could not help it. "You are rather dull, Magician. Why did you waste your earnings like that?"

SEVENTH NIGHT

"Seven, you don't understand," Phillip protested. "He was telling the truth. There was nothing wrong with the powder; it was the people who used it." Seventh Night seemed confused, but Phillip doubted she would ever admit that. He tried to explain in a way that would not be too damaging to her pride. "You see, most of the people who used the powder grew lazy at heart. They had no will to do the work when they found something else would do it for them, and the powder could no longer work for them."

Seventh Night nodded as if she understood. "What do you use it for, Magician?" she asked.

"Music," he said. "It plays a different song for everyone. Usually I find a child's song is the purest, the sweetest. When I'm in need or find my life getting dull, I let a child tell the flute to play."

"Don't you ever tell it yourself?" the sorceress asked.

"No," Phillip answered. "I'm too afraid of what I might hear, or I'm afraid the song will be too short. Besides the kids always get a kick out of it. Would you do it, Seven?"

Seventh Night shrugged and leaned forward

to blow across the mouthpiece of the flute Phillip had held out for her. "Play," she said. She had time to sit back and think about telling Phillip, "I told you so," before the flute began to play by itself. It twirled while it played, suspended in the air. Neithan's eyes grew wide. Seventh Night listened to the music and kept switching her stare from Phillip to the flute to Phillip again. The sorceress simply smiled and laughed at their reaction.

The tune was lively and sweet. Lively enough it was nearly impossible to keep from tapping a foot softly or swaying in time, but sweet enough any listener had to respect the pureness of it. The flute hung in the air playing its tune without missing a note. The music was flawless as if the great composers of all time had spent centuries perfecting it. After the first few minutes, the shock wore off. Seventh Night felt compelled to stand and dance. There was nothing to stop her. She stayed seated as long as her pride could hold her, but the music melted her resistance. She stood and took a few steps away from the others to an empty patch of sand, where she danced slowly and elegantly with an invisible partner.

SEVENTH NIGHT

The others were conscious of her movement but more interested in the tune. When the music started obviously repeating itself, Phillip lost interest. He watched Seven in her graceful dance. It took him a moment to conclude her invisible partner was truly not there. He bit his lip while considering the idea, then he stood and walked beside her. Phillip bowed in a slightly exaggerated manner, and Seven stopped dancing. "May I cut in?" he asked. Seven seemed a little taken aback by the request; then she smiled and without a word offered her hand. Their dance had never been performed and never would be again except by lovers and children who had never learned how.

Neithan and the sorceress watched their companions, wondering whether they had taken leave of their senses or taken the only sensible option. Neithan had left dancing to his brother. The rigid routine of court dancing with its audience had never appealed to him, but this looked like fun, the only sensible thing to do with a clear night and a magic flute. He stood, brushed the sand from his clothes, and turned to the sorceress. "My lady, may I have the honor of this dance?"

"You may, my lord," the sorceress said. She stood and brushed the sand from her simple dress. Soon, they were all dancing and laughing. A cure of a different type, which no magic or potion could substitute.

Then the music changed. It became intense and almost frightening. Seventh Night stopped dancing; no one could dance to the new music anyway. The mood spoiled, the four sat back down and listened to the strange melody. "Why did it change?" Seven asked at last. Phillip shrugged. The sorceress said nothing but listened to the music as if reading it.

The tune turned from frightening to sad. Seventh Night was at the point of breaking the flute when it let out a victorious chord. The music changed back to a more inviting melody. Not the same as before, different, but just as beautiful.

They were too tired to dance so they sat and listened. The tune was less steady than before. At times it would quicken, become more adventurous and every once in a while a sad note. Over all, though, it was too lovely for words.

Seventh Night laid her forehead on her knees to hide a tear. It was silly to cry. She must be tired. She wiped the tear and raised her head.

After the music stopped, the sorceress announced she was tired, and she was going to sleep. Neithan said that was a good idea and followed her to the tents. Phillip returned his belongings to the sack. Seventh Night stood and stretched her stiff muscles. She was not in the least bit sleepy. The music had reminded her of several unanswered questions, and she intended to ask Phillip each one of them for no other reason than retribution. She was irritated with him about something.

Phillip had busied himself making sure the unicorns were taken care of. Seventh Night made a stepping stool out of some thick, flat firewood that had once served as the sorceress' table and watched him over Thunder's back. She crossed her arms on the unicorn's back and tried not to lean too hard.

"Good night, Seven," Phillip said as he started to brush down the grey unicorn.

"Not quite," Seventh Night countered. "You have not been truthful with me."

Phillip did not turn around to answer. "What do you mean?"

"You said you did not know whether or not

you believed in magic," Seventh Night reminded him. "Then you bring out that flute."

"That's no lie, Seven," Phillip said. "I didn't rule out the possibility that it might be something other than magic. A freak of nature, a miracle, maybe a coincidence of the wind and the time and the position being right, maybe some force other than magic."

After she was sure he was not jesting with her, Seventh Night laughed. "Magician, you certainly have some strange ideas."

"That's the common opinion," he reflected. "I don't drink beer or other liquors; I don't smoke a pipe; I don't swear; I don't gamble," for the first time, he glanced quickly at Seven, "or indulge in anything else a good boy shouldn't."

"You don't?" She frowned. "But you told the bandits you won Thunder in a bet?"

"Well, that's not completely true," Phillip admitted, lifting the unicorn's hoof to check its shoe. "Lord Harold wanted to breed some winged unicorns. I grew up 'round horses and had some ideas on how this might best be done. Lord Harold made me a deal...though he called it a bet at one point. If I could breed and raise at least ten winged unicorns, I could choose one.

I did it, and I chose Thunder. Lord Harold was delighted at my decision. No one would buy a black unicorn anyway, too many superstitious. It didn't make a difference to him that Thunder was the smartest and strongest." Thunder looked at Phillip and tossed his head as if to say that much was obvious. Phillip smiled and patted Thunder's neck. "I got the best of that deal."

Seventh Night lifted her eyebrows. "Should I ask where you get these ideas?"

Phillip shrugged. "A group in Gourlin was trying to spread their views before I left, and I agreed with them."

"When were you in Gourlin?"

"I was born there," Phillip said, finally looking at her and taking delight in the brief moment of curiosity in her eyes. "When I was eleven, my father and I traveled with a caravan on route to Tivin. The caravan was attacked by a band of thieves. My father was killed or ran off; I don't know. They didn't notice or ignored me, and after they left, I traveled the rest of the way to Cordance on foot."

Seventh Night was not sure what to think. Her mother hated travel and the treaty with Cordance. She would miss the wedding, and

Seventh Night would most likely only be able to talk to her through letters. That was bad enough, but the thought of either of her parents dying was too horrible. "What about your mother?" she asked Phillip carefully.

Phillip shrugged. "Supposedly she died in child birth, but who knows. My father didn't like to talk about it. Don't look so sympathetic," he warned Seven. "I don't need pity. I didn't know either of them very well, and I've done just fine since then. I don't hold any grudges either, so don't worry about it. If you need someone to lend your sympathy, I know plenty of orphans and paupers I can introduce."

If he did not want sympathy, she was determined not to give him any, but Seventh Night wanted to get off the unpleasant subject. "The bandits knew you," she said. "How? They weren't the same ones that attacked your father's caravan?"

Phillip shook his head and returned to grooming. "When I reached Cordance, I got a job with a merchant caravan. They paid me to help with the horses and play my flute during travels. We rode in a group most of the time, but come fall, one of the merchants had to travel on his own down the same road on which you were attacked. I had gone with him and fell asleep in the wagon.

"While I was sleeping, the same group of bandits that attacked you robbed the man and took the cart into the woods. They discovered me in there and were ready to slit my throat to get me out of the way. At least, they said they were. May have just wanted to give me a good scare. Jonhan, the big bandit that recognized me, was the leader's son. He decided to have some fun before he killed me. He took me by the heels, hung me upside down, and asked why he shouldn't kill me on the spot. I was too terrified to speak, and he started to shake me, asking what was the matter with me. The shaking loosened the flute from my shirt. I grabbed hold of it and took a deep breath. He stopped shaking me, and I blew.

"He practically dropped me. I took the time I had been allowed and started to play. The only thing I could manage was an old nursery tune the merchant had been singing." He stopped a moment to hum a piece.

"I wander here and there,
Withou' a derk to spare.

Someday I'll stop and settle,
Find a wife to fire the kettle.
Bring in a sum quite splendid,
And woefully watch her spend it,
On silks and furs for swine..."

He flushed slightly when he realized he had been singing. Seventh Night gave him a look saying she hoped he played better than he sang. He cleared his throat and continued. "Despite that, they were impressed and let me stay with them. Jonhan declared that was 'good playin' for a little Sprat', and I was never called anything else.

"I stayed for three years. Learned all kind of interesting things such as pickpocketing, lock picking, and stew ingredient picking. In other words, I did a lot of picking." Seven grimaced at the bad pun. "Apology offered for that," Phillip said. "I was a good pickpocket, though, but I never kept anything I took. I'd always end up running after the person and telling them that they had dropped whatever I had taken. Eventually, I got tired and morally unnerved by the crook's life and left. Jonhan's father wasn't in the best health when I left, so I suppose he's the leader now."

"A village," Seven repeated to herself. "An entire village of thieves?"

Phillip nodded. "Hidden in the forest. It's small, not really big enough to be called a village, more of a hamlet. For the most part, the bandits are just normal people, a ruder, uneducated, less refined type of normal, but people just the same. They only robbed every once in a while when someone was foolhardy enough to travel through alone."

"Like me," Seven offered.

"Exactly. Oh, Seven, I've been meaning to ask you something." Phillip stopped grooming and faced her. She gestured for him to ask away. "How does Tivin get by without taxes?"

"By the skin of our teeth," Seventh Night answered. "The deal is that as long as the towns manage their own up keep and the royal family is provided for, we will not use taxes. The laws are more specific than that, but that's the basic idea. If the people did not meet this condition, we were to go back to the old system. It was a nice plan in theory, but my grandfather made one mistake when he set it up. Without the taxes, we do not have enough money for an army or soldiers to enforce any taxes to raise the money to get one. The little army we have is supported by the farms belonging to my father. The nobles have their own soldiers, but in the case of war they would most likely be kept back to defend the noble's home instead of the country.

"That is the reason this marriage is so important. Tivin will adopt Cordance's taxes. The nobles will not be too thrilled about that, but they will like the access to Cordance's harbor. The sea is being used more and more for trade. And anyone who wishes to complain can do so to Cordance's army." She smiled as if the thought pleased her.

"Sounds great, but it'll take some getting used to," Phillip said. "Answer me one more question. You told Neithan or...You said your carriage wheel broke, and the man made one too small. I know I'm not an expert at these things, but didn't you have a spare or something?"

Seven frowned. "That is the odd thing. We did have several spares in storage, but they were all stolen. If that were not enough...I do not understand the blacksmith. He has been with us for years; he never makes mistakes like that."

"Sounds like sabotage," Phillip offered.

"Those were my thoughts also," Seven

agreed. "That's why I tried riding in disguise. I suppose I should have told Neithan right away, but he seemed so happy to see me...Kaleb that is...I didn't want to worry him."

"Even after the poisoning? You know they were about to blame you for it, before I interrupted."

"Were they?" Seventh Night sighed. "To be completely truthful I forgot about it in the excitement."

Phillip smiled sympathetically at her. "You don't look excited. You look tired."

Seventh Night suppressed a yawn. "I am not in the least bit."

Phillip chuckled. He walked around to her and pulled her off the makeshift stepping stool. "Goodnight, Seven." She shook her head half in protest, half in assent. They walked out together into the new morning.

Seventh Night squinted in the glare of the sun off the sand. The desert looked even more unwelcoming in the day. She pulled her hood up to help shade her eyes. "I wonder if this is what death looks like."

"The desert isn't dead," Phillip said. Seventh Night wondered if the sun was affecting him.

"Come on," he said. "I'll show you." He took her by the arm and pulled her after him. Phillip led her behind the tent to a short cactus which was just opening its blooms. Magenta flowers with thin yellow strips, similar in size and shape to the morning glories which had grown outside Seventh Night's window, slowly revealed themselves.

Careful not to prick himself, Phillip picked the largest bloom and presented it to her. "A flower for my lady," he said. Seventh Night was not sure whether he was trying to be gallant or comical, but she accepted the cactus flower with a smile. She put her nose to it and found it to be a sweeter scent than expected. "Thank you," she said, admiring the petals.

Phillip took the moment and kissed her squarely on the lips.

At first Seventh Night was too surprised to do anything, but then she slapped him. "Never!" she hissed at him. "Never, kiss me like that again!"

Phillip was an incredibly annoying mixture of intelligence and simplicity. His answer only proved this further to the Princess of Tivin. "How should I kiss you?"

SEVENTH NIGHT

Seventh Night balled her fist. For a moment, she just glared at him. It had no effect on his steady gaze, so she stomped her boot and let out a frustrated noise somewhere between a grunt and a scream and stormed off to her tent.

Phillip watched her go and wondered whether he should be proud or ashamed of himself.

CHAPTER VIII

A HAPPY ENDING

Prince Kaleb slept peacefully now. The fever had faded away days ago, but the perfect still that followed had not given the Magician Gadolin much hope. The prince was cold, his breathing slow. They had not been able to get a drop of water or morsel of food into him, so it was a wonder the prince showed any signs of life at all.

Fearing the worst, Gadolin had maintained his banishment of everyone but the king and queen from the tower. The king had only found time for short visits, but the queen had taken her turns at vigil, optimistically embroidering the edge of the wedding veil while she watched her sleeping son.

It had been seven nights since the prince had been poisoned. If things had gone smoothly, this would have been a day of celebration, a wedding day. Instead the castle was in a state of unrest and suspicion. The king had refused to let anyone leave until his son returned and his investigation was finished. Contrary to Sir Afphan's prediction, there was no report of any servant, soldier, or noble fleeing their post.

A messenger had brought the news that Tivin's king and his traveling entourage had arrived at Fortesdale and were passing the evening at Lord Harold's estate. Lord Harold had vouched for the character and cleverness of his new apprentice, and Neithan was steady and reliable. But the wisdom of allowing the princess to ride with them came more in question with each passing moment.

The sun was rising over the mountains when the magician heard steps in the hall. Gadolin watched from the prince's bedside as they came through the door in order of height.

Seventh Night, then Phillip, followed by a strange redheaded woman he did not know, and finally Neithan. They were still in their traveling clothes. "Did you find her?" he asked.

Phillip nodded and gestured to the red haired woman. Gadolin stood and cleared his throat. "Madam, do you believe you can cure him?"

"I believe I could," the sorceress said. "But that might prove embarrassing, so she'll do it." She placed a hand on Seventh's shoulder. Gadolin's brow furrowed with confusion and skepticism.

"I'll explain later," Phillip said.

Seventh Night bit her lip nervously. "What if I can not?" she asked the sorceress.

"The world ends," the sorceress teased. Seventh Night's eyes widened, and she quickly amended herself. "Don't worry about it. Remember the flute. Anyone who can produce music like that is full of love."

Seventh Night took a deep breath. She took several steps toward the sleeping prince and turned back around. "Could we be alone?" she asked almost timidly.

"You, you, you out," the sorceress said pointing to the magician, the magician's apprentice, and the other prince in turn. "But I want to watch." Before Seventh Night could object, she continued. "This is just like the fairytales. I told you the cure; you owe me. I'll stand to the side and be quiet." Seventh Night threw up her hand in a submissive gesture. Silently, Neithan followed Gadolin out the door. Phillip lingered a moment.

Seventh Night continued to Kaleb's bedside and sat beside him on the spread. Phillip turned to leave, and the sorceress caught him by the shoulder. "You're not going to stay?" she whispered.

"No," Phillip answered softly and slipped out. The sorceress shrugged and returned to watch the show.

Seventh Night hesitated. It was not that she did not want to kiss Kaleb; she did. But doubts returned. What if this did not work and the sorceress really was a mad woman, as she had first thought? Or worse, what if the sorceress was genuine, but she was as coldhearted as the winter winds? Often she thought things more than she felt them. Seventh Night took a deep breath; only one way to know.

SEVENTH NIGHT

She kissed him and waited.

Slowly, Kaleb's eyes opened. He yawned and propped himself up with his elbows. Seventh Night threw her arms around his neck. "Good morning," she whispered, fighting tears. Shortly, she conquered them and sat back, and Kaleb looked at her in confusion.

"What happened?" he asked blinking sleep from his eyes.

Seventh Night smiled at him. "It is a long story."

Finally Kaleb recognized her. "Princess," he said touching her cheek. "You're even more beautiful. I have so much to tell you."

"I know...Kaleb," she said. Kaleb stared at her for a moment, then smiled and embraced her. They held each other, whispering their love. The sorceress smiled from her watching place and bounced on her heels. She loved happy endings.

ACT II
MONSTERS & MAGIC

CHAPTER IX

WHAT THEY LEAVE OUT IN FAIRYTALES

His reunion with the princess was cut short when Kaleb noticed the tall redhead watching from across the room. Seventh Night pulled back to explain her presence. While she was explaining, Neithan knocked on the door wanting to see if he had awakened. Kaleb naturally welcomed his brother inside, though he was a little surprised to see him with others around.

Neithan was followed by the young man who

had ridden into the castle with Seventh Night. The youth glanced in to see that Kaleb was awake, but otherwise hung back at the door and kept an eye on the hallway. Gadolin came into the room, brushing past his apprentice. He took Kaleb by the shoulders. His bright, wrinkled eyes became misty. Kaleb laughed off the old man's concerns but started feeling all the aches as the rest of his body awakened.

"I better go and let you dress," the princess said and laughed at her own dusty, unfeminine attire. "I need to clean up."

She skipped to the door and stopped at the redheaded woman. "Perhaps we should...?"

"What?" the woman replied in mock surprise. "Are dirty rag dresses not fashionable now? Oh dear."

"I didn't mean..."

"Oh, I'm not offended," the other woman laughed. "By all means, dress me."

Neithan grabbed a long cloak from the dresser and gave it to the princess to hide her soldier's costume for the trip downstairs. Seventh Night draped the cape about her shoulders, and it hung to the floor, giving the illusion of more feminine apparel. The two women disappeared out the door, and the youth followed them into the hall.

With the ladies gone, Gadolin began addressing Kaleb's recovery. They helped the prince stand. Kaleb found his legs more wobbly than he had hoped but managed to stay upright. After he promised Gadolin that he would follow all his advice, the old man left to tell the king and queen the good news.

Once they were alone, Neithan embraced his brother tightly. Kaleb realized then how serious his condition must have been. He returned the embrace awkwardly. When Neithan released him, Kaleb asked him questions about what had transpired. Neithan explained in his way, with few words and fewer details.

"What they leave out in fairytales are the bed sores and the muscle cramps," Kaleb told Neithan later. He paced around the bedroom, rolling his shoulders, stopping occasionally to twist his leg in defiance of a particularly stiff muscle.

Neithan stood before the mirror, shaving his

stubble, while Kaleb tested his muscles. "They have any idea who was behind this?" Kaleb asked.

Neithan stopped to clean his razor and shook his head. "I assume Gadolin would have said."

"What about this new apprentice of his?" Kaleb continued. "He arrived the day I was poisoned, and if I understand the story, left the castle before he was searched."

Neithan frowned uncertainly. "Why would he do that?"

"To bring that sorceress here," Kaleb suggested.

"No," said Neithan.

"It's just a theory," Kaleb said. "But he didn't look happy to see me awake."

"Then why would he take us to the one person who knew how to wake you?" Neithan asked.

Kaleb shrugged and sat down on the end of the bed. "Why would anyone give me a sleeping potion?" He rubbed his neck muscles and looked at his brother with eyes that seemed to apologize for his indisposition. "It clearly wasn't intended to harm me. You made it back by the scheduled wedding day. They didn't even manage to delay the wedding."

SEVENTH NIGHT

"The nobles agreed to wait until you're fully recovered," Neithan assured him.

Kaleb smiled. "That's much appreciated. I'd rather be in best health for my bride. What do you think? A fortnight?"

"If that's what you need," Neithan agreed. "I could use a rest myself."

"You browned your skin in the desert," Kaleb noted.

"I'll stay down in the caves for a bit," Neithan said.

"I'll try to take some sun in the gardens," said Kaleb. "We'll even out."

Neithan wiped his face with a warm, wet cloth, patted it with a dry towel, and sat beside his brother.

"How did Seventh Night take the news?" Kaleb asked, studying his hands.

Neithan chuckled. "She fainted when she first saw me, but she was already under a lot of strain. I think she took things very well, considering. Seemed to be glad it was you she was marrying."

Kaleb covered his face with his hands in a tired gesture. "I wanted to be the one to tell her, to end the lie."

SEVENTH NIGHT

Neithan placed a reassuring hand on his twin's back.

"The two weeks I ask is more for her than me," Kaleb continued. "I need to make sure everything is fully explained. You made it clear that she's only to be bride to one of us?"

"I think so."

Kaleb sighed. "That would be any sensible lady's first concern, of course. I know your character, Neithan, but you're new to her. And it is your birthright."

"If we didn't fear it might invalidate the treaty, I'd let you marry her openly," Neithan said. "You've had to sacrifice your own name for mine. It's a small sacrifice in return, and I'm glad to make it for you."

Kaleb studied his brother's earnest expression and allowed a slow grin. "I hope you always feel that way, for I'm far too greedy not to take advantage of your generosity."

Neithan laughed. "I hope you get a chance to talk to this sorceress we brought back. I think then you couldn't suspect her. She's...very clever. The magic she can do is remarkable."

"So you've seen her do more than prescribe cures to fairytale complaints?" Kaleb asked.

Neithan nodded. "She's impressive."

"And attractive?"

Neithan shrugged.

Kaleb gave him a thin smile. "Pretty faces fade, brother. Our princess, my princess, is a woman of good wit and character. This sorceress may have earned her banishment. You are too quick to trust."

Neithan returned a tired smile of his own. "I'll give up a bride for you, Kaleb, but you must allow me to choose my own friends."

Kaleb placed his arm around Neithan's shoulder. "I'm merely being protective, Neithan. Someone did try to poison us after all."

After a week's constant ride in the desert, Seventh Night enjoyed the cool stone of the castle. She slept late when possible; her father's arrival demanded fresh feasts and state meetings. The queen arranged a dance to help restore everyone to a festive mood; though there were food tasters to remind her that the poisoner had yet to be caught. She saw a lot of Kaleb and could already distinguish between him and his brother, but time alone with him had been limited to quick whispers.

There was an open carriage ride around the main streets of Pinnacle City to reassure the common people that their beloved prince was well and that his bride had arrived safely. Kaleb held her hand through the entirety of the procession, and he felt warm and strong.

Phillip hovered around Gadolin and smiled whenever she glanced at him. She helped him find a book he had been sent for one evening in the library, and he had been so polite and unassuming she was ready to forgive him for his bad judgment. They had both been tired after a long journey.

She would not wish harm on Kaleb again, but she was a little glad for their time in the desert. It had given her a chance to get to know Neithan, and having a little adventure that ended happily was fun in retrospect. She had certainly learned more about the world. There was magic, there was life in the desert, and there were some good people that came from Gourlin.

More through accident than planning, she found some time to explore the castle that was to be her new home. The palace in Tivin was large but regular in its layout. The castle at Pinnacle was a maze of sections and corridors sitting on top of the secret maze that laced through the mountain.

The castle had been so busy, it was nice to find a quiet corridor. Curious, she opened closed doors, knocking gently first to avoid disturbing anyone. The first two yielded quietly to her touch. There was a room for scribes, full of quills, shelves, and small tables, sitting empty. The scribes had most likely been given the week off for celebration. The next room seemed to be serving as a large closet. Odd pieces of dusty furniture were stacked together to one side, while extra buckets and barrels blocked the window. The princess made a mental note to inventory the contents later and see them put to better use.

She knocked on the third door down the hall and again got no answer. She tried the door, but it refused to budge. An unpleasant tingle crept over her shoulder and down her back. She wiggled the handle to no avail. The panic began rising. Her rational mind told her there was no need for it. She should move on to the next door or find someone with a key, but the hall was empty. She pushed the door, pulled at it, and with a last grunt of frustration hit it. Now her hand hurt, and since there was no one about, she allowed herself a whimper.

"Is everything all right?"

She knew the voice, and it made her wince again. "I'm fine," she said, keeping her face turned away to hide her embarrassment.

"You're shuddering," Phillip said, placing his hand on her upper arm.

Seventh Night forced a laugh. "The door's locked. I had a moment of frustration."

"Do you need into the room?" Phillip asked.

Seventh Night shook her head. "No, I—I just don't like locks," she admitted. She could feel Phillip continuing to stare at her. He was like a dog with a bone when he wanted to know something, and she knew he would not let it go. "It's silly. They just...I really don't like locked doors. I have a key to everything in Tivin."

"I'm afraid of drowning," Phillip said. Seventh Night looked up at him curiously. "I mean I'm not afraid of drowning right now, but I never learned how to swim properly. The idea of deep water and fast current...not being able to breathe. Those are nightmares that hang with me the next morning."

"People die from drowning," Seventh Night said with a small smile. "People fall off cliffs and get bitten by snakes and spiders. Those are natural fears; no one dies from locks. But they make me feel like I can't breathe."

"Did you get trapped in a locked room?"

Seventh Night shook her head. "No. My nursemaid used to threaten to lock me in the tower if I was bad though. She never did, but the idea frightened me."

"Scary tower?"

Seventh Night shook her head again. "I used to play there. It was just the idea of the lock, of not being able to leave."

Phillip glanced at the door handle. "It's still bothering you, isn't it?"

Seventh Night started to dismiss the idea but caught herself and nodded.

Phillip surprised her by dropping to his knees and motioning for her to do the same. "I'll teach you how to pick the lock," he explained.

"Wouldn't it be easier to find someone with a key?"

"There may not always be a key."

Seventh Night checked the hall again. "This

is not a dignified occupation for a princess."

"And that temper tantrum I caught you having was dignified?"

Seventh Night flushed again and tucked the fabric of her rose red dress under her knees as she knelt.

"I don't have my normal lock picking tools with me..." Phillip began,"...but, I think we can use..." His eyes searched her hair, and his deft fingers pulled out a hair pin. "You can spare this for a little bit."

Seventh Night opened her mouth but gave up on rebuking him. It seemed as productive as telling the tide not to make waves.

"There are better tools, but this will work in a pinch," Phillip explained. "Here. Look." He bent the pin, inserted it into the lock, wiggled and twisted, asked for a second hair pin and a third, explaining as best he could the reasoning behind his experiments as he went. Seventh Night did her best to follow, wishing she could see the hidden mechanics inside that he was describing. After a while, he placed the pins in her hands and asked her to give it a try.

"Why did they bother teaching you lock picking and pickpocketing if the thieves from the forest only attacked lone merchants on the road?" Seventh Night asked while she squinted at the lock and twisted the pins inside it.

"Oh, well, they'd have us sneak into Pinnacle City too. They just were more careful not to draw attention since there were soldiers 'round."

Seventh Night grimaced. "I think it's horrid. Teaching children to steal. They ought to be rounded up."

Phillip took a slow breath. "You're probably right, but don't ask me to lead you to them, okay? They did shelter me for three years."

"No," the princess agreed. "I wouldn't ask you that."

"Try angling it this way," he said, moving her hand and the pin into a new position.

There was a satisfying click sound. Seventh Night pulled on the latch and the door cracked open. She laughed and took an easy breath.

"Good, I can train you with proper picks next time."

"How long did it take you to learn?"

Phillip sniffed. "A few weeks, but you have a better teacher."

"You're a little arrogant," Seventh Night admonished, but she gave him a grateful hug.

"Thank you."

Phillip returned the squeeze but resisted the urge to prolong the embrace. "I was joking. I was twelve and a little distracted."

They helped each other to their feet and peeked inside the now unlocked room.

"Scrolls?"

"Probably records," Seventh Night said, pulling the door shut. "I should have left it locked."

"I can tell Gadolin. He'll fix it," said Phillip. "I think he knows all the secrets of the castle."

"Does he know his apprentice is a lockpick?"

Phillip shrugged. "Lord Harold arranged things for me, but I don't think it ever came up."

"How did you meet Lord Harold?"

"Linten," Phillip said. "After I left the forest, I tried traveling down the coast. He was there buying supplies, and I overheard him talking about his stables. He wanted to get into the business of horse breeding, winged unicorns specifically. I'd been brought up in the stables, so I started talking to him about it."

"Just pranced up to a nobleman and started chatting?"

"Lord Harold doesn't judge men by the amount of land they own."

"I didn't mean... Lord Harold is a very affable man, but not all the noblemen I know are so gracious. I've noticed most commoners approach with caution and youths only when they're summoned."

Phillip grinned and shrugged. "I had no idea who he was. I just heard him talking about unicorns and had something to say on the subject. I'd always wanted a pegasus."

"You have something to say on every subject." Seventh Night started replacing her hair pins. "I miss Toshk."

"You should take a ride on Thunder. He'd like the exercise."

Seventh Night smiled. "Maybe after the wedding."

Phillip shifted uncomfortably. "Neithan said Kaleb was a bit of a flirt."

"Good day, Magician." Seventh Night inclined her head a bit and turned on her heels.

CHAPTER X

COURTSHIP

Seventh Night stalked back in the direction of her room. She believed the magician's apprentice meant well, but every time she started to think he might be a good friend, he would say something to prickle her. Avoiding him was unlikely to be an option. He was already entrusted with her princes' secret, and as Gadolin's apprentice, he would be taking the old man's place eventually.

She turned the corner and found the prince waiting at her door. She patted her hair, wishing she had time to check the pins' replacement in a mirror before she had met him. "Prince Neithan..." she said, remembering it was best to use the public name for both of them until she was sure of privacy.

Kaleb knew this too but looked a little disappointed. He quickly recovered and returned her smile. "I thought you might like to take a walk in the gardens."

"Very much so," she said eagerly. "Would you wait a moment?"

He nodded, and she hurried into the room to fix her hair in the mirror and check there was no lingering dust on her knees. She wanted to look her best for him, but it seemed a greater disservice to leave him waiting in the hall too long.

When she reemerged from the room, Kaleb made no remark but graciously offered his arm. She smiled as she placed her hand on it. It was easy to smile around Kaleb. He had such perfect manners. Maybe she could get him to train Gadolin's apprentice.

"How is Neithan doing?" she asked quietly. "I haven't seen much of him."

"I think he's more at ease than I am," Kaleb answered in the same low volume. "What do you think of this sorceress you've brought back?"

"I'm grateful to her," Seventh Night said. "But she makes me uneasy. Perhaps people from Gourlin are less refined in their manners, but she's too easily changeable. I worry about the influence she's going to have on Phillip, Gadolin's apprentice. He came to study magic, and she knows things Gadolin can't teach him."

"How did they get along when they met?" Kaleb asked.

"Very well," Seventh Night told him. "He was certainly far more respectful to her than me." Though she reflected they had been asking the sorceress for a favor, and Phillip had been friendly enough when she had stopped ordering him about.

They walked out through a side door directly onto the garden path. There was a sort of balcony with a stair leading directly into a garden outside the guestroom where Seventh Night was staying. Her father had access to the same garden from his room. But this path led farther up the mountainside to other gardens, some for practical purposes, others simply for their beauty.

SEVENTH NIGHT

Seventh Night knew the queen took particular pride in her gardens.

"And this apprentice?" Kaleb asked. "What do you think of him?"

"He's infuriating," she said. "And clever. But not as clever as he thinks he is." Kaleb laughed. "I think he had an unusual childhood," Seventh Night continued. "He lets his tongue run away with him, and he's...very opinionated." She felt she was saying too much.

"Can we trust him to keep my secret?" asked Kaleb.

"I'd trust him with my life," Seventh Night said and realized what was really worrying her fiancé. "I forgot you've barely met them. Phillip's loyal in his way. Lord Harold would never have sent him if he couldn't keep a secret, and the sorceress... I think she's just looking for a place to belong. She's brash, but she's kind. You should have seen how happy she was with the dresses I found her. I feel safe with both of them. And I think if we treat them kindly, we have no reason not to expect kindness in return."

"Neithan likes them," Kaleb said, slipping his arm around her shoulders. "But I wanted a second opinion. I've never had so many people know I exist before."

Seventh Night slid her arm around his waist, enjoying the closeness but wishing she was a little taller. She felt like a child beside a tower. "I've been thinking about that. I wish I could marry you with your own name, but I realized if everyone did know about you, I might not get to marry you at all. I understand Neithan is older."

Kaleb paused. "He is, and it's a thought that crossed my mind as well." He wrestled with some internal discomfort for a moment, letting his hand slip from her shoulder but find comfort in her fingers. He favored her with a charming half-smile. "I hope that means you prefer me to my brother."

Seventh Night squeezed his large, strong hand and found herself smiling without effort again. "I like Neithan, but he's very quiet. You have an easy tongue, and I like how you talk to me."

Kaleb's smile grew as he led her into a flower garden. Summer was waning, but there was still enough warmth to preserve some blooms. There was a fountain fed by a narrow mountain stream that trickled into a small pool by the retaining wall. A smattering of pear trees filled the air with a pleasant scent. The prince took a seat on the stone bench in the center of the garden, which allowed him to look up rather than down at her. "My lips are at your service, princess."

Seventh Night laughed, but a memory of lips and irritating magicians reminded her it might be best not to let a doubt stew without giving her prince a chance to defend himself. "You've been accused of being a flirt," she said as lightly as she could.

Kaleb showed a gallant amount of forbearance. "Neithan calls it flirting. I call it pleasant conversation. I believe the women of the court have as much to say as men do, and sometimes a good deal more. So I talk to them and attempt to be charming. Neithan prefers action to conversation. And I think that's part of why he's never been comfortable with women." Kaleb spoke lightly, but his eyes were earnest.

"He was delighted to discover he had a brother. It let him dodge any princely duty he found distasteful, and I was happy to let him. Any excuse to get out of the caves. He's a shy fellow by nature. So anything that involved speeches or social occasions other than the hunt became my domain.

"The first time you came, he was very nervous about meeting his prospective bride, and I was very curious, so it seemed natural to us." Kaleb covered her small hand with both of his. "We weren't sure what to expect when you arrived. I was watching out the window, and this pretty little slip of a girl stepped out of the carriage. And I think I must have a better imagination than my brother, because I had no trouble picturing the woman you would grow into. When we talked, you spoke like a woman, nowhere near as silly as most girls that age, and I... I had never felt such burning envy towards my brother.

"Neithan's a kind soul, and I knew it was wrong to fester any resentment towards him. He's always treated me fairly. So I confessed what I wanted, and my very accommodating brother said that if I loved you, I ought to have you." Kaleb was watching her for a reaction, but she had too many conflicting thoughts to allow any expression. Kaleb released her hand. "People of our rank rarely have much choice in who they marry, and I understand this is an arrangement. The choice between two identical brothers forced to share the same identity may not be much of one, but it's all I can give you. And it is yours, my princess. I want to be your husband, and Neithan gives it his blessing. But I wouldn't force you into that arrangement. If you had preferred the simplicity...if you do prefer the simplicity, of marrying Neithan for private life as well as public, I would leave."

Seventh Night touched the side of Kaleb's face, letting her fingers slide through his chestnut hair. "Where would you go?"

"Somewhere far away where I could use my own name." Kaleb shrugged. "My brother and I share a lot, but there are limits. I had considered leaving before I met you, but I didn't want to leave if you would have me."

Seventh Night felt the pink creep into her cheeks. The eyes were the first thing that told her which brother was speaking. Neithan had a tendency to look down or over her head, while Kaleb looked at her like she was the most beautiful thing in the world. "That's why I would prefer you as a husband," she said. "Even if it's a little more complicated."

Kaleb smiled. He was very handsome. Seventh Night joined her hands behind his neck, under the chestnut mane, and kissed him.

Night had fallen, and the princess was starting to doze when the light rapping at her door woke her. There was a maidservant sleeping in the adjoining room, and the princess was tempted to ask her to deal with whomever was at the door. The soft knock repeated, and she flung aside the curtains and pulled on a dressing gown. She ran her fingers through her hair on the off chance it was Kaleb and walked quickly to the door.

Phillip stood outside, holding a bag. "I was hoping you were still up. But if it's too late..."

"Of course it's too late," she hissed at him.

Phillip had the grace to look apologetic. "I just finished my chores for Gadolin and—."

"You know, you are not the only moral man in the kingdom," Seventh Night snapped at him. Phillip blinked at her, mouth halted midword. "My father has never smoked a day in his life. I know plenty of men who don't gamble, and Neithan and Kaleb both are the picture of moderation. He's been completely faithful to me, and it was a great disservice to him to suggest otherwise." She did her best to keep her volume down, but she allowed all her frustration with Phillip's arrogance to seep through.

"I never said I was..." Phillip said slowly, looking very wrong footed, which pleased her. "I don't..." He paused, momentarily at a loss for words, and this pleased her too. "I never said other men weren't moral or moderate. I don't think that...but it's...it's unusual in Cordance to abstain from all the things I do completely. That's all I meant."

"You sounded rather proud when you said it," she challenged him, though her voice had lost its heat.

"I'm not ashamed of it," Phillip said. "Keeps me out of trouble, but I don't think it makes me better than other men...well, not most of them anyway. And I never accused your prince of being unfaithful, but Neithan had said it...and I thought you ought to know."

"I talked to him about it," Seventh Night said, more easy in her mind now that she had her say. "Neithan's very reserved. I think he considers a smile a flirtation."

Phillip wisely said nothing.

"Why are you here anyway?" asked the

princess.

"I brought some different locks and picking tools," he said, indicating the bag. "I thought we might continue the lesson."

Seventh Night smiled in spite of herself.

"But if it's too late..."

"No, come in." She stepped back to let him enter. There was a sitting area with a table between the door and the fireplace. Phillip spread his locks and tools on it, and Seventh Night lit some candles.

Prince Neithan sat on a wooden crate in the cave they had given for the sorceress's workshop, watching her organize her books. They had offered her a room in the castle, but she said it was safer to keep her books and magic supplies in a hidden place. Gadolin had taken her on a walk around the castle grounds and escorted her to one of the feasts and the dances, but she had spent most of her time in the caves, settling in.

Neithan consulted Kaleb briefly every evening but knew his brother wanted more time with his bride, so he also spent most of his time in the caves. As Gadolin was old and the room needed to remain secret, Neithan volunteered to move in what furniture the sorceress required. She said it was silly and dangerous to use magic for what could easily be done by hand, though she could light fires with a few words and a finger snap.

Not that they needed many fires. She had done something to the stones so that the room was quite well-lit without them.

The prince could not easily run about the castle moving furniture to secret passages, so he had cobbled together shelves using scrap boards which Gadolin had ordered servants to bring to his chamber under the pretext of using them for extra firewood.

His carpentry skills were limited, but Neithan was fairly proud of the result. They were still standing. The sorceress had watched him build. She would hold something if he asked, but otherwise she was quite content to sprawl in a comfortable chair he had smuggled down from his own rooms while he worked. Sometimes she read while she did this; other times she would merely watch, catlike, making the occasional question or comment.

She enjoyed directing him on the position-ing of the furniture. He suspected she had him move some items far more than necessary, but he liked being useful. When he was not moving or building, he watched her sort her vials and perform magic. She talked a lot while she did this, and he did not understand half of what she said. But he found it fascinating.

"Do you like to read?" she asked abruptly.

"Not particularly," Neithan said.

The sorceress glanced at him with a cocked eyebrow. "Can you read?"

"Of course."

"I'd heard the literacy level in Cordance was deplorable."

Neithan said nothing.

"So is this what you do, just sit around in a cave all day while your brother plays prince?"

"I try to do something useful," Neithan said. "When I'm bored, I run."

"Oh that sounds very useful," the sorceress quipped.

Neithan shrugged. "I think Kaleb reads sometimes."

"It's good to know the monarchy isn't com-pletely illiterate," the sorceress said, dropping back into her chair. "Your library is lovely. I don't see how anyone could have so many books and not read them."

"I've read some of them," Neithan said.

"I think I'm going to stay here until I've read every book in your library," the sorceress said.

"That will take a long time."

"There's no hurry. It's not like I have anywhere else to go." She tapped her finger on the chair arm. "I spent enough time in the desert. Are you anxious to get rid of me?"

Neithan shook his head.

"I'm thinking about stealing Gadolin's apprentice." The sorceress continued to watch him with her green cat eyes. "I've never had an apprentice before. If Phillip can play music, that will help him learn magic; they're similar in nature. Rhythms and tempos. The world sings to us if we can learn to listen. Do you ever hear the sun sing when dawn breaks?"

Neithan shook his head again.

"Do you play any instruments?"

"No."

The sorceress sighed. "I will say Gadolin knows a little more useful information than your average magician. Not any magic, of course, but chemicals and medicines. Those are certainly important. Some of them are very similar to magic. But he lacks any sense of rhythm. He doesn't understand the art of the thing. I think I might be able to learn both. Maybe I can teach Phillip, while Gadolin's teaching me. What do you think?"

Neithan had not had time to form any thoughts on the subject. He tried, but the sorceress did not have the patience to wait for him.

"I guess I ought to talk to it over with them, but maybe I should wait 'til after this wedding. Things seem rather busy now."

Neithan nodded, and the sorceress sighed.

CHAPTER XI

CARRIED AWAY

Seventh Night held her head steady as the hairdresser ran the stiff brush through her raven locks. Helen, the seamstress, was painstakingly sewing small white roses into a wreath for her head. The Princess of Tivin could not remember being this picked at and fussed over, save the first time she was presented to Cordance's royal court. She winced as the hairdresser pulled too tight, quieted the woman's sincere and numerous apologies, and held fast to the chair as the hairdresser carefully wove larger versions of the wreath roses into her hair.

After an eternity, the hairdresser finished coaxing every hair into place, and the seamstress placed the wreath and veil on her head. The dress was made of the finest materials. That translated to Seventh Night as the bodice itched and the skirt was too slick. The perfumer stood idly by waiting to add the finishing touch, but Seventh Night wanted a moment alone before she started smelling like a walking bouquet.

"We have been at this a long time. Take a moment's break. I wish to get a breath of fresh air." Her attendants hesitated, and she clapped to dismiss them. The women hurriedly backed out of the chamber. Seventh Night sighed and walked out onto her balcony that led into the garden. She leaned…no, no movement with a corset was a lean...she carefully bent forward at the hips and crossed her arms on the stone wall.

It had been a stressful two weeks of wedding preparations and feasts. She was tired of crowds and only truly enjoyed her stolen moments alone with Kaleb and the late night she spent with Phillip learning the fine art of lock picking. Despite her most earnest prayers, Seventh Night's mother had remained home.

She had not seen much of Neithan or the sorceress. When she asked, Neithan said he had been helping the sorceress set up her things in one of the mountain chambers. Seventh Night wished she had had more time to speak with Neithan, but she had no regrets in regards to the sorceress. Phillip had been working hard at his apprenticeship, but somehow managed to find a few minutes every day to pester her.

The garden smelled fresh and alive. Afternoon sunlight filtered through the trees and lit the open path like a heavenly stair. Small birds fluttered from tree branch to tree branch, twittering contently. The bees buzzed from petal to petal of the lingering blooms scattered throughout the greenery. All was surrounded by a high wall. The air was slightly misty with the humidity. Seventh Night blinked and found the mistiness was caused by her own tears. She wiped away one droplet, but others followed.

She heard the soft creak of the door and quickly wiped away her tears. Without turning around, she knew her visitor. Footsteps came closer and stopped beside her. "Today's the big day, huh?"

"It is," she replied quietly.

"Tell me, Seven, what's wrong?"

"I am fine," she said. "It's all just moving a little fast."

Phillip put a warm hand on her shoulder. She almost wished he would hug her, the other servants seemed afraid to touch her, but that would probably crush something and throw the hairdresser into a fit. "What else?" he asked.

"I wish my mother was here," Seventh Night said with a shrug. "I shan't be able to see her again, most likely. I can only speak to her through letters. I have never been far from home for long, and now I shall never return..." Her voice failed her, and she fought back another tear.

"Is that all?" Phillip coaxed.

Seventh Night stood and looked at him for the first time. "Is that not enough?"

Phillip shrugged and leaned back against the stone. "I have a hard time believing you couldn't arrange a visit or two." He flitted his gaze up the castle walls and at the clouds and brought it back to rest on Seven's face. He studied her for a moment. "You don't love him. Do you?"

Seventh Night stared back at him. "Of course,

I love him," she said, feeling unnecessarily defensive.

"There's an old saying in Gourlin," Phillip said. "'A fire left unkindled soon burns out.' Admit it. It's not what you expected."

"What is?" Seventh Night countered. "And we have an old saying in Tivin: 'absence makes the heart grow fonder'." Phillip was unmoved. She sighed and turned back to the garden. "There is simply so much at once."

"If you need time, I can take you out of here," Phillip offered. "One of the tunnels leads out of the garden. I could hide you somewhere for a while, maybe in the thieves' village. You could have the time you need. You could stay with me or explore the world a bit or even come back here."

Seventh Night laughed. It was an amusing thought, almost tempting. She looked at Phillip's straight face. "You're serious, aren't you?" Phillip nodded. Seventh Night felt anger swell up in her. "You keep down talking royalty. But this is the difference between royals and commoners. We have to think about more than ourselves and sometimes even our kin. The kingdom, the people we are 'oppressing', come first. I have

SEVENTH NIGHT

to think about the future of the kingdom. I am an only child. There is no one else to take my place. Even you must be able to see that."

It was Phillip's turn to look away. "I see it," he muttered. "But they could join the kingdoms some other way, Seven. I don't see why you have to be part of the bargain."

Seventh Night crossed her arms over her chest. "Has it occurred to you I might want to get married?"

"Yeah, but to him," Phillip grimaced. "He has a mouth with six sides. I know some of it's been forced on him. But I've been around every flavor of crook and con artist in my life, and he's—" Phillip studied Seventh Night's expression and thought better of what he was going to say. "...a perfectly wonderful guy. I'm sure you'll be real happy."

"Yes, he is wonderful. He is honest and hand-some and sweet and clever, and I love Kaleb." She felt a certain satisfaction in saying his name. "You should have more respect, Magician."

"Phillip," he corrected her. "You've known me nearly a month now. Why do you still call me that?"

"It annoys you." She smiled. "And, you

keep calling me Seven."

Phillip shrugged. "It annoys you. You two are a funny looking couple at best. He's so tall and bulky, and you're, well—not." Phillip chuckled. Then he stopped, and his expression changed. "You know, I love you."

"You'll get over it," Seventh Night said.

"Maybe."

"You best go," she managed. "I have to finish getting ready."

Phillip leaned over to kiss her, and she put up a hand to block him. "Just on the cheek?" he asked. Seven hesitated, then nodded her approval. Phillip kissed her on the cheek and walked back inside.

Seventh Night sighed and descended the steps to the garden. Phillip had succeeded at giving her guilt pains, but there was nothing she could do. It was his own fault. She had done nothing to encourage him; in fact, just the opposite. He would have to get past this. Hopefully once he saw her happily settled in her married life, it would be easier to let go.

As she walked the path, the garden became shadowed by a cloud passing over the sun. A breeze picked up and died away. Tonight everything would be settled. She would be married to Kaleb, and Phillip could turn his attention back to his magic. He could have that sorceress for all she cared. Seventh Night caressed her veil thoughtfully and looked up.

Her breath stopped, and she stumbled backward in horror. Two hideous birds, each the size of a cottage, were perched on the wall, blocking the sky. Solid brown with undersized yellow beaks, they stared at her with large, hollow eyes. One of the birds spread its wings and swooped down. Seventh Night screamed and threw up her arms, uselessly trying to ward off the creature. Claws grasped her around the waist and jerked her off the ground hard enough to loosen her veil. Seventh Night found it hard to breathe in the creature's grip; the last thing she remembered was her veil falling like a snowflake to the ground.

Phillip rushed back through the princess's chamber, nearly knocking over the small table where they had their lockpicking lesson. He reached the balcony in time to see her body fall limp in the monster bird's claw. The ladies-in-waiting came up behind him and gasped, shrieked, or gawked. Phillip ran down to the garden, picked up a rock, and threw it in vain at the buzzards. When the rock fell back to the ground, he took out his frustration on a nearby tree. Soldiers rushed into the garden, and Phillip rubbed his sore fist.

The women, all at once, tried to explain the situation to the soldiers. One of the archers raised his crossbow, targeting the bird's large body. "Don't!" Phillip shouted as he knocked the crossbow so that it pointed earthward. "You might hit Sev—the princess." The archer sneered at the insult to his skill but agreed the risk was too great. Even if his aim was true, the bird was now high enough that the fall might kill her.

Phillip squeezed through the helpless soldiers and squawking women. He ran back through the chamber and the hallways to the stables. Phillip grabbed a water flask and his sack and saddled Thunder. He flung open Thunder's stall and led him to the courtyard. In the distance, he could still see the birds. If he hurried, he might be able to catch them when they landed. Thunder stretched his wings and backed up so to have room for taking off.

A hand grabbed Thunder's bridle; another

hand gripped Phillip's wrist. "Where are you going?" the sorceress's voice snapped at him.

"Let go," Phillip demanded, trying to free his wrist. "If I don't hurry, they'll get away."

"Let them," she said calmly.

Phillip stopped struggling and looked at her in shock. "What?" he asked, not thinking he understood her clearly.

"I said, 'Let them go.' You'll never catch them, and if you do, what then? One swoop of those claws would kill you. See, there are two of them. The second to guard the first." The sorceress released his wrist.

Phillip glanced longingly at the fading dots on the sky. "I could follow them," he said in a defeated tone.

"Do you know how far they'll go?" the sorceress challenged.

"Thunder's strong," Phillip retorted. "He can take it." The unicorn snorted and stomped his hoof for emphasis.

"Can he fly across the sea?" the sorceress countered. "Those are terrocks. There are none in this region. There aren't any on this side of the sea. They had to come from the Wizards Land." Phillip frowned at her in confusion. "I'll explain inside," she told him, and grudgingly Phillip dismounted.

SEVENTH NIGHT

CHAPTER XII

A VERY LONG TIME AGO...

They gathered in the library. The king, Gadolin, Neithan, Phillip, the sorceress, and Kaleb stood or sat in a rough circle. Kaleb was still dressed for the wedding and had learned of Seventh Night's abduction before he had had a chance to shave. Neithan was dressed in common garb and clean-shaven. But the otherwise exact likeness was uncanny. The sorceress sat beside Neithan wearing her nicest dress, simple in cut but bold purple in color. Gadolin stood at the king's right-hand side, and

Phillip sat beside Gadolin.

The king cleared his throat. "Now," he said to the sorceress. "I believe you had something to say."

"Yes, sire, the birds that took Seventh Night are terrocks. They're found only in the Wizards Land, across the sea. Someone from there must have sent them, or someone brought them from there. I tend to think the former, since they were headed in that direction." The sorceress finished and leaned back in her chair. The king stroked his beard, his eyes lowered.

"What's the Wizards Land?" Phillip asked.

"Many years ago," the sorceress began, "long before we were born, there were real magicians and sorcerers here on this side of the sea." Gadolin frowned but kept his peace. The sorceress did not want to insult the old man, but she did not consider him a real magician. Real magicians used real magic. Gadolin, like most of the so-called magicians, was a doctor who could do parlor tricks. She was not about to apologize for something that was true, so she continued.

"The evil ones as well as the good lived along side everyone else. But it came to a point where the evil magicians made a greater name for themselves than the good, and the people came to fear all those who used magic. The leaders of several countries got together with some good magicians and sorcerers. Someone had discovered a land across the sea. The kings convinced the good magicians to chase the bad magicians there and to live there as guards to see the magicians never returned.

"As I understand it, it was quite a war, but finally the good magicians got them all across the sea or killed them in the process. Any that might have been left are long since dead."

"You said your father was a magician," Neithan pointed out.

"Yes, well, you see it has been a very long time since the magicians crossed the sea. Many of them were curious to know how things were here. My father and another were sent here in secret to scout around and report back. While he was here, he met and married a woman, my mother, and here I am," the sorceress said and folded her hands. Living as a hermit she had never had to sit this long, and she found herself restless.

"You said there was another," Kaleb spoke

up. "Who was it?"

"I don't know," the sorceress said. "Sar—Sarge—Sargy—something like that." She furrowed her brow in thought, then brightened with remembrance. "Sargon. Yes, I'm sure of it; Sargon was the other one."

The king paled under his beard. "Sargon?" he repeated.

"Do you know him?" the sorceress asked.

"No," the king said. "It sounds like a name I've heard before, nothing more." The sorceress nodded, finding that as easy to swallow as a cactus. "Neithan," the king continued, "organize a search party. We can't sit around with our hands folded. It's almost dark now, so be ready to begin tomorrow. Send a messenger ahead to make sure the ship is ready if you need it." Neithan nodded.

"I wish to go along," Kaleb said.

"That would not be wise," Gadolin objected. "The two of you should not be seen together in public."

Before Kaleb could say anything, Phillip interjected. "I don't know," he said. "If he kept that fuzz and wore soldier's clothes, maybe grunt a little more when he spoke and didn't stand right beside Neithan, he might be able to pull it off."

"Yes," Kaleb agreed. "Your apprentice has a point, Gadolin. And though it sounds childish, I must pursue my love. To sit idle while my princess is in danger is too much for me." Phillip rolled his eyes. "Father, will you give your permission?"

"Yes," the king consented. "But be cautious."

"Sire," Phillip said. "I wish to go too. Seven's a good friend; I want to make sure she's alright."

"Your studies," Gadolin reminded him.

"I'm not sure I could concentrate until I know she's okay," Phillip said. He knew good and well he was not fooling Gadolin in the least bit, but the ancient magician said nothing.

"I'd like having you along," said Neithan.

"It is settled then," said the king. "You are dismissed to prepare." With the king's words, they filed out the library door, except for Neithan and Kaleb who slipped through a secret passage hidden behind a bookshelf.

Phillip waited for Gadolin, so that he could have a word with him, but the old man spoke first. "I can't say much for your tact, boy, and I don't approve of you going off like this. But

I have no control over it. You are preoccupied; tell me what's troubling you."

"Master Gadolin," Phillip said as they began walking. "The king seemed to know this Sargon. Who is he?"

"Come to my lab," Gadolin told him. "We will talk there." They passed several corridors in silence until they came to the stairway leading to the lower levels of the castle. They passed the door that led to the dungeon. Even though the chamber had not been used in ages, its various devices of death lying about the empty rooms caused a cold shiver up Phillip's spine. The end of the hallway was lit by two torches. Phillip pulled on one torch and stepped back as the stones separated, revealing the entrance to Gadolin's laboratory. After they were inside, Gadolin pulled the cord that returned the wall and torch to their places.

Gadolin walked about the room fiddling with various objects. Phillip sat down upon a stool and waited. The old man went about his business in silence, but Phillip was patient.

The chamber had been carved into the mountain. The walls were stone, and the ceiling was high. Clear water that had seeped through the rocks from a mountain stream dripped into a large basin at the edge of the room. On the opposite wall, a large stone fire pit still burned and cast its glow upon the chamber, though the magician had lit candles to bring better light to the worn, wooden table.

Gadolin took a book from his shelf and dusted it off. He opened it on the table and began to inspect the pages.

"Master Gadolin," Phillip spoke up. "About Sargon?"

Gadolin closed the book and rubbed his eyes. "I would not take the time to explain this to you, if I did not fear it had something to do with the princess." He took a deep breath before continuing. "Two years before Neithan was born, the Gourlin desert was not nearly as large as it is now. There was a stretch of forest between the King's mountain and a small desert the Gourlins claimed. We were never friendly with Gourlin, and the proximity was a great concern.

"That year there were rumors of an upcoming attack from the Gourlins. The soldiers were preparing to defend the kingdom, but the king sent men out looking for more powerful methods to deal with them. The search became more urgent when reports came in of a great number of Gourlin soldiers and mercenaries massing together at the edge of the forest.

"A traveler named Sargon came to the castle claiming he could solve the king's problem. Sargon showed the king three seeds, each about the size of a walnut. He said that if they were planted in certain places, the seeds would destroy the enemy.

"The king was skeptical but told Sargon that he could have whatever he wanted within reason. Sargon said his request was simple. He had no children of his own, and if the king would give him one of his, he would be content. The king pointed out that he had no children and that he and his wife were getting on in years. Sargon told him that was of no consequence. Then the king said that even if he did have a child, Sargon could not possibly have the first born for the first born would be heir to the throne. Sargon said that that was well with him. The king did not believe that he would have any children or that Sargon's plan would work. He told Sargon that, if he was successful, he would give him jewels and gold to fill two trunks, and that if he and his wife ever had a second child, Sargon could return the two trunks completely filled and claim it.

"Sargon agreed. The king sent three spies to plant the seeds in the places instructed by Sargon. The spies planted their seeds and hurried to return to Cordance soil. The next night the seeds sprouted. Thick thorny vines covered everything. They crushed and suffocated, killing everything, including the Gourlin soldiers. Then everything that the vines killed turned to sand. After a few days, so did the vines themselves.

"Sargon took his treasure and disappeared for two years. At the news of Neithan's birth, he came back to return the trunks and claim his payment. He was told to leave and refused. Sargon sat outside the castle door for two days, then on his own accord left without the trunks. He hasn't been heard from since. This may be his revenge, claiming the king's daughter-in-law as the promised second child."

"Do you think he could have known about Kaleb?" Phillip asked.

"It's not likely," the old magician said. "But possible. What isn't?"

"No one noticing a desert that wasn't there before," Phillip answered. He could not help wondering if some of the sand he had walked on might have been someone's brother.

"They probably noticed in Gourlin," Gadolin said. "But remember, from the Gourlin side they could already see a desert. Very few in Cordance could see past the mountain range. The king had everyone who knew what had taken place take a vow of silence. So while there were certainly strange stories about a doubled desert spread, no one knew why. There were rumors and questions, but no answers. I imagine the rulers of Gourlin did not wish to advertise that they had lost so many men without a trace."

"Do you think this Sargon would harm her?" Phillip asked.

"I can't answer that," Gadolin sighed. "A king's daughter is a valuable hostage. Death steals her value, but if he's been behind the plot to disrupt the wedding..."

Phillip rubbed his temples, inwardly berating himself for leaving her alone. "What would he gain by causing trouble between Tivin and Cordance?"

SEVENTH NIGHT

Gadolin re-opened his book. "There's nothing logical about revenge, Phillip. Or love for that matter."

Phillip sniffed, not sure he agreed, but it was not time for philosophic discussion. "Why didn't the King—?"

"Tell his sons he had sold one of them to a wizard?" Gadolin finished. "Guilt, I think, but that is the king's business. You and I are secret keepers, and I want you to keep this secret unless it is absolutely necessary to tell it."

SEVENTH NIGHT

CHAPTER XIII

AND VERY FAR AWAY

Seventh Night awoke to the sound of a bird cawing. She rubbed her temples, propped herself up on her elbows, and looked at her surroundings. Her bed had thin white curtains bunched up at the rails. The walls were a dark gray stone. One window stood open, letting in light and air. Outside it was cloudy. The room was scantily furnished. Besides the bed there was a small oval table and a rich brown wooden bench.

With a rush of adrenaline, Seventh Night

remembered all that had happened to her. She sat straight up. The corset allowed no other position. She was still in her wedding dress, but it was crinkled and her veil was lost forever. The flowers in her hair were crushed from where she had lain on them. She went through the task of pulling them out while she collected her thoughts.

While it was not impossible that she had been rescued, she thought kidnap more likely. The giant birds had come for her directly, leaving no time to raise an alarm before she took her walk in the garden. To her knowledge, there were no such creatures in Cordance or Tivin, which indicated they had come from elsewhere. Reason suggested they would return to the place they had been sent from, as that was commonly the habit with trained birds. But returned to where? And who had sent them?

Most likely the same power behind the other attempts to disrupt her wedding. Cordance had plenty of old enemies, and though Tivin did not have many enemies, neither did it have many friends. Her mind listed the most likely suspects.

Uritz was a mountainous country on Cordance's northern border. They had seven princes, all but the eldest still in want of a wife, and a terrain that might accommodate giant birds. But there were several spies in Uritz from Cordance and vice versa. It seemed unlikely none of the spies would have noticed a giant bird flying around, and there had been no reports of anything out of the ordinary.

She knew very little of Gourlin, other than the strong enmity between them and Cordance. There were very few traders that braved the desert when there were easier roads to the north and south, making reports scarce. She knew Gourlin received tribute from most of its neighbors, but they had made no move west in decades. It could have been them, but if they had beasts that powerful, it seemed unlikely they would stop short at a mere kidnapping.

Perhaps they had done more damage. She had been unconscious. She wondered if Kaleb and her father were all right. Neithan and Phillip and, surprisingly, the sorceress also held her concern.

The same argument for Lampshmith held as for Uritz. Trade between Tivin and Lampshmith was frequent. They might not be comfortable with Tivin's merge with Cordance, but they had few places to hide giant birds.

Muori had never displayed enmity. It was a small, fairly neutral country that holed itself up with a large wall that surrounded the entire kingdom. They did not trade often, and Muori's king politely refused all invitations to visit or be visited. They were too small to support birds of such size. She could think of no other likely suspects. The north was too wild and the south too peaceful and prosperous. Seventh Night narrowed the possibilities down to Gourlin…or some unknown.

The princess pulled the last of the petals from her hair. She decided the window offered the quickest clue to her location, so she walked over and looked out.

Dark, dismal, and gloomy were the first terms to come to mind. It was not just the rows of black clouds that made it seem that way. The window was high up, most likely in a tower, and to add to the sense of vertigo, the structure in which she was held stood on a rock rise, which allowed Seventh Night to see a long way off. The grass in the field all around was dead or dark as if burnt. The trees far beyond the field reminded Seventh Night of the haunted woods from fairytales she was told as a child. They were dark and forbidding. Even the air seemed thick with despair, but that was most likely the humidity. Seventh Night had no more idea where she was than before.

She was turning from the window when there was a loud pounding on the door. She froze, uncertain whether to run and hide. There were no decent hiding places, and they knew she was in here anyway, so she stood her ground. Her fear melted some with realization. If they planned to kill her, they would have done so already. She smoothed her dress and straightened her posture. She was a princess, and she would act like one.

The door began to open. Some of Seventh Night's courage slipped. After those birds, there was no telling what sort of hideous thing would enter. A man entered. He was so unimposing, she almost laughed. The man was not much taller than she was. He was far from muscular and looked twice her age. He had dark hair and eyes and a complexion which most definitely did not come from working outdoors. He wore finery, an outfit of purple and gray. The man tried to smile pleasantly, but it ended up as more of a sneer.

"You are awake, I see," he said.

Her confidence returned. "Where am I?" she demanded. "Why have you brought me here?"

"Hardly a polite way to begin a conversation, Princess," he said.

"I did not intend to start one," she said. "I simply want my questions answered. Who are you?"

"You should show more reverence. I am King Sargon of the Wizards Land," he told her.

"The what?" she asked.

"The land across the sea from Cordance," he said. "That is all you need to know. You will not escape. Even if you do, you will be unable to return home."

Seventh Night had stepped away from the window. She was now less than three feet from Sargon. "We shall see," she said and bolted around him for the door.

"Martyr!" he shouted. Seventh Night ran through the doorway. She began to run down the hallway, but something blocked her path. She looked up and gave a shriek. Seventh Night recognized the creature as a cyclops from stories, but those stories had not frightened her half as much. The creature stood about nine or ten feet tall. It was broad shouldered, and its muscular chest was bare. Red skin covered its body. The one large, green eye glared at her. The cyclops spread its lips apart to release a low, rumbling growl and revealed a frightening set of needle sharp teeth.

Seventh Night backed up and tried to run the other way. Sargon caught her arm and wrestled her back into the room. He shoved Seventh Night toward the bench. She stumbled, tripped on her dress, caught her balance, and sat down to catch her breath. "What was that?!" she screamed.

Sargon gave her a nasty smile. "You just met Martyr," he said.

"Martyr?" she repeated.

"He was once a man who crossed me. He paid for his cause," Sargon said. "You will too if you do not be careful." He called for his beast. The cyclops would not fit entirely through the door, but it extended a massive arm holding a tray of food. "I have arranged for your breakfast." Sargon took the tray and placed it on the table. "Be a good child and stay in this room, and no harm will come to you." With that he walked out and closed the door.

SEVENTH NIGHT

Seventh Night heard the sound of a key turning and ran to the door. She wrestled with the latch and pounded with her fist, but it was locked tight. She sighed and leaned against the heavy wood.

The lock made her nervous, so she went to the window for a breath of air. The scene outside was far from pleasant, but it was open. She noticed that a wide moat surrounded the castle. The water flowed and stirred. A long shadow pushed foam against the rocks. Suddenly a serpent, half as wide as the moat, reared its head. It stretched its neck up toward the window and seemed as if it would reach it. Seventh Night did not scream but slammed the shutters closed and fastened them. She sat down on the bench and decided to try the breakfast. It was more than adequate. She was halfway through when she wondered if Sargon had been the one to poison Kaleb and lost her appetite.

She pushed the tray away and put her head in her hands. This was not fair, she thought. She knew good and well life was not fair, but that changed nothing. This was still not fair. Everything had started to go smoothly and according to plan. At sunset, she would have been married to Kaleb, and Tivin's worries would be gone. Her dear, sweet Kaleb... She wondered if he knew what had become of her. Would he come for her?

That was how it went in the storybooks. The prince rescued the princess, and they lived happily ever after. That was ridiculous, but so were giant birds, cyclops, and moat monsters.

She wondered if Phillip had seen the birds. Phillip! The lock. She ran her fingers through her hair, searching, hoping, and found what she needed. She pulled out a hairpin that had held a flower.

It was time to see if she had learned anything.

It took her two dozen attempts and three hairpins before she heard the click of the lock.

Seventh Night sat back on her heels. It had worked. The door was no longer locked. Suddenly the room did not seem so bad. She did not want to stay, but where would she go? The world outside the window became more frightening. Sargon had promised she would not be harmed if she stayed put. Then again, Sargon was a kidnapper, possible poisoner, and not the sort of man that could be trusted. There was no telling what a person like that would do if he was angry.

Seventh Night looked at the door in terrible realization. The door was unlocked, and she had no way to lock it back. Someone would return eventually to check on her. If they found the door unlocked, Sargon would take further steps to secure her, and then it would be too late to escape. There was no choice now other than to follow through with her attempt.

Seventh Night stood. Several layers of underskirt had been put beneath her dress to make it seem fuller, but they served no purpose now. She pulled them off and hid the garments under the bed. She could run faster without the extra weight. Of course now her skirt was too long, but she fixed that by bunching up the fabric in her hand. She cracked the door open. It creaked loudly, and Seventh Night froze. After some time passed and she still had not heard any movement outside, she peeked through the crack. She saw no one. She opened the door enough to stick her head out and saw no one the other way either. Carefully, she opened the door wide enough to slip through. Just as carefully, she closed the door with a thump. It echoed down the hall. She froze again, expecting Sargon or the cyclops to come tearing around the corner. No one came. Seventh Night inched along the wall but soon realized that her wall hugging was slowing her down and she could be just as easily seen.

She came to a turn and, soon after, a door. She opened it slowly. As soon as she was sure no one was inside, she slipped into the room closing the door behind her. The room looked as if it had been vacant for years. Cobwebs filled the corners and dust covered the floors, but that was the least of her concerns. She had no idea where she was or how big the castle might be or how she was going to get out.

Her heart still pounded rapidly. She decided to rest a moment. A dusty trunk lay in the middle of the floor, and an ornate key lay on the dressing table near it. Seventh Night blew the dust off the key before picking it up. She turned it over in her hands. It was a gold key with the inscription "D. & L." The end looped into a three-leaf clover shape. Seventh Night tried the key in the trunk. It fit, and she turned it. She opened the lid and brushed the dust from her fingers. The trunk was filled with dresses and little personal items, a necklace, a ring, and a needlework sampler. The way the dresses had been thrown in instead of folded made it seem that someone had packed her things in a hurry and then left without them. Strange. Of course, they could have simply been sloppy. She shut the trunk and relocked it. Then she returned the key to the dresser.

Her heart had stopped pounding so quickly. She opened the door and slipped out of the room. Eventually she came to a staircase. As she descended, she reflected on how large and empty everything was. The stairs came to an end, and she began down another hallway.

Seventh Night was about to turn a corner when she saw the light of an approaching torch and heard footsteps. She ducked inside an open door and hid behind it.

"After we've checked on the princess, I will use the mirror again." She heard Sargon say. "That idiot failed to disable Prince Neithan, but the harm can be controlled. No one should reach the castle, but it is your job to stop anyone who comes this far. Martyr, do you understand?" A low grumble. "Stupid creature, I'll explain it again later." Seventh Night waited until the last flicker of torchlight disappeared. The halls seemed that much darker. She began down the corridor from which Sargon had come.

A few staircases and several corridors later, it became quite clear to Seventh Night that she was lost. She began to panic and run. Sargon had most definitely discovered her absence by now and was no doubt hunting for her. A labyrinth of halls surrounded her. She was not sure whether she should worry more about dead ends or running around in circles. She came to an intersection of passages and stopped a moment to catch her breath. Still panting, she spun around in a circle trying to decide which tunnel to take. Everything looked the same, one hallway like another hallway, one turn like another turn. While standing still, she heard footsteps again pounding on the stone. She looked down to make sure they were not her own.

Canceling the possibility of taking the tunnel the footsteps were coming from or the one she had just left, Seventh Night chose one of the remaining passageways. She ran down the corridor until she spotted a door and bolted for it. Her dress fabric slipped from her hand, and she tripped on it. She hit the stone floor hard. She almost cried out in pain but by some miracle held her tongue. She picked herself up and ran for the door again.

One of her slippers slipped off. It had been tied on with a ribbon, but the simple bow knot had worked itself loose. She almost screamed from frustration but again held her tongue. She started to retrieve the white slipper, but the other set of footsteps sounded closer. Forgetting the shoe, she hastened for the door. Once inside she closed the door quickly, only remembering at the last moment not to let it slam.

The footsteps grew very loud. Seventh Night pressed her ear against the door crack. The footsteps passed the door. She let her breath out slowly with relief.

"Martyr! You fool, get back here!" She heard Sargon's voice say through the door. "Look, she's been here. She's lost a shoe. She must have heard us coming, or she would have retrieved it. Check that room."

In horror, Seventh Night took a step back and looked around the room. It was a library, big and open without any furniture save a single writing desk and a book pedestal. There was nowhere to hide.

Chapter XIV

Hidden Things

Phillip paced about the garden from which Seven had been taken. He was restless. The search party would leave soon, but not soon enough. The sorceress was coming along. Neithan would play the role of the prince, and Kaleb the role of a gruff soldier. Phillip wished he had never suggested the disguise. He did not want Kaleb to come along. Kaleb annoyed him to no end. The prince was suave, honey-tongued, and handsome, perfect for a beautiful princess like Seven. Phillip could not stand him.

SEVENTH NIGHT

He stopped pacing and stared at the sky. This was impossible. When would he wake up and discover this was all a dream? He was back at the tavern; Seven was only a messenger, not a princess; there was only one prince; the sorceress could be the real Tivin princess; there were no monstrous birds or real sorcerers; Seven could be his; and everything would be perfect. He sighed. Until then, he would play along with this dream.

His gaze dropped back to the ground, but as it dropped, he saw something that caused him to look back up. A spot of white hung on a tree branch. It was Seven's veil. Phillip hurried over and pried it away from the tree. He touched it to his cheek and held it like a treasure. It was not the same as holding Seven, but it was as close as he could get at the moment.

"Phillip," a voice called from behind him. Phillip jumped. He dropped the veil and moved it behind a bush with his foot. That was his treasure. Kaleb could not have it.

Phillip turned around. "Neithan?" he asked. The prince nodded. "Is it time to go?"

"Almost," Neithan said. "I have something for you."

SEVENTH NIGHT

"What is it?" Phillip asked.

Neithan held up a gleaming sword. It was not fancy, but it looked new. "Just in case," he said and handed it to Phillip. Phillip took the sword and flashed it around. For a moment he imagined raging duels and courageous rescues. It seemed like a good sword, but he knew nothing of balance or swordplay.

"Thank you," Phillip said, "but you should know, I've never used one."

"I'll teach you," Neithan offered and handed Phillip a sheath to put his sword in. "I need to go check on the preparations."

"I'll catch up to you in a moment," Phillip told him. Neithan nodded and walked away. Phillip laid the sword on the ground and fastened the sheath to his belt. Gingerly he lifted the sword off the grass and slipped it into the sheath. He returned to the bush where he had hidden the veil and picked it up. Carefully he folded it into a small square and slipped it inside his shirt. With a fresh determination, he headed out of the garden.

SEVENTH NIGHT

Sargon opened the door. The library was large and empty. He scowled. He was expecting a shriek of terror, instead silence. No, he would not accept it. The princess had to be here. "Martyr," Sargon called. The cyclops squeezed through the doorway. "Find the princess," he ordered.

The cyclops groped unproductively around the room. Sargon pulled out his sword. He walked over to the writing desk and held his sword so that anyone hiding underneath could see it. When that failed to produce a whimper, he looked beneath the desk. He had hoped to find the princess with eyes squeezed shut and shaking with fright, but again there was nothing.

A large window had been placed in the library when the castle was built to shed extra light into the room. Sargon had had it covered with thick curtains. He smiled, knowing he had won the game. "Martyr, the curtain." The cyclops muttered a growl and swiped back the curtain with his massive arm. Light poured into the library. Though diffused by cloud cover, it made Sargon wince. His wince twisted into something darker as his eyes adjusted and he could see no silhouette. He stormed out of the room.

Martyr began to follow, then turned his head back. His slow mind was puzzled by something, a smell or a hunch, but Sargon screamed for him. Martyr let out a low sigh and turned to follow the angry little man.

The very simple and straightforward reason that Sargon did not find the princess in the library is because the princess was not inside the library. In the most precise sense she was not inside the castle either. Balancing on the ledge outside the window, clinging to the castle for dear life, Tivin's only heir wished she was farther away than that.

Seventh Night squeezed her eyes shut as another spurt of wind tugged at her hair and gown. She tried not to think about the way her stocking felt slick against the smooth ledge, not to think about how slipping off that ledge would send her plummeting down to the moat, not to think about how hitting the water from this height would be practically the same as hitting solid ground. Despite her efforts, she was very aware of every sensation: the cold sweat on her brow, the merciless itching of her bodice, the light wind that suddenly seemed so threatening.

Her left hand tried to hold the corner where the stone gave way to the window. Her right arm stretched above her head; her right hand clenched a crevice in the outer wall that made a decent handhold. She squeezed tight and tried to listen for signs that Martyr and Sargon were still there. But she had not been able to hear anything over her heartbeat and the wind. She had been able to see the flash of movement when the curtain was flung open, but any other motion was obscured.

Her sense of time was unreliable, so she tried to play her mind through all the possible places they could look. The library was a good-sized room, but it had few worthwhile hiding places. She was fairly certain that if they had not discovered her by now, they must have left. Even if they had not, her arms were tiring, and she still had to climb back to the window.

Taking great care, she edged herself back towards the window. Releasing her handhold was difficult, but she did not want to stay out on the ledge any longer, and she refused to let herself fall. Murmuring a simple prayer along those lines, she reached her hand out to push the window. The blessed thing swung inwards.

Why a window of this size and at this height would swing open, much less inward was beyond her, but at the moment she thought its installer to be an absolute genius.

She dropped inside and resisted the urge to curl up on the floor and enjoy its relative security. The Princess looked down out of the window again before closing it and wondered at her own sanity. She doubted the magician's apprentice would have thought of going outside the window or would have attempted the ledge even if he did. She smiled at the thought of besting him and smiled more at besting Sargon. It was comforting to have some sort of advantage in that she could hide better than he could look for her.

Seventh Night pulled the last of the hairpins out of her hair. She could not hide forever. Her stomach growled, reminding her that she would have to find something to eat eventually. If only she had some way to defend herself...

The writing desk caught her attention. Her father had always kept a sharpened dagger in his desk drawer for emergencies. She searched the desk. There was no dagger, but she found a quill and small pouch in which to carry it and her hairpins. She kept these in case of another lock. She also found a paper. The ink was smudged, but she was able to make out most of what it said.

Havanderier is dead. It is hard to believe that such as Sargon could defeat him. I fear there was deceit involved. His death fills the land with such sorrow even the sky is weeping. Havanderier was the greatest — — Wizards Land ever had. His praises will be sung for years, but sung in secret. Soon—— will come to claim his prize.

Delenora is gathering her belongings. We must leave before —an——s arrives. I fear dark times——

The writing ended in a large blob of ink where the writer had pressed the quill too hard.

Seventh Night wondered what the document meant. Sargon was mentioned, but who was Havanderier? The writer was correct in one respect. With a man such as Sargon in power, these were dark times.

She returned the paper to the desk. Her shoeless foot was cold and sore. Gritting her teeth, she cracked the library door open. No monsters came roaring after her, so she slipped outside. A worn white slipper lay in the hallway. Sargon had left it. Seventh Night smiled and began to retrieve it. But what if he had left it on purpose to bait her, Seventh Night asked herself. Her toes crunched up to remind her how uncomfortable they were. She could not walk barefoot for long. Other people could, but she was not used to it. As if sliding into her own coffin, Seventh Night put the slipper back on, double knotted the ribbon of both shoes, and took off running.

She managed not to panic this time. When she felt she had reached a safe distance, she slowed to a walk. She recognized the passage that she was taking and chose a different route. Seventh Night lost track of how long she wandered, but she took her time and carefully chose her path. It seemed to her that she was making progress. At least she was heading down. Once she reached the ground floor, it should not be difficult to find some kind of exit.

Most of the windows in the castle were shut or covered and hard to notice, but as Seventh Night went further into the depths of the castle, she realized she had not seen any windows, shut or otherwise, for a long time. She wondered if she had overshot the first floor and gone into the lower levels. Seventh Night was about to give up and head back when she spotted light coming from down the corridor. Her feet froze to the floor. Had she walked straight into Sargon and his beast? But the light did not move, and no noise came from the corridor. Seventh Night found her courage and walked toward the light.

The end of the hall split into two opposite directions. Both were lit with torches mounted on the walls. It took her eyes a moment to adjust. Then Seventh Night followed one of the paths to a door at the end of the corridor. She looked back to make sure no one was coming and opened the door.

A stairway leading to the floor gripped the wall of the huge cavern. She saw no torches or windows, but the room was well-lit with the exception of a dark shadow beneath the stairs. Seventh Night made her way down the steps. She clung to the wall for there was no banister, and it was a long drop. The floor was better polished and swept here than in the rest of the castle. In the center of the cavern a waist-high wall of stone surrounded a pool of water. Near the pool stood a mirror on a pedestal. It was encircled by an elaborate gold frame. Along the wall were tapestries and a dozen suits of armor. The armor was not as well-polished as the floor, but it still seemed to whisper of brave warriors and mighty battles.

Seventh Night walked around the room and wondered what its purpose was. She stopped in front of the mirror. The glass was of a quality rarely seen. She looked at her reflection and sighed. She was glad Kaleb did not see her like this. Seventh Night combed through her tangled hair with her fingers and wondered what Sargon had meant by "use the mirror". Her thoughts were interrupted by a creak that echoed through the cavern. She spun and saw the door starting to open. Without a second thought she ran and hid behind a tapestry. The tapestries were hung from rods extended from the wall and draped to the floor, which concealed her slight figure as long as she kept her back pressed against the stone.

From her hiding place, she heard the footfalls of Sargon descending the steps, but she did not hear the distinctive tread of his cyclops companion. She crossed her fingers and pressed her back against the wall. Sargon's footsteps stopped. Silence echoed in the large cavern. Sargon stirred the water in the pool. He took his time walking to the mirror. Seventh Night watched him through a slight crack between two banners.

She half expected him to whisper magic words like the sorceress had. Instead, Sargon said, "Show me Kaleb."

Sargon's reflection wavered, and Kaleb's reflection replaced it. Seventh Night inhaled sharply. He was dressed in a soldier's outfit, but it was unmistakably Kaleb . . . or Neithan.

In the reflection, Kaleb paced back and forth. The prince stopped and stared straight at Sargon. Seventh Night wondered if he could see the villain. "Greetings, Kaleb," Sargon said.

"What have you done with her?" Kaleb asked. His brown eyes glared at Sargon critically. Seventh Night furrowed her brow. He had not asked who Sargon was.

"I have done nothing to your precious princess," Sargon snapped. "It was necessary to delay the wedding."

"Granted," Kaleb said. Not *how dare you* or *you fiend*, he simply said *granted*. "But why was

I not informed of the change in your plan?"

"I did not think it was necessary," Sargon retorted. "You have to admit it was effective though."

"It would have been more effective if your agent had not botched the first part," Kaleb pointed out. Sargon began to object. "I received the poison, Sargon, not Neithan. I was lucky some simpleton knew where a sorceress lived."

"But there are no sorcerers on your side of sea," Sargon said.

"Apparently there is one," Kaleb said, "the daughter of your traveling companion some years back."

"Mortagin's daughter," Sargon said thoughtfully. "If she is anything like him, this could be a problem."

"The princess said she could change form," Kaleb offered.

"A shifter? Even worse," Sargon said. "Keep a close eye on her. What was the response of your brother?"

"We are heading out in a search party soon," Kaleb said. "The sorceress is coming along. She recognized your birds. They are considering attempting to cross the sea, but I'll do my best to dissuade them."

"A small party would be easier to manage," Sargon told him.

"Agreed," Kaleb said. His expression softened. "How is Seventh Night?"

Sargon shrugged. "Healthy enough to break out of her room. She's somewhere in the castle, unless she jumped out of a window."

"She escaped?" Kaleb asked disapprovingly.

"It's a temporary situation," Sargon assured him. "When I find her, I'll collar that impudent little neck of hers."

"Sargon, you damage a hair on her head, and I swear I'll—" Kaleb started.

"I know, I know. I won't permanently damage her," Sargon promised. "She's too valuable an asset, even if she is a woman."

"Just take care of her until I get there," Kaleb snapped. "Good day." With that, Kaleb's reflection vanished, and the mirror returned to normal.

"Oh, I'll take care of her," Sargon hissed and started back to the stairs.

Seventh Night's head spun, her stomach tied into knots, and her knees threatened to give way. No, it was not possible. Kaleb. He was a traitor. Everything about him was a lie. No sweet line could undo what she had just heard. He would poison his own brother, honest, pure-hearted Neithan.

Assuming Neithan was honest and pure-hearted. Clearly she had failed in her assessment of princes.

Phillip, he had to be real. No one could make up someone like that. The sorceress was probably believable. No wait, she was a shifter. Perhaps she had changed form to look like Kaleb, and everything they said was done for her benefit. Seventh Night tried to comfort herself with that possibility, but it was a hollow comfort. His mannerism, different tones he took, little things that could not be copied convinced her that he was the man she had thought she loved.

She wanted to cry, but no tears fell. They simply collected in her eyes and fogged her vision. Seventh Night wiped them away. She was a princess, the princess of Tivin. She had to do what was best for her kingdom. Right now that seemed to be getting rid of Sargon. She could not do it on her own. She wished she could warn Neithan and Phillip. Seven stepped out from behind the banner. She felt cold and angry. How could Kaleb do this to her? She wished she had never seen that horrid mirror. The mirror! Its smooth glass and gold trim gleamed seductively. Seventh Night licked her lips. It was too fitting. The mirror that broke her heart might save her life.

Seventh Night hurried over to the mirror and grabbed it as if ready to shake it into working. She stopped and let her hands drop away. Holding the mirror might deter the magic somehow. She tried to stand the way Sargon had stood.

"Show me the magician," she told the mirror, daring it to disobey her. Her reflection wavered as Sargon's had. When the picture cleared, she saw what appeared to be a stable but no Phillip. She was about to give up, when he paced into view. "Magician, Magician," she called. She tried to yell and keep her voice down at the same time. Either Phillip did not or could not hear her, for he did not respond.

"Phillip, please," she said. This time he seemed to hear something. Phillip looked around and scratched his head. "Magician, listen to me!"

"Seven?" he asked.

"Yes," Seventh Night answered. "It's me."

"Where are you?" he asked.

"Across the sea," Seventh Night told him, "in some place called the Wizards Land. You need to tell Neithan and hurry. He knows you are coming."

"Who?" Phillip asked.

"Sargon, the wizard king," Seventh Night said. Phillip looked straight at her and some of the color in his tan face faded. "Are you alright?" she asked.

"Yes," Phillip said, stepped closer, and bent down. "But you're reflecting from my sword."

"I'm using a magic mirror Sargon used," she said hurriedly. "Stay quiet and listen to me. I am in a castle. I believe it is on some sort of rise. There is a moat monster and a cyclops and who knows what else. I escaped my room, but I do not know how long I can continue hiding. Sargon was the one who poisoned Kaleb. I heard that from his own lips. You need to find him and destroy him, or I fear the future of Tivin and Cordance will be grim." She took a deep breath and allowed a moment for the news to sink in.

She did not want to continue, but someone had to know the truth. "But I fear he is the least

of your immediate worries. Kaleb—"

"Seven!" Phillip called as her image faded. The sword became as it had been. He felt a bit overwhelmed, but then a fresh determination flowed into his veins. "I'm coming, Seven," he whispered. Taking the sword in hand, he stood and ran out of the stables.

CHAPTER XV

IMPOSSIBLE THINGS

The soft sound of water slipping had not caught her attention, nor could she see anything in the mirror, for its surface was filled with Phillip's image. It was in the polished frame of the mirror that she got the impression of something moving, and even then she could only tell it was large. Her breath left her as she turned slowly, hoping that she had not been found by Sargon or his cyclops.

They had not found her, but that was little comfort. The dragon like head was as wide as three well-muscled men standing shoulder-to-shoulder and just small enough not to bump the sides of the pool as it rose up. For half a second Seventh Night felt frozen as the dragon head rose gradually out of the water revealing its serpentine neck, its reptilian eyes as transfixed on her as she was on it. She backed away, stepping softly past the mirror to the nearest suit of armor. The armor did not hold a proper spear, but a parade banner pole with a pointed end. In hindsight, this was advantageous for she was not well-muscled and the banner pole was not nearly as heavy as a spear. Besides, she was as adept with a spear as Phillip was with a sword, so the whole exercise was as much for show as anything.

Disengaging the pole from its grasp, she caused the armor's gauntlet to clatter and fall. Seventh Night clutched her weapon in a most unprofessional manner. Her back to the wall, she eased her way toward the stairs.

The serpent-dragon head had risen enough so the height of its neck was now that of two men. It swayed slightly but kept its eyes transfixed on her. It seemed to Seventh Night much like that snake in the desert, only far more terrible.

SEVENTH NIGHT

Her foot found the first step, and she began the awkward climb, the banner pole grasped in her hands and her back pressed against the wall. The serpent-dragon continued to sway, sometimes coming closer, then moving back again, always keeping its eyes fixed on her. It rose no higher though, and eventually Seventh Night reached the door at the top. Now out of reach, she decided the banner pole was an ungainly thing to carry around and let it drop down into the room.

In the council chamber of Pinnacle Castle, which served double duty as a war room, Neithan studied the map spread out before him as Kaleb spoke. "We should send a small group into Uritz, and the rest of us should head south," he said and drew a line with his finger on the map.

"But the terrocks were headed west," the sorceress insisted.

"They could have turned," Kaleb pointed out. "We can finish a search on land faster than we can cross the sea."

"Do you know how wide the sea is?" the sorceress asked.

"No," Kaleb admitted. "But all we have is your word that this place exists to begin with. We might spare a small party, but anyone who goes will be sailing into the unknown and cut off from the rest. Why should we risk the main force on the word of a banished Gourlin?" The sorceress balled her fist and took a threatening step toward the prince.

Phillip burst into the room. "I know where Seven is," he announced.

"Where?" Neithan asked. He was just as happy that Phillip had broken up the argument between his brother and the sorceress as to hear he had news.

"Across the sea in the Wizards Land in some castle on a rise," Phillip said.

"Hah!" the sorceress crowed triumphantly.

"How do you know?" Kaleb asked.

"Seven told me," Phillip said, holding up his sword.

Kaleb blinked. "That's impossible."

"Nothing's impossible," the sorceress shot back. She blinked and turned to Phillip. "How did she tell you?"

SEVENTH NIGHT

"She said something about a magic mirror," Phillip said. "I heard her voice and saw her face reflecting from my sword."

"I've heard of a mirror that is supposed to do that," the sorceress said. "Did she say who had kidnapped her?"

"It was Sargon," Phillip said. "She escaped, but I think he found her again. We need to hurry."

"You can fill us in as we go," said Neithan.

She wanted to jump out the window. The castle felt like an infinite thing that would continue to grow and twist the longer she stayed, and the window appeared to be the quickest way out. Only the straight drop and jagged rocks below stopped her. At least Seventh Night knew she was back above ground now. Maybe if she circled around the floor, there would be a more inviting exit. There had to be a way in and out. She almost questioned that last thought but pushed the doubt aside. Even if it was not true, there was no benefit in worry.

It was something inward that caught her eye,

however, a grand hallway with high arched ceilings that would have swallowed the grand dining hall of Pinnacle castle, but the size was not what caught her attention. It was the color. Most of the castle was grey or brown stone, the walls roughly hewn, and the floors flattened by wear, but the floor of this grand hall was glossy black and white marble. The white walls were smooth and cool to the touch. Lining the walls were life-sized portraits of women, most in bright, handsome dress but some in peasant garb, all of them sad and haunting. The room was heavy with magic to the point that even she could taste it. The air smelled of dry lightning.

Seventh Night felt compelled to enter the eerie hall. She walked softly down the center of the large room, her footsteps soundless. Despite the strangeness, the hall was or had been meant for guests. It was built to impress and invite, built for receiving, and for guests to come in there had to be an entrance. The thought excited her, but her eyes kept falling to the paintings. They were not right. The portraits were all the same style, very realistic. The backgrounds were all the same empty gray.

And they seemed to be changing. The hands,

the expressions, shifted every time she looked at them. She felt like their eyes were following her.

The eyes of one portrait in particular grabbed her. She sidetracked from her trek down the middle and approached it. The tall woman had the dress and bearing of a true lady. Her perfect complexion was pale, her brown hair swept back into a soft bun, but her dark eyes were infinitely sad and compelling. "Who are you?" the princess murmured. The sound of her own voice seemed to temporarily break the spell. She looked away to the far end of the hall, slightly dismayed by its length.

Her eyes returned to the painting, but now the woman's arm was stretched out to her. Seventh Night let out a yelp and stumbled back. She tried to run, but the length of her dress slowed her, and her feet became sluggish. She was not entirely sure what she was running from. The painting had moved, but its surface had remained flat. She tried to calm her breathing when she noticed an even more peculiar frame. This one held no woman, only the swirled grey background. She felt drawn to it. The secret to the enchantment was in the empty portrait, or behind it, but she knew it was there.

She stepped towards it cautiously and rested her hand on the adjacent pillar. As her other hand reached forward to touch the canvas, the air filled with a thousand urgent whispers. Her fingers were ready to brush the surface. Only instead of brushing it, they went through. Her hand followed; then she realized it was pulling her. Her eyes widened with understanding. She gripped the pillar with renewed vigor, but it seemed inadequate against the pull. She had no will to scream and only felt a horrible resignation.

Her hand slipped from the pillar.

CHAPTER XVI

THE CYCLOPS

Sargon had left Martyr to look for the princess on his own. The cyclops was happy with this because he did not like the angry little man yelling at him, and when Sargon was there, Sargon yelled at him.

The castle was very, very big, and Martyr hoped it would take him a very, very long time to find the princess. He walked down one hall and then another, up one stair and down another. He opened door after door. Very few were locked. They did not need to be locked.

Martyr did not understand why they needed to be closed either, but he knew Sargon would yell if he left the doors open. So he closed each one he checked.

And after many halls and stairs and doors, Martyr smelled something. It was the same smell as the room with all the books, only it was not a book smell. He was tired of opening and closing doors, so he followed the not-book smell.

He followed it through many more passages and down many more stairs. He followed it to the room with the mirror and the big water monster. He was not fond of the water monster, so he was happy that a fresher scent led a different way.

Vaguely it crawled through his mind that he was supposed to feed the monster.

Right now the scent was more important. He followed it through more passageways and up more stairs. He followed it to the room with all the paintings. It was there he found the princess, her arm halfway through the canvas.

Martyr snorted and shook his head. Princesses were not very bright; even he knew better than to stick his hand into an enchanted painting. He ran over before she got pulled in any further and wrapped his arm around her waist. It took a good tug to get her out.

Since she was held pretty securely under his arm, he carried her that way, and set off to find Sargon.

The tiny princess should have been happy to have gotten away from the painting, but she pushed and kicked and wriggled.

Martyr felt satisfied about finding the princess, but as he walked on, something bothered him. He did not want to give Sargon the princess. He did not like Sargon, but if he did not do what Sargon asked, Sargon would yell. But, when he had the princess before, he had yelled a lot too. More than that, the way-deep-down voice did not want to give the princess to Sargon.

Having done all that walking to catch her though, Martyr did not want to just let her go. He thought about it some more until he found an idea he liked. Happy, he ran past the kitchen and into the room with all the barrels. In the back wall of this room was a little wooden flap door. Martyr dropped the princess inside.

As she slid away Martyr reflected that she was a lot softer and a lot nicer to look at than

Sargon, but she kicked a lot and screamed almost as much as Sargon yelled.

Seventh Night slid down a slick, steep tunnel. She would have admitted to being confused and frightened if she was not so winded. More abruptly than the slide began, it ended. Seventh Night found herself flying through the air. She considered screaming, but as she saw the water rushing up to meet her, she decided inhaling would be wiser.

She slapped into the water.

It closed around her, and for a moment she was awed by how the sky looked from underwater. The awe was short-lived as her desire to breathe came to the forefront. She had never learned how to swim, but she had read about swimmers in books. Hardly the same, but she knew enough to kick and move her arms and try to head for the light.

By some miracle, she managed to break the surface. She gasped for air and tried to figure out where she was. It did not take her long to decide she must be in the moat and needed to get to land before the moat monster reached the same conclusion. After much kicking, grasping, and gasping, she reached the shore.

She lay there for a minute, shivering and coughing. Though certainly happy to be out of the castle, looking at the high cliff and the shape moving in the water reminded her that she was lost and alone in a strange land, and the man she had trusted and loved had betrayed her and everything else she loved.

Though the movement in the water spurred her to move away, she paid little attention to where she was going.

It was in this manner that she wandered into an orchard. Gradually it dawned on the still dripping princess that the very strange thing about this orchard was that there was nothing particularly strange about this orchard.

Birds sang, and the sun shone through the branches without the constant cover of clouds. The trees were green and bore a pretty, pale orange fruit. It even smelled good. This of course reminded Seventh Night that she was very hungry.

Before she could do anything about her

stomach, her attention was drawn to a small boy about nine who was jumping under a tree. Not sensing anything particularly malicious about him, she approached.

"Hello?"

The boy stopped jumping and looked at her. "Hiyo, can you reach it?" he asked.

"What?"

"The gabaya," the boy said. He put his hands on his hips and looked at her expectantly.

Seventh Night looked over her head at the ripe fruit on the branch. She would never be tall, but she was taller than the boy. She reached up and plucked one and gave it to him. The boy beamed and took a bite.

"Why are you all wet?" he asked through his mouthful.

"I fell in the moat," Seventh Night said simply.

The boy grinned and swallowed. "*Masei, masei, masei*," he said and circled his finger in the air. A wind came up, nearly strong enough to knock her over. When it subsided, she was practically dry.

The boy laughed at her dropped jaw and ran off.

SEVENTH NIGHT

"Wait! Please!" Seventh Night called. Her legs were too tired to run after him, and he did not turn back. She sighed and picked a fruit for herself.

"THIEF!"

Seventh Night turned her head toward the new voice. The wiry man it came from did not look threatening, but the sharp pitchfork in his hand did. Not really interested to see what happened when he caught her, Seventh Night threw the rest of her energy into running.

CHAPTER XVII

THE PRIDE OF CORDANCE

It took Neithan's party a day and a half to reach the seaport. The Cordance seaport was located in Cordance Bay. The bay stretched for over two miles, but most of the seaside community lived near the central docks. They had formed a village called, in traditional Cordance originality, Seaside. The village was divided into three basic areas: the merchant area with stores and taverns; the slums for the forgotten, the old, the crippled, and the good-for-nothings; and opposite the slums the homes of the fishermen and sailors' wives. Seaside was the fastest growing village in Cordance. Not that it was growing all that rapidly, just faster than other places.

For the most part, trade was carried out over land. Men had fished near the shore for thousands of years, but sailors had just begun to tame the waves on a larger scale. They were building bigger ships and sailing farther out to sea and further down the coast. The more foresighted people knew that ships would soon dominate the trade routes. The roads were simply not good enough.

Phillip did his best to keep Thunder at a slow pace. He pulled on the reins again, and the unicorn snorted and shook with displeasure. Phillip knew he wanted to run and stretch his wings. He did not blame him, but they had to keep in their proper place in the procession. A crowd had gathered on the side of the road. They respectfully took off their hats as the prince passed by. Phillip thought he saw one man spit, but no one else seemed to notice.

When they reached the docks, those on horseback dismounted. Phillip patted Thunder on his muscular neck and found Neithan, who was speaking with the captain of the king's flagship.

The *Pride of Cordance* lived up to its name. The vessel dwarfed all the surrounding ships. It stood a couple of stories above the water, without counting the mast. An extra long dock had been built exclusively for the *Pride*. All Phillip could see from the shore was the rear of the ship and the tall masts.

Neithan noticed Phillip standing there. "Captain Onnell, this is Phillip. He'll be coming along." The white-haired captain was not a very impressive looking man, the kind that could be easily lost in a crowd, but Phillip had learned not to judge by the exterior.

Phillip gave a courteous answer, which the captain returned along with a nod. What he lacked in looks, the captain made up for in voice; he had a strong, stern voice that made someone think twice before disobeying. Then Phillip asked Neithan, "Do I have time to take Thunder for a walk? He could use the exercise before being cooped up on the ship."

Neithan nodded. "We're leaving first thing tomorrow."

As Phillip walked away, he heard the captain

saying, "You're not going to let that thing on my ship?!"

"Yes, Captain," Neithan said. "It's a strong horse. It might be useful when we reach the Wizards Land." Grudgingly, the captain nodded his consent, unwilling to contradict the prince.

The sorceress carried her sack across her back and her bow and quiver of arrows in her hand. She had not packed her whole lab like before, only one book of magic, some clothes, and a comb. She pushed back a copper curl the wind had blown in her face and headed toward the ship.

She had not gone two steps before the captain yelled at her. "You there!" he snapped. "Where do you think you're going?"

"To the ship," the sorceress said patiently.

"No," the captain said. "I won't have it. I simply won't have it."

"Won't have what?" Neithan asked.

"Prince Neithan, who is this woman?" Captain Onnell demanded.

"She's a sorceress who's coming to help us find the princess," Neithan said. He realized his mistake as soon as he finished the sentence. He should never have said sorceress.

SEVENTH NIGHT

The captain's round face began to change color. "Sire, I can almost suffer the black horse and even a woman out of respect for your Highness, though all they do is get in the way, but I will not have a witch on my ship!"

"I'm not a witch!" the sorceress shot back.

"Captain," Neithan said calmly. "I understand your concerns, but she is a good sorceress. She is the only one who knows anything about the Wizards Land. She *is* going." The captain started to protest. "If you have a problem," Neithan cut him off, "I will simply have to find someone else to sail my ship."

The captain's face changed color again from red to white. "It is not that I mind, Sire," he said hurriedly. "It's the crew. Sailors are very superstitious. Having a woman on board is bad luck, the black beast makes it worse; if they were to find out she did magic, there may be a mutiny."

"Then I suggest we keep the sorceress part quiet," Neithan said. "And maybe it's time the sailors got over their superstitions."

"Yes, Sire," the captain said reluctantly. Neithan nodded satisfactorily and went to make sure that all the supplies were being loaded.

SEVENTH NIGHT

The captain gave the sorceress a nasty look. "Welcome aboard."

Later that evening, the sorceress stood on the upper deck of the *Pride of Cordance* and looked out at the night sky and the bobbing waves. She took a deep breath of sea air and crossed her arms on the railing. The sea rolled out its open arms. In the dark, it was difficult to tell where the waves ended and the night began. The stars played across the sky with the motherly crescent moon to watch over them. The sea sang its siren song as sailors checked ropes and swapped stories.

The sorceress noticed Neithan walk up beside her but said nothing. "What are you thinking?" he asked.

"I like the sea," the sorceress said. "It's kind of like the desert, except made of water, and the dunes move, and it's not as hot. I like the smell and the breeze. I wonder what it's like further out."

"The same," Neithan said. "Except the waves are bigger, the wind stronger, and you can't see the shore."

"Sounds great." The sorceress looked at Neithan. "You're not out here to talk about the waves are you?"

Neithan shrugged. "You need a name," he said.

"Why?" she asked.

"Because sailors are superstitious," he answered. "I'm taking a risk bringing you on board in the first place. If I call you sorceress all the time, it will make it worse. And I don't want to have to keep calling you 'hey you' either."

"Then call me Hayoo," the sorceress suggested.

Neithan grimaced. "Is that what you want to be called?" he asked.

"No," the sorceress laughed. "You can't get a joke can you?"

Neithan shrugged.

"You're not very talkative either," she teased. "I want a man who can carry on a conversation."

"I pity the man you marry," Neithan said. "You'll talk him to death in less than a week."

The sorceress looked a little taken aback, then smiled admiringly. "Good one," she said. "Maybe you're smarter than I give you credit."

"Thanks," Neithan said sarcastically. He

turned to leave.

"Wait," the sorceress said. "I didn't mean that."

Neithan turned back around. "I know," he said.

"Then why are you going?" she asked.

"I'm tired," Neithan said.

"Oh," the sorceress said. "Goodnight, then." Neithan started to leave again. "Do you know where Phillip is?" the sorceress asked.

Neithan stopped and waited a few seconds before turning back around. "He's spending the night on shore," he said.

"Oh," the sorceress said. "See you tomorrow then?"

"Yes. Goodnight," he said with a note of finality.

"Goodnight," the sorceress said and returned to watching the sea.

The moment dawn spilled across the water, the town of Seaside came to life. Fishermen rowed their boats out of the shallows. Shops opened and vendors poured onto the streets hoping to offload their merchandise to the soldiers and departing sailors. A small crowd formed at the docks to see the *Pride of Cordance* off.

Phillip watched them gather from the ship. He weaved through the busy sailors and spotted Neithan. The prince was discussing a matter with Captain Onnell. Phillip found a vacant place at the rail where he could listen to their conversation.

"Did Thunder cause any problems with the crew?" Neithan asked the captain.

"Three quit on the spot when they saw that demon horse," Onnell replied. "Two did not come back from the slums last night."

"Will that cause us any problems?"

"Not likely," Onnell said. "Four more signed up when they saw your witch."

Phillip looked around and found the sorceress. She had told Phillip earlier she refused to be useless. At the moment, she was busy talking to one of the sailors. The sailor handed the rope to her in annoyance and said something. Phillip decided he needed to learn how to lip read. The sorceress took the rope from the sailor and helped him pull.

Phillip felt a tap on his shoulder and turned

to see Neithan towering over him.

"Are you settled in?" Neithan asked.

Phillip nodded. "There wasn't much to settle." He lowered his voice. "Did Kaleb get on board?" On further consideration, Kaleb had shed the role of a soldier and became a sailor. He had ridden ahead of Neithan and the soldiers to find a position on the ship.

Neithan nodded. "He's somewhere below."

Phillip looked out at the waves uneasily. "Is the water always this choppy?" he asked.

"No," Neithan said. "Today's pretty calm."

"Wonderful," Phillip muttered.

Neithan smiled. "Are you seasick?"

"No, no," Phillip assured him. "I'm fine."

CHAPTER XVIII

THE CRYSTAL INN CITY TAVERN

All her life, Seventh Night had been taught the importance of presentation. The proper way, the graceful way, the diplomatic way were ingrained deeply into her subconscious. All this focus on etiquette however had left her with little physical strength or practical knowledge of how to fend for herself when she was not within the secure walls of a palace (something her desperate ride to Pinnacle had taught her, and then she had at least had Toshk as companion and protector). Training in the royal ways did make her very willful, and now it was by sheer will power that she stumbled through the city.

Her mother would have been appalled by her lack of grace and timid manner as she made her way down the street. She had found buildings and some semblance of civilization. She only hoped that she could find a sympathetic soul.

A door to a decent sized building flung open in front of her. Two men and a woman burst out onto the street laughing. The smell of cooked meat and other edibles wafted out. Looking up, Seventh Night saw a sign.

CRYSTAL INN CITY TAVERN

The prospect of food and a bed led her inside.

A fire crackled in the hearth, and she drank in the warmth. The tavern seemed to be doing a good business. Most of the tables were occupied. The rise and fall of voices made her realize how unsettling the quiet, emptiness of the castle had been.

A large, bearded man stood behind a counter that was part of the back wall. Seventh Night made her way there, nearly tripping a few times.

When she got to the counter, she leaned upon it.

"I'm hungry," she said.

"Well, what do you want?" the man said, echoing her posture.

"I don't have any money," Seventh Night explained to him and glanced down at her hands. Her crest ring had managed to stay on her finger through it all. "But you can have my ring."

The man took the ring with little ceremony and bellowed to someone behind him. "Vyn, soup!" He turned back to Seventh Night. "Go sit."

Relieved that he had accepted her payment, Seventh Night found the nearest empty table and sat down. She was too tired to notice the curious glances that came her way. She laid her head on her hand and studied the imperfections in the wood.

"Hiyo," said one of the two men who had sat down in front of her without her notice. "What's a pretty little thing like you doin' out on her own?"

Seventh Night raised her head and looked at them wearily.

"Wha's wrong darlin'?" he continued. "You

lose your tongue?"

"I'm tired," she said. She had no energy for pleasantries or arguments.

The first man looked over at the second. "She's tired," he repeated sympathetically.

The second man smiled and nodded sympathetically. Then the second man spilled some powder out into his hand. He blew it in to Seventh Night's general direction. She waved her hand at the powder and coughed.

"Who you stayin' with, love?" the first man asked, before she could start to get up.

"No one," Seventh Night said with a little scowl.

"You'll have to let us find you a place," he said helpfully.

Seventh Night did not like the sound of that at all and frowned a little more while she studied the men. The first one might be called attractive if a bit scruffy. The second much less, though they both seemed to be roughly the same age.

The scruffy, attractive one reached out his hand, and ran his fingers along the hair beside her face. "Can't leave nice young ladies all alone at night," he soothed. "It's not safe."

Before her brain could send the signal, her

hand snapped up to knock his away. Before she could make any further objections to his behavior, a heavy soup bowl thunked onto the table.

"Are they bothering you, child?" a female interrupted. The speaker, Seventh Night found as she looked up, was an unusually tall woman about twice the princess's age dressed in a practical brown dress. She was worn in the way of someone who had no aversion to work but was not weighed down by it. Her brown hair was frizzy with a grey tint and pulled into a sensible tail. She held herself with the confidence of a noblewoman, and her gaze bore into the two men.

The first man raised his arms innocently. "We were just being friendly, Mother Vyn."

"I saw how friendly you were being," Vyn shot back. "Leave her alone."

"Now, don't be sore, Vyn."

"And get out of here," Vyn continued. "I don't want to see either of you around here for a while."

The man opened his mouth again.

"Out," Vyn repeated.

Reluctantly, they both rose from the table and

left the tavern.

Vyn shook her head. "You all right, hon?" she said, as she sat down.

Seventh Night nodded.

"Eat your soup," Vyn instructed. "It will fix you up."

Seventh Night obeyed, and Vyn studied her.

"Do you need a place to stay, child?" Vyn asked gently.

"I was hoping you would have a room," Seventh Night said. "I don't know what the ring is worth here. But I don't have any other money..."

"Don't worry about it," Vyn said. "I have a room for you."

Vyn left and returned with some bread and milk to go with her soup. Seventh Night found herself eating with a graceless relish that reminded her of being ten years old again and starved after a horseback lesson. Vyn sat beside her, nibbling on some bread, and seemed to find something mildly amusing in the way the younger woman was eating.

After Seventh Night finished, Vyn took her upstairs to a small room. It was the least luxurious bedroom in which the princess had ever stayed, but the simple fact it contained a bed made it a beautiful sight.

Vyn led her to the chair beside the bed and instructed Seventh Night to sit. "Goodness, child," she said softly. "You must have had a busy day. Let Mother Vyn clean you up." She took a cloth from her pocket, dampened it with water from a small washbasin, and started gently wiping Seventh Night's face.

The princess thought this to be a little odd but not particularly threatening. Besides, other things seemed more important. "What was that powder?" she asked.

"Probably Chalcain," Vyn said. She dipped the cloth back in the water. From the look of it, Seventh Night must have been a little dirtier than she had realized. "It makes you more open to spells and suggestions for a while. You should be all right in the morning."

Seventh Night nodded. That made a little sense.

"Where are you from?" Vyn asked.

"Tivin," Seventh Night heard herself answer.

"I'm not familiar with that town," Vyn said. "Is it far?"

"Very far."

SEVENTH NIGHT

Vyn took Seventh Night's hand and began dabbing her arm. Seventh Night saw blood on the cloth and noticed some small scratches she did not remember getting. Her eyes made a lazy circle around the room. Bed. Wall. Chest of drawers. Door. Washstand.

"Now into bed," Vyn said as she folded back the covers. The chair was close enough Seventh Night need not stand. She simply rolled onto the bed. Vyn coaxed off what remained of her white slippers and covered Seventh Night with the blanket.

Vyn sat in the chair and smoothed Seventh Night's hair away from her face. "Did you run off from your wedding?" Vyn asked.

Seventh Night shook her head sleepily. "Carried off," she murmured, half asleep.

"That's too bad," Vyn said softly.

"Worst part is that he was right," she mumbled, then she slept.

SEVENTH NIGHT

CHAPTER XIX

MYTHS ABOUT MERMAIDS

Three days later, Phillip stood at the bow of the *Pride of Cordance*, straining his eyes for any sign of land and wondering if he should risk a turn in the crow's nest.

"Slow going, eh?" a gruff but familiar voice said from behind him. Phillip had not seen Kaleb since he had arrived on the ship, not that he had been looking. Kaleb joined him at the rail. He wore a hood and a patch over the left eye. Between that and the bristles on his chin, he played his role rather well. Though Phillip thought the accent needed work.

Phillip shrugged in response. "You look terrible," he commented.

"I thought that was the point," Kaleb replied smoothly in his own voice. He stroked his beginnings of a beard. "I told Seventh Night once that I was thinking of growing a mustache. She said that was fine, but if I did, I could forget about marrying her. Of course, she was laughing when she said it."

"Probably the thought of you with a mustache," Phillip offered.

"There's a lot of complaining among the sailors," Kaleb said. "They are worried about being this far from land."

Phillip shrugged. "If I thought it would do any good, I'd complain too, but all we can do now is wait."

"Storm to starboard!" someone shouted. Phillip hurried to the starboard side of the ship and searched the skies for clouds. Kaleb glanced that way, then disappeared below deck. On the horizon Phillip saw a black, ominous looking cloud. Despite the distance he could see the storm churn violently and the occasional flash of lightning. He watched for a while to see if it was coming closer, but the storm hovered in its place north of the ship.

The sorceress and Prince Neithan stepped up beside him. "Does it look bad?" the sorceress asked.

"Yes," Phillip said. "But it's not coming any closer."

"Good," the sorceress sighed. She made a quick, graceful turn and hopped up to sit on the rail. "If I hear one more complaint about being bad luck, I'll—I don't know—do something."

"Speaking of bad luck," Neithan said, "how about Winefried?"

"Yuck!" the sorceress said.

"Matillie?"

"Double yuck."

"Janny?"

"Too childish."

"Loriga?"

"No."

"But that's my mother's."

Phillip grinned and shook his head. Since they had set sail, the prince and the sorceress had been playing some sort of name game. Neithan threw out name after name, and the sorceress refused them.

"Do you have any idea how much further it is?" Phillip asked her.

"Not the slightest," she admitted. Neithan paused a moment and stared at the storm clouds, searching the depths of his mind for something. "To be honest I'm getting a little stir crazy myself," the sorceress continued. "If I knew how to swim, I'd jump in the ocean."

"Play with the mermaids," Phillip suggested jokingly.

"What are mermaids again?" the sorceress said more to herself than anyone else.

"They're these women with fish tails," Phillip told her. "Old Omthais has been telling stories about them at night. Their king was insulted by some men, and they took it out on all mankind. Foundering any boats that came in deep water and drowning those men that fell in the sea. They liked to come to the surface and taunt the sailors before they knocked them over."

"Why did they stop?" the sorceress asked. "They did stop, didn't they?"

"Apparently the mer-king's daughter didn't like them taunting the sailors before they killed them. So he promised her they'd stop that part.

If the sailors could see a mermaid, they wouldn't tip the boat. It's supposed to be good luck now to spot a mermaid. But!" he said with a wicked grin. "They still drown those that fall in the sea." With that he grabbed her arm and made a motion as if he were going to push her off the ship.

Startled, the sorceress gripped his arm. Phillip laughed. The sorceress threw him a dirty look, then she laughed as well.

"Have you ever seen one?" she asked.

"No." Phillip shook his head. "I don't think they exist."

"But it's good luck to see one," she said.

"According to Omthais."

"I've got it!" Neithan said, slapping the rail with a satisfied palm.

"Got what?" the sorceress asked.

"A name," he said triumphantly.

"Spit it out," she said.

"Andomare."

"Andomare?"

"Yes," Neithan said. "It means wild fire in an ancient language."

"What do you think?" she asked Phillip.

"I don't know," he said. "What's it for?"

"Me," the sorceress said incredulously, as if she could not believe he did not think the whole world revolved around her. "Do I sound like an Andomare to you?"

"I could get used to it," he said.

"Alright," she said turning to Neithan. "You can call me Andomare."

That night, Phillip slipped into the smaller of the two rooms where the sailors slept. He needed to speak to Kaleb, but he had no idea what he wanted to say. Not that the need to know was urgent; Phillip found the room empty.

In a way, he was relieved. He had been saved from stuttering around endlessly before he figured out what his point was. He started to turn around and leave, but something caught the corner of his eye. At closer inspection he found it to be a map. Creased where it had obviously been folded many times, it showed the kingdoms surrounding Cordance from Gourlin to the Wizards Land. Each of the kingdoms possessed a number, Cordance-two, Tivin-three, Uritz-four, Lampshmith-five, Muori-six, Gourlin-seven, and so on. Phillip found the map odd. He had started to put his finger on the reason, when Kaleb entered the room.

"What are you doing?" Kaleb asked when he saw Phillip holding the map.

Phillip tried not to look guilty. "I was just admiring your chart."

With a set jaw, Kaleb held out his hand for the paper, and Phillip handed it over to him. Kaleb carefully refolded the map. "I would appreciate it if you consulted with me before rummaging through my things," Kaleb said tightly.

"I offer apology. I didn't mean to pry," Phillip lied. "It's very interesting," he continued. "What do the numbers stand for?"

Kaleb hesitated. "I keep a journal of what I know about the different countries. I use the numbers to remember what country goes with what information."

"That's a good idea, much more convenient than using the country names," Phillip said, managing to keep the sarcasm in his head and out of his voice. "Is that the Wizards Land drawn in on the left?"

"A rough sketch," Kaleb said. "We know it's somewhere to the west."

SEVENTH NIGHT

Phillip opened his mouth to speak, but a shout muffled by the wood came from the deck. Phillip hurried out of the room. Kaleb tucked his map away and followed.

The light of the full moon spilled upon the waters making the crest of the waves visible. Phillip found Omthais leaning over the railing, pointing vigorously, and looking like a delighted child. Phillip ran over to him. "What's happened?"

"Mermaid!" Omthais exclaimed breathlessly. "In all my years...It's a mermaid!"

Phillip looked where the old sailor pointed. A fish tail vanished below the waves. He had decided not to spoil the old man's dream by pointing out that it could just be a big fish, when he saw a silhouette like an arm break the current. Something reminiscently human broke the surface before diving below the waves. He waited with Omthais until it seemed the creature would not return.

"In all my years," Omthais murmured. "In all my years...wasn't she beautiful."

With only moonlight to see by, Phillip could not be sure, but he had to admit it looked like it could have been a mermaid. He looked around for Neithan or the sorceress, Neithan or Andomare he corrected himself, but they were nowhere to be seen. Kaleb had disappeared as well.

Neithan had been on deck when the cry of mermaid rang out. He had looked over the rail in time to see the mermaid break surface, golden hair glistening in the moonlight. The sight should have fascinated him, but instead he found himself thoughtful as if the appearance had been a riddle. He had a feeling...

While the rest of crew was fixated on watching over the starboard side in hopes of seeing the mermaid again, Neithan walked to the port side. He saw one of the rope ladders draped overboard and smiled. He went to retrieve something from his cabin and returned.

After a few minutes, the rope ladder tensed as a dripping Andomare climbed to the top. "Enjoy your swim?" he asked when she reached the deck.

Andomare gave him a warning look. Her copper-red curls were weighed down with water, and a droplet rolled off her nose. She sat down on the deck, exhausted. Neithan wrapped the thick blanket he had brought around her and sat beside her. She smiled at him.

"Why did you do that?" he asked.

Andomare shrugged. "We needed some good luck," she said.

Neithan put a hand on her shoulder. "But you can't swim?" he reminded her.

"Oh, it's much easier to do with a tail," Andomare explained. "At first it took some getting used to, but I watched the fishes, there are some really big ones down there, and after a while, I figured it out. It's real pretty under the surface. I wish you could see it. Some of the fish sparkle like silver, and some things down there don't look like fish at all, but I think they're alive. There were these funny things on the bottom of the ship. They were like little rocks with tongues."

"Barnacles," Neithan said. "Most ships get them."

"Really," Andomare said with a curious look. "Do you think they're a disease ships get or little creatures?"

"I don't know," Neithan said. "Probably little creatures since you can find them on things other than ships."

SEVENTH NIGHT

Andomare pulled the blanket tighter around herself and rested her head on Neithan's shoulder. "I'm tired."

Neithan stood and pulled her up. "I'll take you to your cabin."

The sorceress regarded him with emerald eyes and smiled. She pulled the blanket over her head to hide her wet curls, and Neithan led her beneath the deck.

SEVENTH NIGHT

CHAPTER XX

MOTHER VYN

The first morning that Seventh Night awoke at the tavern was actually an afternoon.

She found a simple dress hung over the end of the bed. She tried it on and managed to make it fit reasonably well. Since there were no other shoes, she put her now-not-so-white slippers back on her feet.

When she crept downstairs, she found only a couple of people sitting in the tavern's public room. She started to sit down herself when she heard voices from the room behind the counter. One of them sounded like Vyn, so she put her ear to the door and pushed it open slowly.

"She can stay if you like, Vyn, but she has to do something useful."

"You're impossible, Yalan. The child has obviously been through a lot. She needs charity, and she seems like such a good little thing."

"Vyn, she's a young woman, not an infant. I'll grant you she seems respectable, but respectable people like to earn their keep. That's how they stay respectable people."

Seventh Night cracked the door open far enough that she could see Vyn sit down and cross her arms. "You should see her hands," Vyn said softly. "She wasn't made to work."

"How about it, girl?" the large, bearded man asked Seventh Night, startling her. "You willing to work?"

"Hush," Vyn admonished him. "Did the dress fit, hon?"

Seventh Night nodded and entered.

"I'm sure she has a name, Vyn," Yalan said.

"Of course. What's your name, dear?"

"Seven," she answered. She did not want to give her full name, even if they were trustworthy.

"How pretty," Vyn said.

"It's a number, Vyn," Yalan snerked.

Vyn made a face at him. "It's a pretty number. They could have called her Five."

Yalan laughed. "Well, Seven, I can offer you room and board for chores. What can you do?"

"Beg pardon?"

"You cook, sew, or know any useful spells?" he asked.

Seventh Night took a seat and frowned. She had attempted sewing once and accomplished nothing more than sore fingers. "No," she admitted.

Yalan raised his thick, dark eyebrows. "You ever swept a floor? Washed dishes? Done the laundry?"

She shook her head and tried to think of something she could do that would be useful to these people. She knew a few languages, names of the constellations, philosophy, political ideas, history, the proper etiquette for Tivin and surrounding countries, how to ride a winged unicorn, and had a general idea of how many things were done. She knew how to be a proper princess and what the needs of her kingdom were, but she had no idea how any of it could be useful to these people.

"What did you do all day at home?" Yalan asked.

Vyn gave him a small kick. "Can't you see she's a *lady*? You do remember what that is, right?"

Yalan narrowed his eyes at her. "Yes, Vyn. It's what you're not."

Vyn glared back, and for the first time Seventh Night sensed their banter had gotten a little mean.

"I'm an only child," she interrupted. "I think my father tended to dote on me a bit much."

"Nothing wrong with that," Vyn said with a note of finality.

Yalan huffed. "She's yours, Vyn. Just don't forget to do your own share." He stood and walked out.

"If I didn't love that man, I'd have to strangle him," Vyn sighed.

"I didn't mean to cause any trouble," Seven apologized.

"Don't worry about it," Vyn smiled. "If you weren't here, it would be something else. You missed our fight over the turnips earlier."

SEVENTH NIGHT

Seventh Night did worry, though, just not over the fight. It bothered her that Yalan thought she was useless, more so that he might be right.

The second morning Seventh Night awoke at the tavern, she went downstairs in search of breakfast. She found it, along with a busy Vyn in the back kitchen.

"Mother Vyn," she said between bites. She had learned that was how everyone save Yalan was expected to address the woman. "I do want to be helpful. I'm afraid I just don't know what I can do."

Vyn stopped what she was doing for a moment and looked at her. "I suppose I could just get you to help me with my chores, if you don't mind. I guess Yalan has more sense about him than I do, but I do remember how to take care of a lady. It would feel strange."

"I'm not really a lady here," Seventh Night said. "If I were, I would pay you properly for letting me stay, but since I cannot, I feel that I must do something for you." She smiled. "To stay respectable."

So Vyn took her through her day's routine. Seventh Night tried but got the feeling that she was slowing Vyn down as much as she was helping her.

Mother Vyn seemed quite happy with the arrangement, though. Seventh Night did her best to get Vyn to talk about the city and land in general but took care not to reveal how out of place she was. The sort of things she talked about did not sound particularly important or magical at first. Eventually she tried some more direct questions.

"What sort of spells do you know?"

Vyn did not react as if it were an unusual question. "Nothing grand," she said. "Just some practical things."

"Like what?"

"I have a cold spell that's pretty useful."

"Could you show me?" Seventh Night asked.

Vyn took her back to the kitchen and opened a deep chest. Seventh Night could feel cool air drift out from it. The insides of the chest were frosted and filled with various types of food. Midwinter, it would not have been a strange sight, but this was late summer. She thought it was quite wondrous but tried to dampen her awe.

"The cold spell is actually on that stone under there," Vyn explained. "I will have to recast it in a few days." She closed the chest. "It has come in very handy as valuable as food can be."

"Is food scarce?" Seventh Night asked.

Vyn frowned. "Not recently; depends how foul a mood takes him."

"Who?"

"Sargon, of course," Vyn said.

"It's terrible for a king to deny his people food," Seventh Night murmured to herself. She hoped her escape did not put him into a foul mood. She did not want these people to suffer on her account.

"I also know a simple sleeping spell," Vyn continued. If she had heard Seventh's comment, she did not want to discuss it further. "And one to keep out the rats, which is very important for a properly run tavern. It would have been very expensive to have someone else come and do it." Vyn dusted her hands together and swept her gaze about the kitchen as though checking for signs of rodents. "What sort did you learn at home?"

"I—" Seventh faltered. "I was never very good at it. I tried a few times and could not manage anything." Which was not completely a lie. Alone in her room, she had playfully attempted to imitate some of the sorceress's chants, and nothing had happened.

"Oh," Vyn said sympathetically. "That does happen to some. You may simply be trying too hard. It can be difficult for beginners, but you are young."

Seventh Night nodded.

That night she went to bed unhappy, because now Vyn thought that she was incompetent as well as useless.

The third morning that Seventh Night awoke at the tavern, Vyn loaned her a neat apron, found her some decent shoes, and insisted on fixing her hair.

Vyn sat behind her charge and brushed out her tangles. "It's been a long time, but I do remember how to take care of a lady."

"You have before?"

SEVENTH NIGHT

"I was an attendant to the Lady Dumas," Vyn said nostalgically. "Before I left the castle."

"Why did you leave?"

"Same reason everyone else did," Vyn said. "I suppose that was before you were born."

There was something sad in her voice, so Seventh Night decided not to ask any more questions. At least not for the moment.

When Vyn had fixed Seven's hair to suit her, they went downstairs for breakfast. After breakfast, they would go to the market, which Seventh Night assumed was the reason for the attention to her appearance. She had to trust Vyn's assurance that she looked nice, for there were no mirrors to be found in the tavern, no reflective metal at all save a few kitchen knives that were sheathed in wooden blocks when not in use. This was hardly unusual, as good mirrors were expensive, but she did wonder if it was deliberate.

Yalan was already at the table, eating and frowning at stacks of coins.

"Marketing day," Vyn said as if he needed to be reminded.

"Dark skies, Vyn," he growled. "Where does the money go?"

SEVENTH NIGHT

"Well, this stack here," Vyn said, picking up a stack, "is going with me to the market." She dropped the coins into a dress pocket.

Yalan narrowed his eyes at her. "That is not what I meant."

Vyn gave him a tired smile, as if this was a discussion they had had often. "Are we making more than we spend?"

"I think so," Yalan said. "But I thought we had a bit more than this. I'm wondering if someone ran off with it."

"Why don't you check your ledger?" Seventh Night asked as she sat down.

"My what?" Yalan asked.

"Your record of finances?" she tried again.

Yalan continued to give her a blank stare.

"You do not keep a ledger?" she asked incredulously. Yalan's expression answered her question. "Then that is the greater part of your problem." She noticed Vyn looking at her oddly as well. "Do people not keep ledgers?"

"We count the money each month," Vyn said, sounding a little defensive.

"Hush up, Vyn," Yalan said and then focused on Seventh Night. "Explain this ledger thing to me."

She explained. It seemed like such a basic thing to her. Her family owned a great deal of farmland. Keeping track of its income and expenses was necessary to keep it producing well enough to support their small army. She felt silly to have not thought about it. Checking her father's figures had been the one thing she had done that common people might actually consider work.

As Seventh Night spoke, Mother Vyn quickly got over any defensiveness she felt about the subject. She and Yalan liked the idea quite a bit. Yalan liked the idea of keeping a record he could check, and Vyn liked the idea of Yalan having a record he could check.

Seventh Night became happier as well, because she had in her own way finally been of use.

Their trip to market was delayed to nearly midday, but Vyn and Seven finally got underway. Seven was relieved to get outside again. Her small triumph had also helped her alleviate some of her fears, and her curiosity was taking over.

She was eager to see the city.

"Why do they call it Crystal Inn City?" she asked.

"You haven't seen the Crystal Inn?" Vyn exclaimed.

Seventh Night confessed that she had not. Vyn promised they would go while they were out. "The Crystal Inn came first, and the city grew up around it. It's a beautiful place."

The city was impressive. Larger than Pinnacle, it also seemed taller. In the part of the city where Vyn's Tavern was located, the buildings were of fairly straightforward wooden construction. As they traveled, Seventh Night took note of the changes in the architecture. Here there was more stone, there brick, and somewhere off in the distance a cluster of domes, so overgrown there was no way to know of what they were constructed. Besides making for a more interesting walk, it told Seventh Night that this was an older city that had lived through several periods and styles.

She wanted to ask Vyn about all of them, but being too curious about things might make Vyn even more suspicious than she was already.

The market was filled with new distractions.

SEVENTH NIGHT

It was not the first time that Seventh Night had been to a marketplace, but it was her first time without a full escort. In addition this market was a far busier place than the market she remembered. Tivin was by nature a country of quiet people, who went about their business with a calm reserve. This market was crowded and noisy. The people argued and haggled and shouted to one another. If she was in the practice of going to the market regularly, Seventh Night thought she would prefer Tivin's calm, but this was certainly an interesting place.

Vyn put her arm around the younger woman's shoulder so they would not be separated. In her other arm she carried a large basket. As Vyn moved through the market, buying and haggling over various food items and essentials, Seventh Night watched the strange people and the odd items the shops offered.

She spied a table of women who she noticed were given generous space by the surrounding tables and carts. "Who are they?" she asked Vyn.

Vyn glanced at the women distastefully. "Witches," she said. "Thanks to Sargon we have to tolerate them."

"Is there a difference between a witch and a sorceress?" she asked.

The look Vyn gave her told Seventh Night two things: the first that there was a difference of significance, and the second that any girl of her age, even if she was a sheltered, silly girl who could not work magic, should know the difference.

"Where are you from?" Vyn asked her very seriously.

"*Very* far," Seventh Night answered, still aware of the crowd.

"I think when we get home you need to tell me about it." Vyn apparently understood this was not something to discuss in a public.

Seventh Night nodded. Her interest in the market drained. They finished Vyn's errands and returned to the tavern.

Yalan groused as Vyn pulled him away from his chores, but Seventh Night sensed he would not have come at all if it were not for Vyn's serious expression. Seventh Night would have preferred to keep him out of things, but Vyn and Yalan, however they might argue, were a unit. If you told one, you told the other. They went into a small room with some chairs and a fireplace, and Vyn shut the door. "Seven is going to tell us about herself."

And she did, briefly, focusing upon the most recent events. She told them about the wedding and her kidnapping and escape. She told them about using Sargon's mirror to send a message, but she could not bring herself to tell them about Kaleb's betrayal.

"I don't like being lied to," Vyn said when she finished.

"Don't sulk, Vyn," Yalan admonished her. "You're the one who wanted to take her in before you even knew her name. Besides, put in the same position, I'd probably come up with some pretty big clam tales myself."

"I did not lie," Seventh Night insisted. "But I did let you come to wrong conclusions. I am sorry for that, but I thought for my own safety as well as yours I should keep quiet."

Vyn took her hand and squeezed it. "You are forgiven," she said with a smile. "I hope you feel you can trust us now."

"If that's all, I'm gonna get back to work. Can't sit around and chitchat all day," Yalan announced as he stood. "Keep her out of trouble, Vyn. That means keep her inside and don't either of you say a word to another living soul about it."

Yalan left, and Vyn started asking Seventh Night questions. Her eyes shone, and Seventh Night saw that Vyn had decided to enjoy this new secret between them. After Vyn was satisfied, Seventh Night felt free to ask her own questions.

"If a ship was coming from the east, how would they reach the castle?"

"It's not legal to use anything but the most primitive float," Vyn said. Her brow creased as she considered. "The castle is high enough you might be able to see it from a ship, but that height is partly due to some sharp cliffs. So they would probably need to sail south. If they go south and travel on foot, they would almost have to come through Crystal Inn...unless they decided to avoid people altogether." She glanced towards the wall as though seeing something far beyond. "Even so, the only road to the castle leads directly from the center of the city. I suppose they would have to go that way eventually."

Seventh Night could have melted from relief. It could be as simple as waiting here for them.

"I hope the guardian doesn't give them

trouble," Vyn murmured.

"What guardian?"

SEVENTH NIGHT

CHAPTER XXI

THE GUARDIAN

"Land!"

The cry rang and echoed through the morning air. It was repeated a score of times before it reached Phillip's ear.

The *Pride of Cordance* had three large rooms under the forecastle, sunk half above, half below the main deck. A short stair and hall led to the three doors. The center one was the King's Chamber, and to its right and left were the Queen's Chamber and one for royal guests. Phillip jumped out of his bed in the guest chamber (arguably the nicest bed he had ever slept in) and made his way to the windows of the King's Chamber, which Neithan occupied. It was divided into a suite with a table where they took their meals, and by now, he thought nothing of passing through it.

Straining his eyes, he saw a dark color protruding on the horizon line.

"The Wizards Land," he breathed.

"Home, sweet home," a voice startled him.

"I didn't hear you come in," Phillip told Andomare.

The sorceress shrugged and joined him by the windows. "I just hope I was right," she said. "They're going to be pretty mad at me if we came all this way for nothing."

"She's here," Phillip assured her.

"Then so is Sargon." Andomare held his gaze with her green eyes and smiled warmly. "You scared?"

Phillip smiled. "We're still not on dry land, but no."

"Well, I'm scared."

He looked at her curiously. "With all your powers, how can you be frightened?"

"All my powers might be something back

home. But here... I don't know how I compare. Would I be a great sorceress or mediocre, or maybe by their standards, I'm a beginner. You see, I've never really had any formal training."

"Ah," Phillip said. He glanced out the window again. "When we're finished here, where will you go?"

"I'll—" the sorceress stopped a moment, considering. "Back to Cordance, I guess."

"What then?"

Andomare looked uncomfortable. "I don't know. I'll think of something." She turned to rest her arms on the windowsill. "Let's survive this first, then I'll worry about it."

Phillip perched himself on the sill of the neighboring window. "Sounds like a plan."

He heard what sounded like footsteps and a whispered scraping. He turned to find the point of Neithan's sword a few inches from his face. Phillip raised his eyebrows. "Problem?"

"We've been neglecting your training," Neithan said, lowering the blade. "Fetch your sword and come up on deck."

The sailors were in a dramatically better mood since land had been sighted. When Phillip and Neithan arrived on deck brandishing their swords, those who could slip away from their work gathered to watch.

"This will be rushed training," Neithan explained. "Just copy what I do and try to get a feel for your blade."

"So how—?" Phillip let his question fall when the prince spread his stance and raised his sword. The magician's apprentice did his best to imitate. Neithan brought his sword down in a few easy swings that Phillip blocked without difficulty. Phillip smiled, "I think I'm getting this."

Suddenly, Neithan's sword flashed like a demon, and Phillip found himself half way to the ground with his sword a good arm's length away from his hand. "Lesson one," Neithan said. "Don't underestimate your opponent."

The audience of sailors burst into laughter. Phillip allowed himself to sit back on the deck. He thought about reaching for his sword, but he had the feeling there would be another lesson in that. His problem was solved by the dagger that appeared at Neithan's throat.

Andomare's other hand was closed on the prince's sword arm. "Lesson two," she said. "Don't underestimate your opponent's friends."

"Well put," Neithan muttered. It would not have been hard for him to push her off, so she retreated. The move had given Phillip time to retrieve his sword though. "She has a point," Neithan said more loudly to Phillip. "For someone of your skill level, backup is very important."

The sailors sensed it was all right to laugh again. Omthais pounded his leg on the deck. Andomare found herself a perch and winked at Phillip. He gave her a dramatic salute with his sword.

As they continued the exercise, Neithan went more slowly, but made sure that his superiority was clear.

Andomare watched them for a while, but her gaze drifted to the sea and the closing land. The clangs ceased, and she looked back to see that their exercises had ended. Neithan caught her eye, but Captain Onnell appeared and demanded the Prince's attention. She wondered what was on his mind.

She caught sight of Kaleb in the distance,

winding a rope and staring at her with his uncovered eye. She frowned, and he looked away. Andomare opened her mouth and heard Phillip's voice.

"What's that?" he asked.

Looking back out at the water, she saw a huge something moving under the surface. "I don't-aw-ah wah!" she exclaimed as a jolt sent her flying toward the deck. She hit and rolled.

Before she could think about picking herself up, she felt herself pulled up by the shoulders and cradled in Neithan's arms. "Are you all right?" he asked, crouched over her with a worried expression.

"I'm fine," she assured him without taking the time to check if that was true. In other circumstances she might not have objected to the position. As things were, she pushed off his arm, and he helped her stand. "What...?" the question died on her lips as she looked forward. Something with a split tail wider than she was tall and a body like a big worm curled itself around the bow.

"You know what that is?" Neithan asked.

"No clue."

"Get below deck," he told her and drew his

sword.

Andomare started to say something, but this time a noise from the aft stopped her. She turned and saw the other end of the something big make its appearance.

A head with a long neck rose to tower above the deck. A blue fin started behind its eyes and continued down its back to disappear into the water. The rest of it was grey. The head itself tapered into a sharp curved beak. Black lidless eyes sat on either side of its face.

And then a second head rose, identical to the first.

Wasting no more time, Andomare ran below deck.

"To keep anyone from trying to recross the sea, the ancient kings created a guardian, a great sea serpent. It swims the coastline and destroys any ships that try to cross its boundary."

"And I can't warn them."

SEVENTH NIGHT

As the soldiers filed up on deck, Neithan divided them into two groups. He sent half to the bow to dislodge the tail and the rest aft to deal with whatever the heads did. He wanted to rush at the tail with his men, but he knew that was not his place. He had to keep a clear view of the situation, so he stood his ground.

Phillip ran below deck. He did not want to desert Neithan, but he could not leave Thunder trapped if that thing decided to tear the ship apart. The black unicorn was already knocking against the door to his stall. The other normal unicorns were whinnying uneasily.

"Easy," Phillip said. "I'll get you out." He opened the stall door and placed the saddle on Thunder's back. The preparations to leave calmed Thunder.

A grey unicorn began to kick at his own door. Thunder snorted and narrowed his eyes at the grey unicorn. The animal stopped and stood nervously in his stall. Phillip felt sorry for it but did not think letting it loose on the deck would do anyone good.

"Come on," he told Thunder and led him out. "We're going to help." The ship shook again. Thunder stopped and turned back to his stall. Phillip grabbed his rein and corrected him. "Coward."

Thunder snorted and shook his head.

"That's better."

Another rock of the ship knocked a few of the soldiers off their feet. Others, however, were having better luck. One of the soldiers put a decent cut into the tail. Neithan relaxed a little. If the monster proved this easy to injure, they might get through the attack considering it an interesting experience.

His relief was short-lived. The head to his right opened its mouth, screeched, and spat fire across the deck. Someone screamed in pain. Neithan had to jump back to avoid the edge of the flame, and almost lost his footing. "That's bad," he muttered.

Thunder and Phillip arrived on deck to a scene of fire and confusion. Captain Onnell had the sailors who were not hiding deal with the flame by whatever methods were at hand. Thunder gave Phillip a look that said *you better not expect me to go into that.*

SEVENTH NIGHT

"We're going over," Phillip told him and mounted. Phillip turned Thunder to a small empty portion of the deck where they could take off.

He felt someone grab his wrist and looked down to see Andomare, bow in hand.

"Take me with you," she demanded. Phillip gave her his arm and helped pull her up behind him.

Once she was situated, he gave Thunder the command. They ran to the edge of the boat and jumped over the rail. Instead of plummeting toward the water, Thunder gave a mighty flap of his wings and rose into the air. The exclamation the sorceress gave almost made Phillip smile, but concern stole his amusement.

He was very grateful that he had taken time to give Thunder a little exercise each day.

A collection of small cheers and grunts came from the bow. Neithan turned to see the tail release and slide back into the water. The heads drifted back from the boat a few yards, but the way their eyes stayed focused on the ship told Neithan that they were not leaving yet.

SEVENTH NIGHT

The head to port opened its mouth and spat flame at the deck, though less effectively this time.

"Can you get him steady?" Andomare asked.

"If we stop, we'll plummet," Phillip said. "But we can make a big circle."

"Do that then."

When they reached a comfortable altitude, a good distance above the reach of the heads, Andomare let go of Phillip and readied an arrow in her bow. He reached one arm behind him to the small of her back to steady her. Despite the awkward position, Andomare managed to fire without causing any injuries to herself or Phillip.

The arrow hit midway down the neck and stuck, but it only damaged the monster enough to draw its attention to them.

"Try for an eye," Phillip suggested.

"I was aiming for the eye the first time," she said unhappily.

"Practice shot. Try again."

The sorceress nocked another arrow. Phillip could hear her chanting something that he would ask her about later. She let the arrow fly, and this time it hit its intended target.

SEVENTH NIGHT

The fire-head thrashed and spat some flame in random directions. Phillip believed they were safely out of range.

"I wonder what the other head does," Andomare murmured.

In answer, the second head opened its mouth and shot a powerful stream of water across the deck. This was good because it put out a decent bit of the fire the first head had started. This was bad because it had knocked several men down and across the deck, and Neithan had to release his grip on his sword to keep old Omthais from tumbling over the rail and into the sea. Instead of Omthais, Neithan's sword went flying into the water.

The water-head stopped spewing and swooped at the deck. It almost made a lunch out of another sailor, but a larger sailor rammed into the man, knocking both of them into a roll that took them out of harm's way. It took Neithan a few seconds to realize that the larger man was Kaleb.

Hoping to give them a little time to get to cover, he waved his arms and shouted to get the creature's attention. The creature turned its head his way, then pulled back. It looked poised to strike and deciding the best method to do so.

"He lost his sword!" Andomare shouted in Phillip's ear.

Before Phillip could ask her what she was talking about, Andomare pulled his sword from his sheath. "Get down there so we can give this to him," she ordered.

"Who?" Phillip shouted as Thunder decided to make his own course changes.

"Neithan!"

From the tone of her voice Phillip knew there was no reasoning with her until she got her way. He steered Thunder toward the boat and tried for a fast, straight dive across the middle of the ship.

Seeing the nasty black thing that had injured it come within reach, the fire-head gave chase.

"Neithan, catch!" Andomare yelled.

Neithan turned around and took a reflexive step back at the sight of a great, black winged unicorn bearing down upon him. Andomare tossed the sword in his direction. Gracefully he caught it by the hilt and in the same motion took a few steps to his left. This took him completely out of Phillip's flight path as Thunder began to climb again. It also got him clear of the fire-head that lurched across the deck in Thunder's wake.

In a slightly less graceful motion accompanied by an unintelligible roar, Neithan put all his strength behind a sharp edged blow to the neck stretched out in front of him.

The soldiers at the rear ran forward to help, but the fastest of them only managed scratches as the neck snapped back and out of their reach.

Neithan stood calmly and tried to assess how much damage he had done. Apparently the blow had gone straight through, and though it was nowhere near cleaving the head off, it had left a significant gash in the neck.

"Did the yelling help?" he heard Kaleb ask from beside him.

Neithan nodded, not taking his eyes off the fire-head.

Andomare fired an arrow into the fire-head's other eye.

The fire-head began to sway unsteadily, then fell back into the sea in a way that Neithan could not believe was intentional. He wondered what the other head would do.

He got his answer as a stream of water hit his back. He let it knock him to the deck, careful to hold onto his sword this time.

"Somebody went over," Phillip mentioned almost casually to Andomare after the water stream cleared.

"Oh," she said and strained to see. "Get down again."

Phillip complied, taking Thunder lower over the spot where the man fell.

"Hold these," Andomare said, dropping her bow and quiver around his neck.

"What are you going to—?" Phillip began.

Andomare pulled her leg up onto Thunder's back, then jumped off and dove into the sea. Thunder looked back at Phillip questioningly. Phillip shrugged. Thunder shook his head and made a whinnying snort.

Andomare crashed into the sea and tried to ignore the sting as the water slapped back around her. She saw the man sinking into the water. Her eyes adjusted, and she distinguished he was one of the soldiers. He was trying to fight his way to the surface, but his metal helmet and heavy studded leather clothing were working against him.

She formed her legs into a tail and shot toward him.

Neithan picked himself up off the deck, dripping and nearly slipping. He decided that, while the fire-head was more dangerous, he was even less fond of the water-head. He would be very surprised if the same trick would work again; they needed a new way to fight it. He ran his mind through the inventory of items on the ship.

"Tent poles," Kaleb supplied.

The poles they had brought were tall and thin with sharpened ends. Not the most elegant weapon, but something that could be thrown and not missed too badly.

"Get them," Neithan told him.

Having no other weapon, Phillip tried his hand at Andomare's bow. He had a little experience with bows from his time with Lord Harold. He released one in the direction of the creature and missed completely. He frowned and nocked another arrow.

"Practice shot," he muttered to himself.

Andomare put her hands under the soldier's armpits and pulled. He kicked at her, but he was beginning to lose consciousness so he was not very effective. Andomare strained, but even with her tail, she did not think she could surface quickly enough.

Why do they have to be so heavy? she groaned inwardly. Not willing to give up, she studied the man. His helmet and studded shoulder pads were dead weight. She ripped off his helmet and thanked the fates that the shoulder armor was a separate piece from the rest of his clothing as she unclasped it and released it to the sea.

Much lighter, she decided as she kicked toward the surface.

Kaleb emerged with the tent poles, which were slightly taller than he was. Neithan took one and threw it like a javelin. The soldiers took the cue, and each approached Kaleb for a pole of his own. Even with the current distractions, Kaleb remembered who he was. He drooped his head and slouched a little to add to his disguise.

Phillip finally put an arrow into the monster. It made a small hole in its back fin.

Andomare broke surface and gulped air gratefully. The soldier coughed and sputtered.

Seven poles poked out of the neck of the water-head at various angles. Though individually the makeshift spears did not appear to do much damage, the head, with a resigned tilt, retreated back into the sea.

The soldiers cheered. Neithan thought celebrating might be premature but took it as a good sign. Behind him, he heard hooves hitting the deck. He turned around to greet them but saw only Phillip and Thunder.

"Where's Andomare?" he asked.

"She jumped in," Phillip said with a shrug and gave Thunder a pat.

"Jumped in?" Neithan repeated.

"Hey!"

Neithan followed the voice to starboard side and looked over.

"Could you throw a rope or something?"

Andomare shouted.

Neithan nodded and turned back to order for a rope. It was brought quickly, and one end tossed over the side. Andomare tied her end around the waist of the soldier.

"Haul him up first. I've got to get something," she shouted and disappeared below the waves before anyone could comment.

They pulled the half-conscious soldier up and laid him on the deck, where he sputtered back to life. His rusty red mustache dripped water into his mouth making him cough again. Otherwise he was only slightly wetter than the rest of them.

Neithan strained his eyes over the side, looking for Andomare. After a few moments she popped back up.

"Okay, me now," she shouted.

Neithan dropped the rope down for her. She twisted it around her arm and waist a few times, and he pulled her up. When she got to the rail, she threw her dangling arm over with its prize.

"You dropped this," she said, breathing heavily, and let Neithan's sword fall to the deck. Then she pulled herself over and sat down.

"Thank you," Neithan said as he picked it up

and handed Phillip's back to him.

"Are they still down there?" Phillip asked Andomare.

"There was only one," she reported. "One tail with two heads, and it took off that way as quick as it could. But it was bleeding bad."

A few of the men standing around had looks on their faces that told Andomare they thought it very strange that a woman had jumped into the sea to rescue a soldier and had the sense to check on the monster while down there, but since Neithan and Phillip acted as if it were a perfectly normal thing for her to do, they held their tongues.

She gave them a little smile and rested her head on her knees.

Yes, maybe it was very strange.

ACT III
BREAKING THE SPELL

CHAPTER XXII

THE PRINCESS'S NEW POSITION

"Are you a sorceress?" Seventh Night asked Vyn.

Vyn spared a glance at her as she sniffed the large soup kettle. Satisfied, she lifted it off the heat and placed it on the stone hearth. It was time for the evening dinner crowd. Vyn kept so many pots bubbling and roasts roasting with such precision and timing that it was as if watching a dance. Seventh Night did not dare try to help, believing correctly she would only succeed in throwing Vyn off her rhythm. So she stood off to the side with her back resting against the wall, watching Vyn and letting her thoughts wander.

"I'm about as much a sorceress as Yalan is a farmer," Vyn said with a nod to the small vegetable patch outside. In a single movement, she released the pot, turned to the table behind her, grabbed a vegetable, sliced it into even slivers, and turned back to toss them into another pot. "Most people don't go around touting themselves as sorceresses unless they can do something impressive."

Seventh Night thought what Vyn and Yalan could do was impressive but had already expressed as much. Yalan had a spell set in the kitchen, which kept a breeze cycling through and made the kitchen heat tolerable, a true blessing in the summer months. She wondered what Vyn considered impressive, and she worried what that could mean for her friends.

Mostly she worried about Phillip. If Neithan came, he would probably come on the *Pride* and bring soldiers and such.

From what Vyn told her, the Wizards Land had not seen a ship like the *Pride of Cordance* in a long time if ever, which gave her hope that it would be too large for the guardian. She assumed Neithan would come, but she did not know, not for certain. All she knew for certain is that Phillip would come, even if he had to cross the sea on a leaky raft. She hoped he did not do anything that stupid. Of course, he would find a way to bring his black unicorn. She could trust a farmboy more than her betrothed, a thought that knotted her insides. Phillip would come. Phillip would always come. She just hoped he made it.

"Darling, if you'd like to help, you can take this out front," Vyn interrupted her thoughts.

Seventh Night picked up the awkward tray, heavy with its bowls and mugs, and assumed Yalan would tell her what to do with it. It took both hands for her to keep a decent balance.

"Ah, Vyn decided to let you work," Yalan noted good naturedly as she came out of the kitchen. "Take it to those three gentlemen over there."

When she unloaded the tray, the three men asked where Mother Vyn was. She explained that Vyn was in the back, and she was helping out for the night. She retreated back to the kitchen quickly, still a little unnerved from her first encounter at the tavern.

Vyn set out some more plates of food for her, and Seventh Night realized this would be her job for the evening. At first she simply dropped off the meals as quickly as she could, but as the evening wore on and nothing unpleasant happened, she took more time to talk to the patrons. Most were fairly friendly.

While it was not the sort of thing she would like to do for the rest of her life, she found it to be a somewhat pleasant distraction from her own troubles.

She slept well that night. The next day she found herself occupied in the same way with the lunch crowd. Since it was lighter, she took more time to talk to those who came. They liked her because she was pretty and polite and genuinely fascinated by any silly magic trick they could do.

Most of the things she was able to get them to do were simple bits of magic like a spoon dancing to pipe music. One of them was quite proud to show her his ability to make dried leaves burst into flames by a certain snap of his fingers.

"Dried leaves are easy," his companion said matter-of-factly. "I'll be impressed when he can make fresh leaves burn."

"Well, it's not as if dried leaves were in short supply," Seventh Night defended the man gently, which earned her a smile from him and sniff from his companion.

The tavern door creaked open and a hunched over old woman entered. Dressed in dark, ragged clothing, her hair was a disheveled grey mop, she shuffled her way to the closest table, various charms and decorations chinking as she sat.

"What's that old witch doing here?" the fire starter's companion wondered aloud with obvious distaste.

"Is she a witch?" Seventh Night asked, still curious about the distinction.

"She claims to be reformed," the fire starter said. "Calls herself a fortuneteller now. I think she's a bit—" He made a gesture which Seventh Night took to imply mental instability.

Seventh Night looked back to Yalan for guidance, and he offered her a raised eyebrow. Not sure what that meant, she excused herself to find out.

"Girl, come here," the old woman said the moment Seventh Night stood.

SEVENTH NIGHT

Seventh Night did not care to be ordered around, but she wanted to be a good hostess for Yalan and Vyn. She was a bit curious as well, so she walked towards the old woman. "What would you like—?" she began.

"You're not from here," the old woman stated gruffly.

"I—"

"Sit," the old woman ordered.

Seventh Night found herself seated across the table from the hag.

"Maybe..." the old woman hissed to herself. Her eyes narrowed at the princess. "Do you want to know your fortune?"

"I'm not sure," Seventh Night said.

"Give me your hand."

Seventh Night hesitated. It was one thing to sit with the old woman, but to let her touch her...

"Give it!" the woman snapped.

Seventh Night jumped a little and let her hand drop on the table. The old woman grabbed it and pulled it toward her, palm upward.

"I smell the sea on you," the woman whispered conspiratorially. She reached into her rags and pulled out a folded black cloth. She opened it on the table to reveal a golden circular amulet. She smiled almost kindly at Seventh Night. "Do you like it?"

"It's pretty," the princess admitted.

"Pick it up, and you may have it," the old woman said.

Seventh Night did not feel completely comfortable taking the woman's things, but she did want a closer look at the amulet.

Gently she picked it up and immediately dropped it. "Ow!" she shrieked. "That thing burnt my fingers!" When she inspected her hand, she found it only slightly reddened, but it was enough to make her retreat from the table.

The old woman slapped the cloth back over the amulet and looked annoyed. "You're not the one," she groused and tucked the offending necklace back into her clothing.

Seventh Night was still nursing her hand and staring incredulously at the old hag when Vyn stormed over.

"Get out of here and leave my girl alone," Vyn barked at the hag.

The old witch sneered at her but retreated towards the door muttering. "Doesn't matter. Closer, though, closer."

SEVENTH NIGHT

When Vyn was sure the old woman was leaving, she inspected Seventh Night's hand for herself. She found no permanent damage but recommended they soak it in cool water anyway. "Witches dabble in things that ought to be left alone," Vyn muttered in partial answer to Seventh Night's unspoken question.

"Can't run a business if you toss out all the customers, Vyn," Yalan chided as they walked by, but Seventh Night observed he made no effort to get the witch back.

Chapter XXIII

The Hawk's Flight

"Y" ou used all of them?" Andomare bemoaned her empty quiver and shot Phillip a betrayed look.

"I—it was the only weapon I had," he apologized weakly.

Neithan smirked but kept his face turned where Andomare could not see.

"Did you even hit anything?" she whined.

"Yes," Phillip defended himself, though he sounded a little sulky.

Neithan rescued him by telling Andomare it

was time to go.

Three out of four rowboats had been destroyed in the attack, which meant a more limited number could land on shore at a time. The boat held six for the first trip. Two sailors rowed, and two soldiers shifted uncomfortably in their seats. Andomare came because her limited knowledge was all they had. Neithan came because he preferred leading to sending, and no one had rank to disagree with him.

Phillip flew over to shore on Thunder's back before all of them, because after nearly five days he was eager to be off the ship and on dry land.

When the water became wading depth, Neithan jumped out and pulled the boat until its prow rested on the shore. The soldiers exited with less enthusiasm and slogged their way to shore.

Phillip dismounted and expressed his joy by dropping to his knees and lightly touching his forehead and hands to the ground. "I love sand," he said to no one in particular and dusted some of it out of his hair.

The sorceress gathered her skirt, took Neithan's offered hand for balance, and stepped lightly to the ground. She observed Phillip skeptically. "You're odd," she pronounced.

Phillip grinned widely and nodded.

Thunder, free from restraint and unable to resist the open beach, took off at a gallop down the coast. Phillip saw the worried look of his companions and reassured them that Thunder would not go far. No one really thought they could chase the unicorn down anyway, so they had to trust that Phillip was right.

Neithan gave the rowboat a good push, and the sailors rowed back to the ship.

The beach was deserted, and not far off the smooth sand gave way to forest. After a few more trips, the rest of the soldiers and some of the sailors, Kaleb among them, came ashore. By then Thunder had returned, and Phillip set up a post with which to tie him and the other unicorns. Neithan divided them into groups and sent them searching for fresh water and wood to replace the lost tent poles. The rest wandered about, standing guard.

Once all others were occupied, Neithan sat down in a small circle with Phillip, Andomare, and the highest-ranking soldier.

"Where do we start?" Phillip voiced the question.

"The land rises to the North," Neithan said. "It's the most logical place to put a castle if it's nearby at all."

Andomare nodded, but Phillip could see that she did not feel certain that wizards followed conventional logic.

"Even if we don't find the castle," Phillip said. "There may be some sort of settlement where we can get directions."

Neithan nodded, and they all sat around in an uncomfortable silence. The idea of wandering around without any direction in a strange land was unsettling at best.

The sorceress's eyes lit up, and she tapped her hands on her leg like an excited child. With a glance at the officer, she bit back any outburst, and instead whispered something long in Neithan's ear.

"Can you do that?" Neithan asked her.

"I have practice," the sorceress said confidently.

Neithan stood. "Commander, you keep an eye on things here. We're going to take a short walk."

"Sir?" the commander looked at him curiously.

"Phillip, Andomare, and I are going for a

short walk in the forest," Neithan clarified.

"Of course, sir," the commander said in the strained tone of a man not able to get a good handle on his objections.

Neithan let his eyes wander across the beach trying not to look like he was searching for anything in particular. He spotted a grim faced Kaleb sharpening the point on a new tent pole.

"You look like you can be spared," he told his brother in a slightly more royal than usual tone. "Come with us, I'd like an extra set of eyes."

Not leaving time for any questions, the small party entered the forest and put enough distance between themselves and the beach that they were at no risk of being seen. They stopped in a very small clearing.

Andomare put a few additional steps distance between herself and the others.

"Not too far," Neithan warned.

Andomare gave him a little smile.

Phillip opened his mouth to ask what they were doing out here, when the sorceress began to change. She shrunk, folding over and fusing together and becoming a general shade of brown. When the transformation completed, a good-sized hawk shrugged its way out from the neck of her dress.

"Oh," he said, partly in realization of the plan and partly because that was the most dramatic transformation he had seen. Phillip was pleased to see the wide-eyed look on the face of Kaleb, who had never seen any of Andomare's transformations.

Neithan, completely unfazed, squatted down and lowered his arm to the hawk. Andomare stepped onto his forearm, careful not to dig her talons into his skin. He lifted her to his full height, then raised his arm above his head. The hawk bobbed on his arm, and with a great jump, stretched her wings and rose into the air.

Andomare smiled inwardly at the feel of wind. Living alone in the desert for so long had left her with two pastimes. The first involved exploring the considerable library of books her father had left her and practicing the magic they taught. The second was practicing shifting into various forms and sneaking back into town to try them out.

She had experimented on people that way, observed how they treated each form differently, but she liked the power of a stunning beauty best. It let her take little revenges upon those who had injured her in childhood without doing anything at all. She loved towering over men who found her both alluring and frightening and smiling pleasantly in return of suspicious stares from women. Though, in the end such reactions would depress her and make her glad to return to the solitude of the desert.

That was why she liked Phillip and Neithan and even the stuck up little princess. She felt that they would treat her pretty much the same way whatever form she chose.

Which was why her heart leapt a bit, when she saw something that looked more like buildings than forest in the distance. After a bit more study and flight, she made out the faint outline of something that resembled a tiny castle on a rise like Neithan had predicted. Satisfied, she turned and flew the other way to rejoin her friends.

Her mission accomplished, she returned her attention to the wonderful sensations of flying, the wind on her back, the ground rushing past below. She wondered why she did not turn herself into a bird and do this more often.

The arrow that sailed past reminded her.

She flapped back, reversing her direction for a moment, then dived for the forest. She broke her dive and headed in yet another direction as a second arrow flew where she would have been. She kept one eye out for the clearing and the other for new arrows. She found the clearing first and made another dive.

Beneath the relative safety of the trees, she eased off the dive and alighted on Neithan's offered forearm.

He stroked her head and back as one who handled hawks might normally do. "We saw the arrow," he said. "It was too close."

"Did you see anything?" Phillip asked, eagerness creeping into his voice.

The sorceress hawk rolled her neck as if stretching after some light exercise and nodded. She hopped off Neithan's arm to her discarded clothing, stopped, and looked at the men expectantly.

After a few blinks and blank stares, they got the idea and turned their backs.

"I think I saw a town and maybe a castle," Andomare said. They turned back around to see her straightening her dress.

"Maybe a castle?" Kaleb repeated skeptically.

"I didn't go up and knock on the front door," Andomare said tersely. "But it looked like some towers at a distance rather than just a funny shaped rock."

"We don't have time to go chasing funny shaped rocks," Kaleb snapped back.

"We don't have time to argue about it," Phillip interrupted.

"We should return to camp," Neithan said gently and headed in that direction.

Phillip followed him. Kaleb and Andomare had a short exchange of looks, his disdainful and hers an open glare, before they followed as well.

"So you're the evil twin?" Andomare went for the jab quietly so the other two would not hear.

Kaleb glanced at her a bit taken aback, though neither of them broke their pace. "I'm the spare carriage wheel," he said quietly in return.

That defused Andomare a little. She went from being angry to simply sulking.

As they came to the edge of the forest, Kaleb grabbed Andomare's arm to stop her. He waited until Neithan and Phillip had completely left the forest and spoke, "I've watched you."

SEVENTH NIGHT

It was Andomare's turn to give him a suspicious look.

"My brother is very important to me," he said. "And I want you to stay away from him."

"What?" Andomare asked, finding the demand ludicrous for its implied insult and for sheer logistics.

"You know exactly what I mean," Kaleb continued. "He is not as world weary as I am, because I've protected him. I have had to deal with women like you since we were thirteen. You think a pretty face and easy manner is all it takes to claim a prince."

The anger returned to Andomare in full force. "You have *never* met a woman like me," she spat and yanked her arm away. Andomare stormed out of the forest before another word could be said.

CHAPTER XXIV

THE RELUCTANT REBELLION

Dusk began to fall, and the soldiers started a small fire on the beach.

Andomare stood talking to Thunder and untangling the unicorn's black mane with her fingers. Most everyone else was sitting around the fire on remains of the trees they had torn down to make the new tent poles and patch the ship. The smell of cooking fish wafted through the air. Phillip breathed deeply and felt his mouth water. He was feeling energized by Andomare's news, and a general sense of relief settled about the camp. Neithan was propped back on his elbows, watching the clouds with what Phillip thought was unusual intensity.

"They're not moving," Neithan said, not taking his eyes off the sky.

Phillip looked skyward. He had not been paying attention before, so he could neither confirm nor deny Neithan's statement. He did notice however that there were very dark clouds in very definite patches, and none of them seemed to be loosing their water.

They were both still watching the sky when Andomare joined them. "What are you...?" Her question trailed off as a rustling and other voices came from the forest.

The soldiers drew their weapons and stood at ready. Neithan stood calmly. He drew no weapon, but he made sure his large frame was between Andomare and the forest. Phillip followed suit and kept his sword sheathed.

They had a short wait. Not quite a dozen men spilled out of the forest, each stopping when they saw the soldiers waiting on the beach. They were all armed, mostly with bows, but their casual clothing and the fact they were not pointing their bows at anyone, made Phillip think they were a hunting party rather than a group of soldiers.

The two groups stood and looked at each other for a long while. Finally a man with shoulder-length black hair spoke. "You're not from around here," he observed with a rolling accent.

Neithan spared a glance at his own men, dressed in uniforms emblazoned with the rearing winged unicorn crest of Cordance, and noted that even the casual dress of his inner circle was much simpler than the layered cloth of the Wizards Land natives. "No," he replied. "We're not."

The man studied them some more. A change in his expression made Phillip think he had finally taken full note of the ship. "Why are you here?" the man asked.

"Our princess was taken by some of your terrocks," Neithan said. "We've come to get her back."

The man looked to his nearest companion who looked back at him pointedly, shrugged, and nodded.

"We should talk," the black-haired man said.

Neithan invited him to sit down, and they

talked. They soon learned that while Sargon was king, he was not a very popular king. His castle was indeed to the north, but it was nearly impenetrable by direct assault. It was their good fortune that the men who had discovered them were part of a group that had been waiting for an opportunity to take Sargon out of power.

"I can't get you into the castle," said the black-haired man, whose name was Arris. "I can take you to someone in the city who may be able. However, a group of soldiers like this will draw attention. It would be best if only a few of you went with me into the city."

The commander did not like this. Neithan was not thrilled by it, but he could see the sense in the plan. He was here to save the princess, not start a war, and not drawing unwanted attention could be important for both.

"I can and will offer you lodgings for the evening," Arris said, and they accepted his offer.

Unicorns, much less winged unicorns, had never set hoof on the Wizards Land before, so Thunder had to stay at the beach. Thunder did not like being left behind and whinnied like a colt, until Phillip promised him they would not be long and gave him some extra sugar he had been saving.

While Phillip calmed his unicorn, the rest broke down the camp they had set up. At Neithan's suggestion, Kaleb was drafted as a replacement for the soldier who had been burned during the sea monster's attack. The other sailors stayed behind to finish repairs and guard the ship.

Arris owned a manor house and a bit of farmland between the beach and the city. The tired soldiers dragged their way there to spend the night. Arris had room to house them in the vacant building once reserved for farmhands. Vacant because the dark clouds seated over-head had left his farm unsuitable for any crop. Phillip sensed Arris was somewhat taken with Andomare. She was the only one invited to stay in the manor house itself. Neithan dismissed it as a proper courtesy due her gender, since the manor house could offer her a private room and the company of Arris's sister. Andomare accepted the invitation out of curiosity but found herself too tired from the long day to ask any questions.

The next morning Arris and a few of his friends

took the two princes, Phillip, and Andomare to Crystal Inn City. Neithan explained Kaleb's presence to the commander as another person who could fight should this be a trap but not draw the attention a soldier would if it was not. It was a thin excuse, but Kaleb's size seemed to convince the commander that the sailor might be worth something in a fight.

It was late afternoon when they reached the city. Pinnacle City had been the largest Phillip had seen before this. The wooden buildings on the edge of the city as they entered were more tightly packed than the stone and stucco buildings in the center of Pinnacle.

One side of the street they walked was a solid row of two story buildings that shared walls. The other side was almost as tightly packed but with a few more alleys. The street itself was wide enough for seven or eight men to stand elbow to elbow.

They stopped before a door on the shared wall side of the street. Arris knocked, and they waited for a few minutes, trying to look casual. There was no response, so Arris knocked again.

This time a well-groomed man with a touch of gray in his blond beard opened the door. "What do you want, Arris?" he asked, then observed the rest of the party. "Who are these?"

"Visitors," Arris said and lowered his voice to a murmur. "From across the sea."

The older man's eyes widened a bit. "Come inside."

He ushered in the four foreigners. It was only after the door shut that Phillip realized Arris was not joining them.

"Please, be seated," the bearded man said. They took seats on the well-cushioned furnishings around the fireplace.

"I am Leonore," he said as he sat down with the straight-backed casualness of a nobleman and looked at the party expectantly.

"I am Prince Neithan of Cordance," Neithan said in the same tone. "This is my brother Kaleb, the apprentice Phillip, and the sorceress Andomare."

They were all a little surprised by Neithan's revelation of Kaleb's identity, particularly Kaleb.

"Two foreign princes," said a female voice from behind them. "We are most honored."

The woman came into the room with a polished tray holding delicate looking cups and set it on the short table in the middle of the conversation circle. She was as old as the man, most likely his wife. She was dressed in a fine, long, embroidered gown. Her thick white hair fell past her shoulders in smooth waves.

"This is the Lady Delenora," Leonore said.

"Please, my lords," the lady said, her voice as silken as her appearance. "What has brought you to our door?"

Kaleb told the story this time, including the part where the brothers pretended to be one.

"There is a secret entrance to the castle," Leonore said when Kaleb finished. "A tunnel of which I think Sargon is still unaware. We can take you that far."

"Thank you," Neithan said.

"I'm sorry, but who are you?" Phillip asked.

"I was the king's advisor," Leonore said.

"Sargon's advisor?"

"Certainly not." Leonore's voice was lined with disgust. "I was an advisor to King Havanderier from whom Sargon took the throne." He saw the questioning faces of his guests and continued without further prompting. "Havanderier was a very good king, fair and just in all his ways. He came from a line of kings spanning seven generations.

"So that our rulers would not grow dull, it is our practice that any may challenge the king in a duel to the death for the throne. These challenges were far fewer than you may think. Partly because Havanderier was very popular, and no one wanted to be known as the man who slew him. But also because the kings of our realm are raised to be very powerful wizards and have access to the greatest magical devices and knowledge."

"So Sargon defeated Havanderier," Phillip finished for him, attempting to move the story along.

"We believe that Sargon may have illegally used help to kill Havanderier," Delenora said. "Sargon was never a particularly strong wizard. No one thought he would actually win. Havan was planning to let him survive it. Technically you don't have to kill the challenger as long as you are the clear winner. But when all had cleared, Havan was dead, and Sargon stood alone."

"Wasn't anyone watching?" Phillip asked.

"A full out King's Duel is not something you want to observe too closely," Leonore said. "We were watching, but from a distance, and they were out of sight for a while. The terrain near the castle is rocky and mountainous. They started in an open area but moved into a ravine..."

"So you could be wrong," Kaleb said. "He could have won fairly."

Delenora looked at him wide-eyed, and Leonore shook his head. "It may not be completely impossible, but it's close. Havanderier was very strong, and Sargon was not. Whether or not he won fairly, he has abused his power since. The prophecy has taken him to the extremes of paranoia, and our land suffers from his madness."

"He turned an entire forest to desert," Phillip said. "Perhaps he was stronger than you think."

Delenora shook her head. "That was probably just sand root. I'm sorry he loosed it upon your land, but while its creators were very skillful wizards, it does not take much skill to unleash or control."

SEVENTH NIGHT

Phillip heard Andomare murmur quietly, "Just sand root." It occurred to him that she had been uncommonly reserved since they had left the beach. At the moment she was pushed back as far as she could go into the large, cushioned chair in which she was sitting, her hands clasped in her lap. He made a note to ask her what was wrong later.

Neithan returned them to the matter at hand. "What prophecy?"

Leonore and Delenora exchanged glances. Delenora answered, "A reliable prophetess told Sargon that, unless he abdicated the throne, a woman from the sea would bring about his destruction."

"If he thinks your princess could destroy him, that might explain why he's keeping her," Leonore said, though he frowned at the obvious holes in the theory.

Phillip did not like the sound of it either way. There were several things about the story he did not like. "Why hasn't anyone challenged Sargon if he's so weak?"

"They have tried," Leonore said. "But Sargon has completely ignored those who do, and if they persist, he finds ways to silence them. Once he took the throne, he expelled everyone from the castle, courtiers and servants, because 'from the sea' could also mean anyone who lives near the sea. He will not let any woman near him. Some of the more respected sorceresses simply disappeared.

"As king, he has access to all the magic devices and libraries stored in the castle, so that gives him several advantages particularly while hiding within the castle."

"The kings can control the weather?" Neithan asked, obviously still thinking of the strange clouds.

"Creating clouds was something Sargon could do since childhood," Leonore explained. "Before, they were just little ones he would make as an amusement at parties and such. But there are objects at the palace that can amplify a magic spell. Sargon punishes any landowner who resists him by placing a large dark cloud that never rains over his land."

Phillip thought of all the dark patches of clouds he had seen and could understand why that might make Sargon unpopular. "What about those who don't have land?" Phillip asked.

"His other great fascination is with the

creation of monsters," Leonore said.

"Like the sea serpent that attacked us," Neithan ventured.

Leonore shook his head. "The guardian was created very long ago by the ancient kings, but Sargon has most certainly studied their methods."

"How did you get past it?" Delenora asked.

"I don't know if we killed it," Neithan said. "But we wounded it very badly."

"Tell no one," Leonore said gravely. "Fear of the guardian has kept us from your regions for centuries. It is best if we remain that way."

Phillip frowned, "But Sargon came to our kingdom?"

"The guardian may be getting old," Leonore theorized. "Sargon disappeared for several years around the same time as Mortagin. There were rumors that they were attempting to cross the sea, but Sargon challenged the king as soon as he returned. No one had a chance to ask him, and Mortagin never returned."

"Did you know my father?" Andomare asked.

Delenora looked at her as if seeing her for the first time. "You're Mortagin's daughter?"

SEVENTH NIGHT

"That's what I was told," Andomare said with a hint of her usual humor.

"The tunnel," Phillip said, trying to keep the conversation on track. "If Sargon is so terrible, why haven't you sent a force to take him down?"

"The way to the tunnel and the tunnel itself is very narrow," Leonore said. "Not really suited to a large force. Assassins and challengers have gone that way, but none have returned."

"Including our son," Delenora added, her eyes very sad and distant.

"Surely Sargon would guess there was a tunnel if people kept showing up," Phillip said.

"If the only other entrance is the front door, we may not have a choice," Kaleb said reasonably.

"We have checked the tunnel itself," Leonore said. "It was still clear last month."

There was a pause in the conversation, and Delenora took advantage of it. "Please accept our hospitality for the evening," she said. "In the morning, we'll have food and supplies for you and your men ready."

Phillip was not happy about a further delay. He could tell Neithan was not either, but it was important not to offend their new allies, so Neithan accepted the invitation.

Delenora stood to show them to their rooms upstairs, but Andomare stayed behind to ask Leonore some things.

The ousted courtiers were obviously used to receiving guests, though Delenora apologized a few times for not having nicer accommodations for the princes. Phillip was given a small, windowless, corner room. For the two princes, she arranged a larger room with a double bed for each. She did not mention where she planned to put Andomare but excused herself so that she could go downstairs and join the conversation.

Kaleb excused himself politely and closed the door to his room. Neithan and Phillip were not particularly tired, so they tried to amuse each other. They finally decided to go through the small packs they had brought with them and make a list of the sort of supplies they might need.

When they finished, Neithan took the supply list down to their hosts, and shortly after he went down, Andomare came up. Phillip was sitting on the edge of the bed, repacking his sack. Andomare burst into the room and threw herself down on the other side of the bed.

"I'm good!" she announced proudly and smiled at Phillip.

He smiled back at her. "At?" he prompted.

"At magic," Andomare bubbled. "Leonore says that shifters are naturally more in tune with magic than most people. And while most people here know a little magic, they still have to go about normal daily life like back home, so not very many of them really devote so many years to the study of it. While I may not be the greatest ever—I think you have to invent new spells to really be great—he says I've more than earned the right to call myself a sorceress."

She laid back with her hands laced behind her head on the pillow and beamed at the ceiling. Phillip was glad to see that she was feeling better, but he remembered that she had never really given them her actual age.

"I'm very happy for you. So how many years have you devotedly studied magic?" he asked.

"Since I was twelve," she said.

"How long ago was that?" he asked.

She rolled to her side and gave him a jab with her knee in response.

Phillip chuckled. Neithan entered and gave

them an odd look.

Andomare sat straight up. "I'm a good sorceress," she announced brightly.

Neithan raised his eyebrows a little and nodded. "Good," he said and kneeled down to put his own belongs back in their sack.

Apparently wanting more of a reaction, the sorceress tried again. "That means I'm better than most people, even in the Wizards Land."

Neithan continued to pack his things. Phillip saw Andomare's eyes narrow a little and decided it was safer elsewhere. "Excuse me," he said and left the room.

"I found out that my father was a well-respected nobleman and friend to the king," she said, still trying to get a reaction. Neithan moved his head in a way that might be considered a nod, and Andomare fell back with a grunt. "So your brother got the charm, and you got the wit," she said with just enough edge and playfulness to her voice Neithan could not miss the sarcasm.

"Delenora is going to get us some local clothing so we'll blend in a little better," Neithan said, still not looking at her. "And some arrows to refill your quiver."

Andomare glanced at him. He glanced back

at her with his subtle partly amused, partly long-suffering expression, then turned back to his task at hand.

"Hell, I'm mean to you," she said. "You shouldn't put up with it. You're a prince; you could cut out my tongue or something."

"I don't want to cut out your tongue," Neithan said.

"Well, you shouldn't put up with it," she repeated. "You're very nice to me. I should be nicer to you."

"I'd like that," Neithan said and looked at her sincerely with his brown eyes.

Andomare understood she had just walked into a promise that he expected her to keep, and she decided she really did not mind. "Okay," she said, matching his earnestness. "I'll be nicer to you."

Neithan gave her his small smile and went back to repacking. Andomare watched him for a little while but eventually got bored and let her eyes wander. They found Kaleb looking back at her through the open door, his eye patch gone, a vague but unpleasant look on his face. Andomare felt a little cold, because she knew exactly what he was thinking. He was wrong, though. She had every right to be where she was. She raised her chin and her left eyebrow and looked back at him with a mix of innocence and challenge.

Kaleb held her gaze for a little longer, then turned and headed down the stairs.

"I don't like your brother," Andomare said when Kaleb was out of earshot. "And he doesn't like me."

"I noticed," Neithan said with a sigh. He had finished packing and was simply sitting on the floor now. "I wish you got along better."

"He's not the only one," she said seriously. "A lot of people don't like you when they find out you're a sorceress; at least back on the other side of the sea they don't. It's not like that here. I think they'd respect me." She let that hang in the air, but she could see that Neithan knew she was not finished. "I can't decide whether or not I should go back to Cordance when this is done."

"You'll come back," Neithan said. Andomare raised her eyebrow at him questioningly. Neithan explained, "You said you couldn't decide, so I decided for you. You'll come back."

"I love her," Phillip said.

At the other side of the empty table, Kaleb looked up from his map. Dinner was over, and everyone else had retired for the evening. Kaleb had been scratching things in his journal, though Phillip could not read any of it. Phillip had been cleaning his flute far more than it wanted cleaning.

Kaleb looked at Phillip in a very unconcerned way. "Everyone should love her," he said.

"Do you?" Phillip asked him pointedly.

Kaleb laid down his quill. "More than anyone," he said.

Phillip wiped his flute again, not sure what answer he had been looking for. "You should," he said finally and left the room.

He went outside to the small backyard behind the house. The night had cast a blue shadow to the greenery. Small flowers clustered in curved beds beside the dividing fences that marked the separation from neighboring yards. Delenora had told them that many of those banished from the palace had settled in this part of the city.

SEVENTH NIGHT

Even while huddled together for sympathy, they seemed to have the need to clearly mark their territory.

A slightly larger than life-sized statue was the centerpiece of Leonore and Delenora's yard. It was in the likeness of a woman pouring out an empty pitcher onto another bed of flowers that circled the statue's feet. If she had been a living woman, Phillip would not have thought her very attractive, but the figure had a quiet grace he could appreciate. The main function of the statue, Phillip believed, was to show status. To remind those on the other side of the fence, those with a vegetable patch on one side and those with a less impressive garden on the other, that they who lived here were highborn.

Phillip sat down upon the stone bench. From his clothing he pulled a piece of white fabric, fine and sheer as a caterpillar's web. It was carefully folded into a flat square and tied with a string. He untied the string now, unfolding the fabric while he rubbed it through his fingers. Seventh Night belonged in a garden like this surrounded by flowers and nice things. He could not give her that.

Kaleb could though. He could give her nice

things and fine foods and the best of whatever else she wanted. Phillip did not like him, but Seventh Night did. Whatever he might have wanted, the truth was more important. Kaleb was not the outsider trying to steal his beloved. He was the outsider, and the princess was not meant for him.

He played with the veil, folding and twisting it into the shape of a large blossom. He tied the string around the base so it would hold its shape. Phillip stood and laid the white flower in the crux where the statue's wrist met the pitcher. There he left it and took himself to bed.

Later that evening, Seventh Night lay awake. The sounds of a flute muted by the wall of the adjacent building drifted into her room. It was sad, low music, and it made her think of Phillip. He had never played her flute for her himself, and she wanted to hear him play. More than anything right now, she wanted to hear him play.

Chapter XXV

The Elusive Girl Next Door

The next morning Andomare sat on the rug in the front room and stuffed arrows into her quiver. Delenora watched her in a sort of horrified fascination, because she did not think proper ladies should sit on rugs when chairs were available or be so happy about such dangerous toys. However, she was sensible enough to understand that there were more important things than being proper, particularly at such critical times, so she said nothing.

She had had a bit of a debate with Leonore

earlier over the dress for Mortagin's daughter, and she rarely had debates with Leonore. He had wanted Delenora to find a dress appropriate to the daughter of a nobleman. Delenora had reminded him, firstly, that they were not as wealthy as they had once been, and secondly, that appropriate dress for a noble lady was not appropriate for trouncing about the forests and countryside. So instead she had found something very practical, fairly comfortable, and brown with cream colored sleeves as well as tall boots for walking through undergrowth.

Delenora had a harder time resisting dressing up the prince. She had found some clothes for him like a nobleman might wear on a hunt. She wanted to put identical clothes on Kaleb, but he insisted that would defeat the entire point of the eye patch and beginnings of a beard disguise. Instead, she found something very common but very neat for Kaleb and more or less the same for Phillip. Phillip's shirt had turned out to be a few sizes too large, but there was no time to fix it.

Considering that she had only one evening to round it all up and the princes were unusually tall and broad shouldered, she was quite pleased with herself.

"That does it," Andomare announced as she slipped in the last arrow. "Shall we go?"

"I'm ready," Phillip said.

"We will be ready to depart shortly," Leonore answered from the door of the kitchen.

"Do you think it would hurt if we waited outside for you?" Andomare asked.

"Not if you stay within sight of the door," Delenora said. "The city is large enough no one expects to know everyone."

Andomare shouldered her bow and picked up her sacks, one with her belongings, the others with some of the supplies they were taking back. She took Phillip by the hand and pulled him outside with her. They both felt more comfortable in the sunlight.

There was some midmorning traffic. A few carts and booths blocked the alleys on the other side of the street. Andomare did not have any money or need to purchase anything, but she was drawn to such a convenient distraction.

Phillip, apparently far too antsy to enjoy browsing, shifted his bags and rubbed his toe in the dirt. She decided, since no one was paying them much attention, she would not call him on it. She was far more interested in the colorful stones on the cart before her.

Phillip surprised her by suddenly joining her at the cart and feigning interest in the stones as well. "Don't look," he murmured. Naturally, she had to look.

She saw a strange procession. A thickly built man with a short black beard, overdressed for the weather to declare his importance, was riding something like a very hairy overgrown bull. Behind him were some rather nasty looking things like thin black insects with four legs on the ground and two held up to their torso. They were about a head taller than she was.

She held her breath and fought the urge to run back inside to warn Neithan. It appeared her concern might be unwarranted. The procession stopped before the building adjacent to the one Leonore and Delenora occupied. The important-looking man slid to the ground and entered. The huge insects clustered around the door. Relieved but still curious, Andomare read the sign hanging over them.

CRYSTAL INN CITY TAVERN

SEVENTH NIGHT

Inside the tavern, Yalan took note of the overdressed man. He gave no outward sign of concern. Very calmly he stood and walked around the wall to the kitchen behind it, where Vyn was starting the fire and Seven was wiping off the table.

"Graumel is here," he said softly to Vyn.

Vyn paled a little.

"Who's Graumel?" Seventh Night asked just as softly.

"Sargon's chief enforcer in the city," Vyn explained, as she took Seventh Night by the shoulders and hurried toward the staircase. "Go to your room and hide under the bed."

Seventh Night hurried up the stairs. She started to head for her room, but the voices made her stop. She stood next to the top of the stairs, pressed her back to the wall where she could not be seen from the first floor, and listened.

"Where's your girl, Vyn?" she heard a gruff voice ask.

"Our daughter died shortly after she was born," Yalan said just as gruffly. "I don't like it when people bring it up around my wife."

SEVENTH NIGHT

Seventh heard a ring of truth in Yalan's tone, and her heart went out to Vyn.

"I'm deeply sorry for your loss," Graumel said with a weak attempt at sympathy. "But I'm talking about your new girl."

"I don't know what you mean," Vyn said, trying to bluff, but there was a tremor under her voice.

"Pretty little thing, black hair, strange accent," Graumel prodded. "My nephew thought she was quite interesting." He paused between each sentence. "I thought she sounded like someone the king has asked me to look for and return safely to his care. Are you sure you don't remember?"

"Your nephew was mistaken," Vyn said.

"I thought you didn't like liars, Vyn," Graumel shot back. His footsteps never stopped. Seventh Night guessed he was circling to make them nervous, and it seemed to be working.

"How many customers do you have?" Graumel continued after a short pause. "How many sons...daughters?

"Don't!" Vyn pleaded, truly sounding frightened.

The footsteps stopped, and Seventh Night

risked a peek to see Graumel playing with a black whistle. Vyn was seated. Yalan stood behind her, hands gripped on her shoulders.

"Don't make me," he said and leaned toward Vyn. "All you have to do is tell me where the girl is."

Seventh Night did not like the look on Vyn's face. It was too much like someone preparing for a great horror, and she had been here long enough to know Vyn was not easily frightened. The fact that this was on her account made it too much.

"I'm here," she announced as she came down the stairs.

Vyn's expression changed to one of alarm. She tried to rise, but Yalan held her firmly in place. She saw the respect in Yalan's eyes, and a small hint of it in Vyn's under the pained look.

"King Sargon has been worried about you, Highness," Graumel said, oozing superficial politeness. "You must come with me."

Seventh Night took off her apron in a sort of dramatic gesture and looked down on Graumel from the stairs. She could bluster as much as he could. "I'm ready."

"What a beautiful young lady," an old voice said from beside Andomare. She looked to see an equally old woman looking up at her. "A pretty lady must want pretty jewelry."

Andomare smiled indulgently at the sales pitch and at the golden circular amulet dangling from the chain the woman held up to her. Trying to appease the woman and avoid drawing any attention from the insects, she lifted the pendant for closer inspection.

Phillip tried to keep his head down and not pay too much attention to what was going on next door. He realized after a little while that he was the only one on the street not paying attention and that made him stick out as much as anything. A new ripple of movement gave him an excuse to turn around, and he did not believe what he saw.

The overdressed man walked back out the door looking extremely pleased with himself. His hand was on the back of the neck of a small young woman in a very simple, dull green dress, who was trying to look dignified.

SEVENTH NIGHT

The man mounted his beast and pulled the girl up to sit in front of him.

"Seven!" Phillip shouted overcoming his stupor.

Her captor did not even blink but snapped the reins of his beast. Seventh Night was caught between his arms, but she managed to twist around enough to look back past him.

"Phillip!" she exclaimed with the same measure of surprise and relief.

Andomare looked back up at Phillip's exclamation and the response that came after it. The overdressed man snapped the reins again, and the beast took off at a far faster pace than she would have thought possible. The insects trailed behind. Phillip ran after them, but it was a useless effort. About halfway down the street, he realized this, stomped his foot on the ground, and came running back with the same vigor.

When Andomare looked back down, the old woman was gone, and the necklace was still in her hand.

SEVENTH NIGHT

Chapter XXVI

Big, Dark Clouds

Arris had stopped back by sometime the previous evening, just long enough for Leonore to give him some new instructions. During the night he had skipped the soldiers past the city to another sympathetic farm further north. It was there that those who had gone into the city would meet them and be escorted to the tunnel.

Leonore was explaining this to Neithan when Phillip burst back through the door.

"They got her!" he announced, breathing

heavily.

"Who?" Leonore asked.

"Seven!"

Leonore brows stitched together.

"Seventh Night! The princess!"

"Didn't we already know that?" Kaleb said, looking at Phillip curiously.

"He means they just got her," Andomare clarified as she entered more calmly. "This guy with a red shirt, big hat, and lots of jewelry came down the street with some nasty looking insect things. He stopped next door, came back out with the princess, and rode off."

"Why didn't you stop him?" Kaleb demanded.

"I tried!" Phillip exclaimed. "They were too fast."

"You could have followed them," Kaleb snapped, looking at the sorceress this time.

"I can't run that fast either," Andomare snapped back. "And changing in the middle of the street would make me stick out a bit, even here."

Neithan held up his hand to still further argument and turned to Leonore. "Where will they take her?"

"That sounds like Graumel," Leonore said.

"They may stop at his manor, but they are more likely to go straight to the castle."

"Could we cut them off?" Neithan asked.

"If they stop, maybe."

Neithan frowned, not sure whether to continue with the existing plan or try to catch them at Graumel's manor.

"How far out of the way would it be to leave the city by going past Graumel's and checking if they were there?" Phillip asked.

"Half the morning at least," Leonore answered.

"That may be wise," Kaleb said. "We should not risk losing her again if she is so close by."

"We'll go through the castle," Neithan told the floor. He felt the eyes of everyone upon him and looked up to explain. "He won't stop."

They did not stop. They raced straight through the center of town. Certainly not the most comfortable ride Seventh Night had ever had, but she was able to catch a glimpse of the Crystal Inn, which almost made it worth the trip. The castle grew larger as they approached, but she no longer felt the sense of foreboding that she had before. Phillip was here, alive, and the sorceress was with him.

She would be rescued. All she had to do was avoid doing anything stupid to get herself killed and waste their effort. In the most sensible corners of her brain she knew that many things could still go horribly wrong, but she understood now that fearing them did not make things any better. She was tired of crying and screaming and had resolved herself. She would not cry. She would not scream.

There was a single road that rose to the heavy main doors of the castle. Jagged rocks lined its edges, and beyond them it dropped sharply into the choppy moat. Graumel paid little attention to such features but rode straight to the front door. Upon arrival, he dismounted, leaving the princess on the beast's back, and approached the doors.

Had it been only Graumel, Seventh Night would have happily used the opportunity to escape back to the city, but she believed the horse-sized insects blocking the road behind her were the source of Vyn's fear. So she remained seated, her head held high, as though she were merely a visiting dignitary impatiently awaiting entrance.

There was a heavy but simple circular knocker at shoulder height. Graumel used it for four even paced, heavy knocks and waited. After a few moments the door opened, revealing a bored looking Martyr. Seventh Night decided there must be some sort of magic involved in the opening. The door was high enough for a tall man to comfortably ride through on the largest winged unicorn, and it seemed to be made of solid metal. She doubted even the massive cyclops could handle it very easily on his own.

Graumel turned to her, and she dismounted before he could try to help her down. "Here I must take my leave of you, Highness," he said with the same oozy politeness as before and gestured towards the cyclops.

Again Seventh Night moved before he could touch her. At first she had thought the cyclops had been trying to kill her by dropping her in the moat, but with days to think it over, she was far less sure.

While she still found the creature unnerving, he was better company than Graumel. She took a deep breath and stepped inside the castle. Once she was clear of them, the doors swang closed with a loud clomp.

"Bring her here," echoed through the great hall.

The cyclops rolled his eye. He reached out an arm for her, but she dodged back out of reach. "I'll walk," she said, putting as much weight into her voice as she could.

He blinked at her, gave a slight shrug, and pointed a long arm down the hall. She started walking, and he plodded beside her. The cyclops did not look at her directly, but she doubted she could slip off without his notice. Of course, she was hoping for a more direct form of help.

"Could you hide me somewhere for a little while?" she asked softly.

The cyclops made no response, if he heard her at all, and she sighed silently. It had been worth a try.

Neithan and his party met up with the soldiers at yet another farm left barren by a great, dark cloud. Since they were all fairly well-rested, well-fed, and had a guide who knew where he was going, they set forth immediately.

SEVENTH NIGHT

Their path would take them in a wide circle from the west to the north behind the castle. There was a stretch of unwelcoming forest to be followed by the less welcoming foot of the short, jagged mountains that sprawled the north-eastern corner of the Wizards Land. Finally, there would be the narrow tunnel that ran under the moat. First, however, there were the gloomy fields of the farm.

They walked purposefully across the dried, dead grass, but there was a sadness to the land which seeped into all of them. All except Andomare, who was humming softly and twisting one of her arms before her as if feeling for something in the air.

Neithan looked up at the dark sky and let out a heavy breath. "I don't like these clouds," he murmured to Phillip.

"Not exactly cheerful, are they?" Phillip responded.

"Found it," Andomare said in a satisfied, singsongy way. In a more normal voice she asked Phillip if he had his flute with him.

"Yeah," Phillip said, digging the instrument out of his pack.

"Play down the scale," she said. "High note

to low," she added in response to the funny look he gave her.

They had both stopped for this conversation. Neithan was tempted to stop but knew he needed to keep everyone covering ground.

Phillip continued to give Andomare a funny look but complied anyway. He played down the scale.

"Keep doing it," Andomare told him and strung her bow. They received some more funny looks, these from the soldiers, Neithan, and Leonore, as Phillip kept looping the scale. Andomare aimed an arrow at the sky. She kept re-angling the bow until it was almost vertical, then let her arrow fly.

The arrow disappeared into the clouds above. The entire party stopped, because the leaders realized Andomare and Phillip had fallen significantly behind, and looked at the two expectantly. Before they could shout for them to catch up, though, the sky fell.

The water hit in large, fast drops, which slapped the ground and the travelers loudly to begin with and were followed by a more normal steady rain. Andomare laughed, and Phillip let out his own amazed chuckle. Neithan simply resigned himself to the fact that he would get drenched again. The soldiers to their credit kept any thoughts they had to themselves, though they had the look of men who knew they were in way over their heads. Leonore tried to maintain a dignified bearing as the water plastered his hair to his head.

Andomare finished admiring her handiwork and ran to catch up, Phillip on her heels.

"That is not the way to keep from drawing attention," he told her and resumed the walk.

Seventh Night was led to the throne room, another cavernous place with long balconies on either side. A grey stone throne seemed to grow out of the floor, and a second smaller throne sat behind it. Sargon sat upon the larger one.

"I told you there was no point in escaping," he said casually.

"I think I had a far more enjoyable time than I would have locked in my room," Seventh Night matched his tone. "In honesty, you are a very poor host."

As they came closer, Sargon frowned at her.

"You look like a peasant. No one will believe you're a princess dressed like that."

"That was the idea," the princess said.

Sargon continued to frown. He stood and walked past the princess and the cyclops. "Follow me," he said, sounding more than a little annoyed.

He led her through the halls and up the stairs to a small bedchamber similar to the one where she had first awoken in this strange land. "There are dresses in the cabinets; find one appropriate to your station." With that he left the room, closing the door behind him.

The princess looked about uncertainly, not eager to comply with any of Sargon's requests, but she had to admit there was a certain appeal to fresh clothing.

<hr/>

The rain had caused them to quicken their pace, and they soon left the farm. The water ended where their walk through the forest began. After that interestingly wet start, it was a very dry, uneventful trudge. There were enough men in their party crunching through the underbrush to scare off most of the animals. The few they saw eyed them warily and scampered away.

Leonore told Neithan that Sargon seemed to enjoy controlling his monsters as much as he liked making them, so there were not many unnatural creatures running wild.

They made camp not far from a brook at the edge of the forest. It was not quite a clearing, but there was more room between the trees than there had been. As well as a chance to rest their feet, dry their clothes, and warm their hands by the fire, it was their last chance to ask questions. Leonore would only take them to the beginning of the mountain trail, and there leave them to their quest.

So they sat beneath the trees in a small cluster, breaking bread in the most literal sense, and talking softly to each other about things not directly on their minds. "Magic and music are very closely related," Andomare said in response to Phillip's question about why she had had him play his flute. "It's all about rhythms, really, which is why so many of the spells involve chants."

Leonore studied Andomare as she spoke, a mingling of approval and curiosity in his thoughtful expression. Phillip studied him in turn and decided to ask more of the questions that had been rolling in his mind. He wondered why Neithan had not asked many of them, but the prince was very far away even though he sat with them.

"It seems strange," Phillip said when he swallowed enough of his bread to speak. "As unpopular as Sargon is, that so many seem to be willing to help us, but no one has volunteered to go with us."

Leonore turned his eyes to Phillip.

"It does seem like a long time for an unpopular ruler to stay in power," Andomare agreed. "As anxious as everyone is to have him gone, you would think there would be an open rebellion."

"There was an open rebellion," Leonore said. His eyes had a very haunted look. "Small, not very organized, but its end left many believing they would live better if they just waited for Sargon's death."

"How did it end?" Neithan asked.

"The Manti," Leonore said, as though this answered everything. It answered very little for his foreign companions who knew nothing of Manti, and he was obliged to explain. "The black insects you saw are controlled by the black whistle that hangs around Graumel's neck. They were Sargon's first creations after he claimed the throne. The revolutionaries gathered in the center of the city and planned to march on the castle door. More might have joined them, but when Graumel arrived there were forty men gathered. Forty men and ten Manti. None of those men breathed after that day, and none of the Manti were destroyed. You will forgive me if I don't describe it more."

The sorceress covered her mouth with her hand. Phillip tried not to picture it. "Are there Manti inside the castle?" he asked.

"I don't know what you will find," Leonore admitted. "It is not a simple task to create a worthwhile monster. Much time and attention are required, but no one has brought news from inside those walls in over a decade."

They ate silently for a while, but Phillip had never been friends with silence so he broke it.

"Why did you trust us?" he asked.

Leonore smiled. "It is very difficult for a man to lie to Delenora, and very easy for him to talk freely in her presence."

"More magic," Phillip said.

"A gentle magic," Leonore agreed, smiling a little more. "The most beguiling."

Neithan pulled himself out of his quiet. "We need to set the watch in short shifts. I want everyone to be well-rested," he said and looked about. "I don't see Kaleb." He inquired of the nearby soldiers, and one of them said they believed he was taking his time to answer the call of nature. Neithan's brow furrowed, worried but not willing to express it.

"I'll get him," Phillip volunteered.

He found Kaleb sitting near the brook, his back to the trees, and talking softly to himself. He twitched as he heard Phillip approaching, put something into his clothing, and turned and stood. "Did you need me?"

Phillip nodded. "Neithan asked me to check on you. I thought we might volunteer for first watch."

Kaleb shook his head. His expression hidden in evening shadows. "The commander will assign the watches, and he'll want to use soldiers. We're just a couple of civilian peasants who should stay out of the way. The army has ranks for a reason."

"Kind of like life?"

They started walking back towards camp,

more at the same time than together. Phillip crab stepped sideways, so he could keep Kaleb in view.

"Precisely." Kaleb walked at his full height, saving the affected slouch for the camp. "Ranks are given, sometimes earned. You can't simply take them."

"Isn't that what Sargon did?"

"You want to be like Sargon?"

Phillip was less sure what to make of the younger prince every time he saw him. Kaleb's tone was polite, almost friendly, but the words were always so... "I just want to get some sleep," he said.

"Sleep well then," said Kaleb politely.

Seventh Night smoothed the dress she had found. It was green also, but a rich green with equally rich dark red and gold down the front. It was not exactly fresh either. It had the smell of something that had been packed away for several years, but neither mold nor moth had found it, so the princess was content.

There was a looking glass, not as high

quality as the hated one, but clear enough to be of service. Seventh Night found a brush and fixed her hair. In the quiet, she could feel the hum of the castle, layers of magic cast into the stone over the centuries. It seemed to her very lonely.

She finished trying to make herself presentable and looked at the door. With a deep breath, she tried the handle. It was unlocked, but that mattered little for Martyr and Sargon waited impatiently outside.

Sargon led them again, deeper into the castle this time, to a dark room with no windows. He told Seventh Night to sit in a small chair and tied her to it.

"Are you afraid I'll hurt you?" Seventh Night asked as he tightened the last knot.

"Can't have you running off again," he said. She felt his hand in her hair and stiffened. "You might get hurt." He dropped her hair back in place and moved to the table.

The table was covered with vials and measures and small bags and such. It reminded her of how Phillip had described Gadolin's workshop. She heard liquid pouring, and Sargon turned to her, goblet in hand.

SEVENTH NIGHT

"Drink this," he said and held it to her lips.

She sealed her lips and looked at him dubiously.

"That won't help you," he said, but she resolutely ignored the goblet. He smiled as though enjoying a private joke. "I don't see what you're worried about. Your prince will save you, won't he?"

Seventh Night bit her tongue and glared at Sargon.

"As you will," he said with a cruel laugh. He turned back to the table and set the goblet down.

"I don't fear the fearful," she said, wanting to lash back for the injury he had caused. Sargon looked back at her over his shoulder, hoping to silence her with a glare, but had no such luck. She continued, her voice dripping with venom now. "You're a small little man who cowers in an empty castle playing king while others do your dirty work. You—"

His palm struck her face, silencing the insult. Her cheek stung, and her jaw felt a little out of place. But it made her glad to know that she had cut him. She closed her eyes to stop the tears that threatened to come and gather her thoughts.

SEVENTH NIGHT

After a few moments, Sargon pushed a cloth gag into and across her mouth. She opened her eyes to slits. He gave her a twitch of a smile. "I don't want to have to listen to you scream."

He touched something to her upper arm, and she turned her head to look. Then it bit or stung, hard to say which. And Sargon was right; she would have screamed. She tried to even though the gag muffled her sound.

He pulled the thing off, but she barely glanced at it. The room was growing fuzzy, and she felt her body slump. Then everything fell dark.

CHAPTER XXVII

IN AND OUT

"The path to the tunnel begins here," Leonore said. "It is not too difficult to follow; finding it is the trouble."

Phillip agreed. Despite Leonore's announcement, he saw nothing that looked even remotely like a path among the rocks. He glanced at the rest of the party to see equally uncertain looks on their faces.

Leonore did not appear to notice. He walked to a rock and seemed to step into it. Phillip took a few steps forward to get a new angle and saw that the rock was divided by a tall, thin slit. Having demonstrated, Leonore slid back out.

"And now I take my leave of you," Leonore said. He looked at Neithan expectantly, but Neithan was studying the rock. Leonore shook his head and turned to the forest.

"Thank you for your help," Phillip said as Leonore passed. The nobleman nodded a welcome.

"Commander," Neithan said.

The commander nodded and motioned to his men. He went first, turning his body sideways to fit between the rocks. One by one they followed in similar fashion. Phillip soon understood why the prince had been reluctant to lead. His thickly muscular frame caused him some difficulty in squeezing through the gap.

The extreme narrowness only lasted a few feet, and soon they were able to walk normally, though still in single file. The path snaked up and down the mountainside, under rocks and into deep trenches. It was nearly as exciting as the trudge through the forest but with less shade.

That is, until the terrocks came.

"Look!" one of the soldiers shouted and pointed toward the sky.

SEVENTH NIGHT

Two of the enormous birds were circling.

"Keep still," Neithan said.

They all stood very still, their eyes fixed on the circling birds. Currently the path left them with rock hip high on either side, but otherwise they were exposed.

"They're coming!" Andomare announced, trying not to sound panicked.

"Squat, swords up," Neithan ordered and demonstrated the position. They all squatted down and stuck their swords straight up above their heads. Andomare wedged herself even further down between Neithan and Phillip and tried to put her bow together.

The terrocks descended in a sluggish circle. Phillip almost wished they would come faster, so they could get out of their uncomfortable position. Dropping into a sudden dive, the first of the ugly birds came too fast. It scratched at their hiding place, trying to pull them out of their crevice, but the swords made it awkward for the great bird. With their extended weapons their best protection, no one dared to pull back for a good strike, but the bird got a scratch every time it reached for the party. The men were able to dodge enough to avoid the talons for the most part, and only a few sweeps that got past the blades hit flesh rather than leather.

The second bird tried with no more success. By this time, Andomare had managed to arm her bow. She let an arrow fly, and it struck the feathered part of the bird's leg. Not a killing shot, but the terrock screamed a loud, unhappy scream. After one more try, the terrocks left in search of easier prey.

They waited a little while to make sure the terrocks had gone. No one was badly injured, but all were shaken from the misadventure. The commander tried to get them to press on, but Andomare insisted on at least cleaning the bad scratches.

Not eager to wait, Phillip leapt onto the side of their crevice path and walked to the front of the line. Neithan liked the idea and did the same. Andomare satisfied herself by wrapping a bandage around the hand of the young soldier whose scratch was deep enough to be called a gash.

She finished at about the same time Neithan dropped back onto the path. This was a good thing because he did not break stride, and if unfinished she might have been offended.

SEVENTH NIGHT

They continued and had no more trouble with mountain creatures except for a few fist-sized spiders, which were quickly dispatched.

At the point where they all began to think they could stand no more of rocks and sun, the path bent and led downward into a dark tunnel.

"Do you think this is it?" Andomare asked.

"I smell water," Phillip said. "Good chance it's the moat."

"Who has the lanterns?" Neithan asked.

Phillip pulled two lanterns out of his pack and lit them. He passed one of them down the line to whoever was bringing up the rear. As Neithan turned his head to watch the lamp's progress, Phillip started into the tunnel.

The tunnel led down, sharply at first, then gradually. The walls were smooth, but in the way that something natural left things smooth, with ripples and bumps and rounded protrusions. Phillip might have thought it completely natural, except the height and width of the tunnel stayed very regular and the floor was smoother than the rest. It was wider than the path had been; two men could stand side by side uncomfortably.

They walked forward in silence. Phillip kept thinking about the moat overhead and hoped the tunnel had no leaks. It had a cool, moist smell, though he saw no other signs of water.

The tunnel ended with a wall of stone.

Phillip moved the lamp around the edges where the rock met stone, looking for a crack or crease which might betray an opening.

"Is it all walled up?" the commander asked.

"I hope not," Neithan said.

"I can't believe he would bar it with something so permanent," Andomare added.

Phillip found an unlit torch fastened to the wall and smiled. Just like the entrance to Gadolin's lab. He reached out and pulled on the torch. It did not move. "It was worth a try," he said in response to Andomare's raised eyebrow.

Her brow creased as she studied the wall. "It's a wizard's tunnel. Maybe it needs a spell or something."

Everyone cast their eyes about the cave in the lamplight, hoping to see something they had missed.

Phillip continued to stare at the torch. His eyes brightened, "Of course!" he said, drawing the attention of everyone. He dug a tinder twig out of his sack and used the lamp to light it. "It's the only torch in the hall. It has to be here for something."

He lit the torch with the tinder twig. Its glow grew, then flared as the whole torch head caught fire. There was a solid click of something mechanical, and the wall opened.

"Not bad," Andomare said.

Eagerly the party spilled into the room. Relieved from the confines of the tunnel, they found themselves in a large, well-lit storage room with barrels stacked to one side. They stood still and silent, waiting for sound or sign that would signal a trap.

"Move on," Neithan ordered. The commander signaled to one of his soldiers, and the man tried the door. It opened, and he looked out cautiously.

"Do you hear it?" Andomare murmured to Phillip.

He looked at her questioningly.

"All the spells and enchantments on the castle, it's like a symphony," she said in childlike awe.

Phillip had never heard a symphony, but he tried to listen for what Andomare heard. He recognized a hum, similar to the vibrations of his flute when he played, and something like a snatch of a melody, but nothing stronger than that.

Phillip blew out his lantern, stuffed it back in his pouch, and collected the other one from Kaleb. Looking about, he realized the room was lit, but without torch or candle or window of any sort. He supposed it was one of those layered enchantments. The light without source left the stone walls a golden color.

"Clear," the soldier announced.

"Keep sharp," Neithan said as he led them into the hall.

"And don't touch anything," Andomare added and glared at one soldier who was resting his hand on the wall. He removed it, trying to act as if her words had nothing to do with his action.

***

In the far corner of the storage room, hidden by a wall of barrels, the red skinned cyclops stirred from his sleep. Sargon had ordered Martyr to hide in the room, behind the wall of barrels, and wait for a band of invaders. He had explained all this gently, without yelling, and it had been the unusual calm from the angry little man that held Martyr's attention. There was a woman with them, beautiful and tall. While there might be many men in the party, Martyr only had one job. Kill the woman.

Sargon had told him this was an important job and he was sure Martyr would do it well. Martyr was so confused by the gentle tone and the compliment that he had gone down to the storage room, sat down behind the barrels, and contemplated this change in behavior as well as a ten-foot, one-eyed monster could contemplate anything. He sat there in the windowless room, waiting for the wall to open and the men to come. Sargon had sent him to deal with another man who had come this way once, a long time ago. Martyr had not wanted to kill that man any more than he wanted to kill this woman. He was not a violent monster. So when the man had come, Martyr had smiled at him and tried to say hello.

But he had not been a nice man. The man had yelled at Martyr and hit him with a sword. The sword had hurt. Martyr still did not like to think about it. It had taken Sargon months to make his arm work again. The un-nice man with the sword had raised it again, so Martyr had knocked it away and the man with it. He had not intended to break the man, but the un-nice man did not work afterwards. The way-deep-down voice had cried for days.

He wondered if this woman was also un-nice and if she would try to hurt him too. He had helped the little princess, but all she had done was yell and kick and come back to the castle again. The way-deep-down voice had been happy to see her and sad too. Martyr found this confusing. Trying to understand the strangeness of people and inside himself made Martyr very tired, and after many whiles of squatting and thinking and then sitting and waiting, the cyclops had rolled onto his back and fallen asleep.

It was the smell that aroused him. The smell of sweat and leather and metal and people. He listened groggily to the low voices and little sounds people in armor still make when trying to be quiet. He peeked between a narrow gap in the barrels with his one great green eye and watched the men in armor bottleneck by the door, waiting for their turn to pass through. The woman had already gone into the hall. He could see the smallest hint of her hair and hear the snatch of melody in her movements.

SEVENTH NIGHT

He would have to go through the soldiers to get to her. They were turned away. Their pointy swords were out, and the sight of them made him want to knock the men away, even if there was a chance they would break. Martyr thought about picking up a barrel and throwing it at the men. He could knock them down and climb over them to get the woman. He thought this was a good plan.

He rolled to his feet far more quietly than the soldiers moved. He wore no metal to clink or leather to rub and squeak. Before he could decide which barrel to throw, he remembered what reaching the woman would mean. This made him pause and peek through the little gap again. A large man, who was almost a cyclops himself with one eye covered, turned and stared directly at the wall where Martyr was hiding. There was a long pointy sword lifted by his side, held tense, ready to strike, bite, and sting.

Martyr felt afraid and tried to make himself as small as possible, which was not easy for a ten-foot-tall monster. He crouched down and covered his massive head with his monstrous hands. He squeezed his eye shut, then peeked it open. The last soldiers passed out the door and whispered for the almost-cyclops to come along. With a last uncertain look about the room with his uncovered eye, the almost-cyclops did.

Martyr let out a low, grumbling, relieved breath.

Out, said the deep-down-voice. Martyr paused. The way-deep-down voice was rarely so clear. *Out*, it said again.

Martyr stepped out from behind the barrels and spotted the tunnel door which was now standing open. *Out*. He understood, but he hesitated. He was not allowed outside. Sargon would hit and yell if he found out. He might even send the Manti after him. The angry little man had said as much once or twice. He would be fed to the Manti if he did not obey.

Out.

But maybe all the pointy swords and the woman would distract him. Sargon would be very angry if he saw the woman. He might try to feed Martyr to the Manti anyway. *Yes, out*, the deep-down-voice encouraged.

He was a curious monster, though he had little opportunity to exercise that curiosity. It was a narrow tunnel, but wide enough he could walk down it if he hunched over without his shoulders scraping the walls. And so Martyr went. He traveled to the end of the tunnel, ignored the narrow path that led to it, and ventured out onto the uninhabited, rocky terrain where there was no one to yell at him.

SEVENTH NIGHT

CHAPTER XXVIII

THE WIZARD KING

Prince Neithan and his party began a thorough search, one floor at a time. It was slow progress, because while they moved quickly from room to room, they checked every door. They all kept their swords drawn, except Phillip and Andomare. Andomare had no sword, and Phillip had been ordered not to draw his until needed, which had offended him only slightly, as he liked having his hands free.

They found lots of nothing. Abandoned rooms, empty rooms, rooms that might still be in use but were unoccupied at the moment. It was eerie to walk through so many deserted halls. The emptiness was disturbing, the time they wasted checking vacant rooms irritating, and the thought of what might be waiting around each corner was both exciting and unnerving.

They went up another set of stairs, this one a bit wider than those before it. The rooms on this floor looked far more used, or they had been at some time. There was a kitchen with pots and pans scattered about. There was no dust to mark the passage of time, but there had been no dust anywhere else. Nor were there any cobwebs or skittering insects. That made Phillip as uncomfortable as anything else.

"Wow," Andomare said quietly from the doorway.

Phillip went over and peeked around her shoulder to see what was so impressive. It was a grand dining hall that made the one in the castle in Cordance laughable. Two ridiculously long tables, or perhaps multiple tables laid end to end, stretched almost the entire length of the room. A half-circle table with a half-circle of very impressive chairs sat at the end where the little doorway in which they were standing was located. There was another small door directly across the dining hall, and a more impressive set of double doors stood open at the other end of the hall.

"They like things big," Phillip said.

They checked the closest door and found much of the same, back corridors leading towards the kitchen. The double doors led to a hall nearly as wide as the dining room.

"Those look like the castle doors," Andomare said, pointing down the hall to her right at the huge pieces of hinged metal.

"This way," Neithan said, leading them down the other end of the hall. The hall ended at another set of large, meticulously carved wooden doors. Neithan tried the handle. "It's locked."

"That's encouraging," Phillip said.

Neithan gave him a sideways glance.

"Probably means it's something important," Phillip explained.

Neithan nodded. "Commander, the door."

The commander gestured to two of the soldiers.

"You know," Phillip began. "I could—"

The commander made another gesture, and the two men slammed their shoulders against the door, accomplishing a loud thunk but not much else.

"I can pick locks," Phillip said.

Neithan frowned at him, wondering how he had picked up that particular skill. "Try it," he said.

Phillip kneeled before the lock and pulled a few small tools out of his bag. He set to work.

Fifty foot taps later, Andomare nudged him impatiently. "How much longer will this take?" she asked.

"I can get it," Phillip insisted, dodging the question.

Neithan sighed. "We're going to check the rest of the floor and come back to this. There may be another way in." He waved his hand, sending the soldiers to the large door on the other side of the hall from where they had come. Phillip continued to scrutinize the lock. "Are you coming?" Neithan asked.

Phillip made an affirmative noise and rose. Satisfied, Neithan followed the party. Once he had turned his back, Phillip stopped, drawn back to the lock. He had never had a lock stump him before. He kneeled down again, pulled out another tool, and decided to try something a little different.

"What is it?" Andomare asked as they entered the new room. It was an exact reflection in size and shape of the dining hall. Except it was empty of furnishings, and life-sized portraits of women lined the walls.

"I think it's a ballroom," Neithan said.

"It's strange," said Andomare.

They crossed through the center of the room, intent on the doors at the other end. Andomare crossed her arms tight over her chest and looked about for something she could not name.

A high-pitched shriek filled the room. Everyone turned to look at the burly soldier who had made it. He shifted uncomfortably under their stares and pointed at the portrait closest to him.

"It moved," he stammered.

"It moved?" Andomare repeated incredulously and hurried over to the portrait. She gasped as the portrait woman's arm went from her side to stretch out toward Andomare. Move was not the right word; it simply changed from one pose to another.

SEVENTH NIGHT

"Neithan, could you hold me?" Andomare asked.

The prince frowned uncertainly but went to her anyway. She took his arm and hooked it around her waist. Then she planted her own hand next to the portrait. With her free hand, she brushed the surface. Her fingers went through, and she jerked them back. She let out a deep breath and steeled herself.

Andomare plunged her arm into the painting. She saw her own hand clasp the woman's arm and pulled. The painting did not want to relinquish its prisoner, but the combined strength of Neithan and Andomare prevailed. Bit by bit the woman came out of the painting. She stepped through the frame to the ground and fell onto Andomare. The well-dressed woman embraced the flabbergasted sorceress.

"Oh, lady, thank you!" she exclaimed. "Please, save the others. They are all trapped as I was!"

Andomare pushed the smaller woman off her gently and surveyed the portraits lining the wall. They all seemed to be moving now. Several of the soldiers blanched. She exchanged glances with Neithan. "This will take a while."

Phillip bit back a grunt as one of his small tools bent in an unusable way. He pulled it out and dropped it back in his pack. He opened the mouth of the pack a bit wider, looking for something else he could try. His eyes fell upon a small leather bag.

"Idiot," he chided himself and pulled the bag out. Phillip sprinkled the powder over the lock and tried to blow some of it inside.

"Unlock," he commanded it. He heard a soft but definite click. Phillip smiled and turned back to his companions who were no longer there. He remembered they had moved on but could not remember exactly how long ago that was or in what direction. Phillip bit his lip. It was foolish to be on his own here, but if the princess was simply waiting inside, he could not leave her.

Of course it could just as easily be some flesh-eating beast waiting inside to tear his head off. That thought almost made him retreat to find the others, but he had been willing to start this quest alone. Why should he run back to the others like a helpless infant now?

Phillip took a deep breath and opened the door.

It was heavy but well-constructed so it made barely a whisper as it moved. The room was large with the highest ceiling he had seen yet. The whisper of the door echoed through the chamber. There was a faded carpet upon the floor that stretched from the door to the two thrones at the other end.

And sitting upon the larger throne was an unimpressive man in rich clothing. He did not move, but he looked at Phillip, then behind him, with sharp black eyes and smiled. "Did you come all alone?"

"Sargon," Phillip half questioned, half stated.

"King Sargon, my little friend," he corrected.

Phillip scowled, "Where's Seven?"

"Seven?" Sargon repeated.

"The Princess, Seventh Night, where is she?"

"You must be the magician's apprentice," Sargon said.

Phillip was already frowning, or he would have done so. This was not right. Not just the ethical aspects of kidnapping and making a kingdom live in fear. Something beneath it all didn't make sense.

"It must have been a disappointment to find yourself indentured to a magician who knew no magic," Sargon continued. "Particularly for someone with your curiosity."

"Where is the princess?" Phillip repeated, placing his hand on the hilt of his sword.

"Why so much trouble for another man's bride?" Sargon asked with a hint of sympathy. "Surely you came here for something else."

"I came here for Seventh Night," Phillip said and drew his sword. "If you don't give her to me, I will take her."

Sargon laughed. "Oh, yes, I have heard of your prowess with the sword."

Phillip wavered a little. He had hoped to intimidate Sargon on some level, but... And in that moment, Phillip understood something. He understood everything. The kidnapping, the map with numbers, why a foreign king from across the sea would care about stopping a wedding in Cordance. The understanding made him angry. The heat rose in him, inhibiting his speech for a moment.

"What else did Kaleb tell you?" he asked

when his voice returned.

Sargon's face darkened. "I am not told . . . I know," he said. He was trying to sound mystical and impressive, but he was groping for some of his words.

Phillip remembered the others. He had to tell them there was a traitor in their midst. He took a step back, then turned to run for the door. Sargon could think him a coward if he liked. It was not Sargon's respect he sought.

As he turned around Sargon said something loudly, and the door slammed shut, cutting off his exit. Phillip looked back to see Sargon standing. The small man walked around his throne and pulled out a gleaming sword which had been hidden behind it.

"There are secrets within this castle," Sargon said as he checked his blade. "Knowledge to make anyone with the potential for magic a great sorcerer. I am feeling generous today. Put down your weapon and hold your tongue, and I will let you live to study them."

Phillip took off his travel pack and dropped it by the door so it would not hinder him. He had asked Andomare about how wizards fight, since he was not satisfied by Leonore's answers. She had been vague. He suspected it was not her area of expertise either but got the impression that fighting with raw magic was as dangerous for the wielder as the target. Most magic was slow working and not fit for the heat of battle. One might use magic to guide an arrow or sharpen a sword, but the words that could kill were also death for the speaker. This was only slight comfort. He imagined at the very least this meant Sargon's sword was extremely sharp and nearly unbreakable, and the tyrant king held it like someone who had had more than one lesson.

Sargon shook his head and made a tsk, tsk sound. "I remember being young and hotheaded, but not so eager to die. Oh, but you're in love," he said sarcastically. "Women really are an endless source of trouble, aren't they?"

"Little foolhardy bringing one over the sea to your castle, wasn't it?" Phillip challenged.

Sargon merely smiled. "There's a certain poetry to it. Supplying the means to my own downfall." He pointed his blade and looked down its length at Phillip. "What are you? Eighteen? Twenty? I can promise you this much. Whatever you think you want now won't be what you want twenty years from now."

"I want to live," Phillip said, just to be contrary.

"And eat when hungry, and sleep when you're tired," countered Sargon in a sardonic tone. "But the dreams change. Those things you want in between eating and sleeping. All those perfect little illusions in your head turn into realities. Even when you get exactly what you want, it never turns out the way you want it."

"Maybe it's not about getting what you want," said Phillip.

"See there, you've learned something already," Sargon said, testing his blade. "Are you really going to make me kill you over a girl you can't have even if you win? I've killed a lot of men to get where I am. The thrill goes out of it after a while."

"Let me talk to her," Phillip insisted, seeing a glim of hope for negotiation.

"I can't allow that," Sargon said. "You'll only make her unhappy with your theories, and her story won't be nearly as riveting. No, silence is the only thing that can save you."

Phillip shook his head. "She deserves the

truth. I'll fight for that."

Sargon gave a dull chuckle. "Since you insist, I do need to kill a little time, and it really will be far more convenient if I silence you permanently."

"You can try," Phillip returned. "But I've been told I have trouble keeping my mouth shut." He had intended to sound brave and cavalier, but his voice came out in more of a deadpan.

Sargon began the long walk across the room to meet him, his stride and smile quite confident. With less confidence and more guarded steps, Phillip came to meet him.

SEVENTH NIGHT

CHAPTER XXIX

A DUAL

The center of the ballroom was filling with well-dressed women, all chattering quietly, and not so quietly, and asking the soldiers questions they could not answer. To their credit the soldiers had regained their color and put aside their own misgivings to reassure the ladies.

Andomare ignored them pointedly and focused on pulling out the last of the women. "I have never seen them before, but I've read about them," Andomare had explained to Neithan earlier. "They're pockets in reality. Not in the paintings. The paintings are just doorways into them. And there's nothing in them, no floors or walls to push against, which is why they could not get out on their own, and no time so they can't tell us how long they've been here."

"No time," Neithan repeated. "So they could have been here for years."

"Decades," Andomare said. "But I'm not sure all of them realize that, so let's not bring it up yet."

"Agreed."

Andomare determined the pockets were only large enough for a single person, which was why they did not draw her in as well. As they went along, she and Neithan had gotten much faster at drawing the women out, so freeing them all did not take quite as long as she had feared. It still took time, though, and left them with the problem of what to do with nearly thirty confused women.

"Quiet," one of the finer dressed women told the others in a hushed but commanding tone. Her eyes fell on each of them until they obeyed. She turned her eyes to Neithan and Andomare. "We are grateful for our rescue, but you seem to seek something else."

"Our princess," Andomare said. "Short, little thing about yea high. Black hair, blue eyes, rather pale." Neithan bit the inside of his lip so he would not smile.

"I remember seeing someone like that," the lady said. "But while we could see out to some degree, the images have no order. The red beast was with her, but whether he was bringing her in or taking her out, I do not know."

"Commander," Neithan said, calling the man to him. "We can't take all these unarmed women running around the castle with us. I want you to take the men and escort them back to the forest." The commander looked ready to protest, but Neithan did not give him time. "When you get to the forest, leave two men to escort them back to the farm. Arris or Leonore will know what to do with them. The rest of you come back here."

"Your Highness," the commander began in a please-be-sensible tone.

"We'll be fine," Neithan said. He spared a glance at Andomare and knew that was true. For in that moment, Neithan understood something. Something about magic and prophecies, and he knew that he was safer with Andomare right now than with a hundred soldiers. "Now hurry, before Sargon realizes we've freed his captives."

With a grimace, the commander choked down his objections and called for the women and soldiers to follow him. They flowed out of the room in a colorful mob, and Neithan and Andomare found themselves alone.

"Where's Phillip?" Neithan asked.

"Where's Kaleb?" Andomare echoed.

"Kaleb probably got impatient and went off looking for Seventh Night on his own," Neithan said, looking worried. "So he could be any-where. Phillip may still be trying that lock."

They hurried back into the grand hall. They could see the soldiers at one end, making a futile attempt to open the castle doors. At the other end was the carved wooden door but no Phillip.

"Maybe he unlocked it," Andomare guessed. She hurried forward to try the door. "No, it's still locked."

"Maybe he and Kaleb went searching together," Neithan suggested.

Andomare raised her eyebrow.

"You're right; maybe Phillip followed Kaleb."

"Or the other way around."

Neithan took Andomare's hand. "Come on," he said, and they hurried back to the ballroom.

He was young and agile, and those were the only things saving Phillip. Sargon was older and rusty, but at some point in his life he had been properly trained in swordsmanship. It was not the sort of duel that would go down in the annals of history. Phillip spent most of his time dodging and retreating, and Sargon was conservative in his strikes.

Kaleb watched them from the balcony. The magician's apprentice was doing admirably well for a beginner, but Sargon was clearly superior and would win in the end. Kaleb removed his eye patch and smiled. The magician's apprentice was not much of a rival, but he was a rival. And Kaleb did not like to have rivals.

"Wait!" the sorceress said and stopped in the middle of the new corridor they were trying.

Neithan stopped and looked at her expectantly. "Stand over there," she told him.

He moved back to where she had indicated.

"It's been a while since I've been somewhere so quiet," she said half to herself. "Everyone has a rhythm, but it's hard to hear when there are so many other rhythms around. I think Kaleb's should be a lot like yours."

She closed her eyes, listening. Neithan waited patiently. She opened her eyes. "This way."

Phillip tripped over an uneven spot in the stone. He fell down and used the force of his fall to roll out of the way of Sargon's sword, which struck the ground with an unpleasant twang. Somehow, through all this, he held onto his own sword. He brought it up to block Sargon's next strike. When the blades hit, he kicked out with his foot and connected with Sargon's shin.

Sargon grunted and took a few steps back. "That was a crude trick, boy," he hissed. "I'll know better next time."

Phillip scrambled to his feet and took a few steps back of his own.

SEVENTH NIGHT

Sargon rubbed his shin with his free hand. Phillip took the opportunity to strike at his sword hand in hopes of disarming him, but Sargon had not let his guard drop as much as it seemed and met the blow.

Once again Sargon forced him back.

Kaleb's smile faded as he heard footsteps fast approaching and went to meet them.

"Oh, good," Andomare said, slightly out of breath. "Have you seen Phillip?"

"Actually—" Kaleb began.

The sounds of the sword fight reached Andomare's ears, and she ran to the heavy stone balustrade. Neithan gave his brother a curious look as he passed.

Sargon struck high, so that Phillip had to raise his blade to meet it. Sargon hit hard, then instead of pulling back for another strike, he reversed the sword and rammed the pommel into Phillip's hand.

A small gasp of pain escaped Phillip's lips, and he dropped his sword. Sargon knocked his elbow into Phillip's stomach with surprising strength and knocked him to the ground. Sargon pulled his sword back now for a final thrust.

"Phillip!" Andomare screamed.

Startled by the sudden addition of a female voice, Sargon looked up at the balcony. Phillip took the opportunity to retrieve his sword. He reached over to grab his blade and for good measure gave Sargon another kick in the shin.

Sargon spat something incomprehensible and glared at Phillip. "No more," he growled.

Neithan shook his head. "He needs help," he said and tried to judge the drop. He was certain he could survive the jump, but not certain he could so without a broken bone.

Kaleb touched his brother's shoulder reassuringly. "I think he's doing well. We should let him fight his own fight."

Neithan frowned at his brother. "I'm going down there."

"Look," Andomare said, pointing to the other end of the balcony. A door-sized opening led to a small curved staircase; below it on the lower level was an unassuming wooden door.

"It's locked," Kaleb said.

"Not a problem," Neithan said. "I will not leave this kingdom in the hands of such a monster."

SEVENTH NIGHT

Below Phillip was retreating steadily, but he had nowhere to go but in circles. He hurt in several places, and he was sore everywhere else. He tried to catch his breath so he could yell something back to Andomare, but Sargon came forward in a sudden assault. Phillip managed to catch most of the strikes with a vigor born of sheer desperation.

Neithan bounded for the door, but Kaleb got there before him and blocked his path. Kaleb put both of his hands on his brother's shoulders to stop him.

"Let Phillip fight his own battle," Kaleb said.

Neithan shook his head, "He'll die."

"Fine!" Kaleb snapped.

Neithan took a step back, shocked by the fire in his brother's voice. "Let me pass," Neithan returned in kind, angered by Kaleb's bullheadedness.

"I will not," Kaleb said and drew his sword.

Neithan took another step back and looked at his brother in true confusion. "Why are you doing this?" he asked softly.

SEVENTH NIGHT

"You're with him," Andomare answered, overcoming her own shock. "You're working with Sargon."

Neithan searched his brother's face waiting for Kaleb to deny it, but Kaleb simply stared back at him stonily, with the sort of regret in his eyes that came from showing your cards too soon. It was not Neithan's nature to become angry over deep wounds, but he remembered Phillip and lifted his own sword. "Let me pass," he repeated.

Kaleb did not move, so Neithan tried to push past him. Kaleb pushed his brother back and brought his sword up. Neithan's met it. As elegant as the duel below was clumsy, the brothers' fight was the sort of duel that bards sung songs about. They were equally matched in strength and size. Both well-schooled with their blades and had practiced with each other enough to know what to expect.

Andomare nearly tripped as she backed out of the way of their dangerous dance.

Sargon drove a thrust straight for Phillip's chest. Phillip knocked it off course so that it sliced the skin of his upper arm instead. He groaned but refused to let the pain best him. It was his left arm anyway, and he favored his right.

Sargon was inclined to show no mercy now. Having got one cut in he pressed for another. He backed Phillip closer and closer to the far wall, reducing step by step his space to retreat.

Andomare stared, transfixed by the sight of two men with the same face, so dear and so despised, in such a deadly contest. She backed up further till her hand touched the stone balustrade. She brought her hand to her heart and found her shouldered bow instead.

"Phillip," she reminded herself.

She looked back downstairs and drew an arrow from her quiver. She pulled it back, hesitating for a moment lest she hit her friend.

Kaleb took a few steps back from the force of his brother's last blow and saw Andomare standing ready with her drawn bow, murmuring something.

Sargon momentarily stopped his assault to gesture and mutter a short incantation. Phillip's bag that he had left by the door slid across the floor and underneath his feet. It tangled him there so that he fell, landing on his wounded arm, causing him to cry out. Sargon saw the sword held loose in his hand and kicked it away.

"No!" Kaleb cried. He changed tactics and caught Neithan off guard as he knocked him aside and ran for the sorceress. Neithan saw what his brother was doing, dropped his sword, and dove for Kaleb's legs, knocking them both to the ground.

Andomare let her arrow fly.

Sargon raised his sword to put an end to Phillip, but Kaleb's cry caused him to look up. The sight of Andomare's drawn bow trained on him made Sargon take a step back. The arrow found the king's heart.

Eyes wide with surprise, Sargon dropped his sword. The cloth around the wound darkened as blood seeped into it. He staggered back and fell against the wall, and then Sargon did not move. His eyes remained open but saw nothing.

Phillip staggered to his feet and stood there, feeling tired and shaken. "Thanks," he called up to Andomare.

SEVENTH NIGHT
"You're welcome," she called back down.

SEVENTH NIGHT

Chapter XXX

The Sleeping Princess

Kaleb gave up his sword to Neithan so his brother would release him and got to his feet. He clutched the balustrade and looked upon the scene with a broken expression. Andomare looked at him and then to Neithan who was holding both swords with an unreadable expression on his face.

She was not sure he could speak, so she spoke for him. "We need to go down there."

Kaleb looked at her with murder in his eyes. "You witch!" he spat and began to move for her.

With his first twitch, however, Neithan's swords thrust into the space between them, blocking Kaleb from the sorceress.

"Go," Neithan said, his voice low with an undercurrent that allowed for no debate. The anger left Kaleb's face as he looked at his brother, and docilely, he led them down the stairs.

When they reached the floor of the throne room, Andomare ran to Phillip and made him sit down. "Let me see your arm," she said. After a short examination, she pulled the dressing bandages out of her pack. "You idiot, you scared me," she chided him as she wrapped his arm. Phillip did not move but kept his eyes fixed on Kaleb.

Kaleb stepped over to Sargon's corpse and closed its eyes. Neithan kicked the fallen sword away, so his brother would not try to pick it up. Kaleb stepped back from the body. He seemed to have lost the will to try anything.

Andomare finished her bandage. "I'll check it again when we get out of here," she said. She kissed Phillip's temple and ruffled his hair affectionately. Phillip was strong enough to stand on his own, but she helped him up anyway.

"It was all a show," Phillip said, anger catching his throat. "That's why nothing stopped us getting into the castle. He wanted us to come. Kaleb would have challenged Sargon, and they'd've had a mock duel, which Kaleb would graciously let Sargon survive. He'd have rescued the princess, saved the kingdom, and be some big hero." Phillip spat the last word.

Kaleb looked at Phillip. There was something in his eyes, but whether it was surprise, anger, or amusement no one could say. "I would have been king."

"Where's Seventh Night?" Neithan asked.

"She's safe," Kaleb said.

"You'll take us to her."

Neithan sheathed one of his swords and kept the other trained on Kaleb. He made a motion for Kaleb to start walking.

Kaleb led them through new passages and stairways. A few times he paused uncertainly but showed no doubt of the general direction. As they walked he seemed to regain some of his confidence. Eventually, he stopped before an arched doorway and looked back at the others.

Phillip passed them all and opened the door.

SEVENTH NIGHT

The princess lay on a large, tall bed. The light from the window highlighted the curves of her face. Her eyes were closed, and she looked very peaceful. Her hands were folded over her stomach, and her hair was arranged artistically on the pillow.

"Seven," Phillip breathed and ran to her side. He sat beside her on the bed and touched her face lightly. "Seven," he said gently. "Wake up. Everything's alright now."

She did not awake. She did not shift or mumble or brush his hand away irritably. Andomare drifted to the far side of the room. Neithan stood at the door, sword in hand, with Kaleb in front of him.

"Seven?" Phillip's brow furrowed. He stood and glared accusingly at Kaleb. "What have you done to her?"

"She's just sleeping," Kaleb said. "It's the same potion I was given. All I have to do is kiss her..."

"*You're* not going to touch her," Phillip said angrily.

"He may have to," Andomare said from the foot of the bed. Phillip looked at her questioningly. "Women are pickier than men. The love has to be reciprocal."

"What?"

Andomare sighed. "She has to love that person, and they have to love her."

"Why didn't you mention that before?" Phillip asked.

"It wasn't important before," she answered.

Phillip looked at Kaleb darkly. "He doesn't love her," Phillip said. "He wouldn't have done this to her if he did."

"I did this for her," Kaleb protested with more passion in his voice than Phillip had ever heard from the man. "Everything is for her."

"Sabotaging the treaty was for her?" Phillip asked icily.

"Don't pretend to understand politics," Kaleb answered in kind. He was not eager to explain, but the tip of Neithan's sword touched his back, urging him to continue. Slowly, hands held up to show he would not try any tricks, he turned to face his brother. "I needed my own kingdom, so I could marry her with my own name."

Neithan's stare was dangerous and unfathomable, so Kaleb kept talking.

"Our parents gave me to Sargon, payment for protection against Gourlin. I was his heir. He knows...he knew he hadn't done things properly as king. He was a lesser noble who got swept up with the idea of power without really understanding what it means to wield it. Maturity made him realize he had bitten off more than he could chew.

"I've been trained to manage a country. Not long ago he decided it would be better to pass on the crown sooner, rather than wait for his natural death. It was going to be better for everyone, and he could retire. But Sargon didn't think the people would trust me if they knew he'd picked me out."

"Sargon thought he could rule Cordance first," Phillip said. "That's why he wanted a king's child, so he could use them to claim the throne." Kaleb looked uncertain, so Phillip pressed on. He had had the whole trip to think about this. "It didn't matter if they were second born, since he figured he could arrange a convenient death for the first at any given time."

"No!" Kaleb protested sharply and spoke to his brother earnestly. "I can't tell you what went through his mind, and as I said before, his plans changed. I made it clear to him I would be party to nothing that hurt my brother. Nothing was done to hurt you, Neithan."

"The sleeping potion was meant for Neithan."

"The princess was never supposed to reach Pinnacle. There were modifications being made to the carriage to bring her here safely. She..." Kaleb allowed a show of amusement at his own expense. "She was too resourceful and forced a change in plans. Sargon's agent didn't know about me, a mistake. I would have dissuaded him."

"Who are his agents?" Phillip asked.

Kaleb gave a small shrug, and Neithan pressed the tip of his sword close again. "I really don't know. He hid their identities so I would not be tempted to betray him."

"Charming." Andomare stood with arms crossed. "Was slaying the guardian part of the plan?"

Kaleb shook his head. "None of you were supposed to come. If the boat's small enough, the guardian ignores it. That's how Sargon and your father reached our shore." Kaleb looked at his brother. "You didn't want to marry her. This way you could have your own wife, openly, and we wouldn't be forced to share a life anymore."

Neithan showed no delight at this consideration.

"You could have started a war," Phillip said, remembering what Seventh Night had said.

Kaleb sniffed. "Sargon could see further than you could understand from this castle. When Gourlin finishes conquering its southern neighbor, it will come west again. War is inevitable unless Gourlin thinks it has no chance of winning. Cordance and Tivin need strong allies, and what's stronger than a country of wizards?"

"Wizards who are grateful to be freed from their tyrannical king," Andomare supplied. "You did plan out a nice fairytale, didn't you? Well, we've killed the evil king. All that's left is for you to kiss the sleeping princess."

Kaleb narrowed his eyes skeptically at the sorceress. "I thought you might try to claim a crown for yourself."

"Don't pretend to understand me," Andomare retorted.

"We'll let Seventh Night decide," Neithan said. "It affects Tivin more than Cordance."

Phillip's insides boiled in protest, but Kaleb seemed to be their only chance. "Do it quickly," he said.

SEVENTH NIGHT

Kaleb smiled. He walked over to the bed, leaned over Seventh Night, and kissed her lips tenderly. He drew back and waited.

And waited. Concern grew on Kaleb's face. "Why isn't this working?' he asked no one in particular.

"Like I said, you don't really love her."

"But I do," Kaleb insisted. "I do." He looked so pathetic, Phillip might have felt sorry for him under different circumstances.

As things were, his only concern was for the princess. "Maybe she doesn't recognize you with the facial hair. Andomare said women are pickier."

The sorceress sniffed. "That shouldn't make a difference. I didn't mean it in a social sense. It has to do with how the potion effects body rhythms and energy flows. The potion creates a barrier around the mind and slows the body. Love is the energy needed to break through it." She glared at the younger prince. "Could be a terminology problem. Desire isn't love, Kaleb."

"Quiet!" Kaleb snapped. "I know that." He softened his voice and touched Seventh Night's forehead. "Please, my princess, please."

"Maybe Sargon lied to you and used something else," Andomare suggested.

Kaleb shook his head, but he did not seem certain.

Phillip crossed to the other side of the bed. He had thought he might carry Seventh Night, but his wounded arm protested when he put his hand under her head. Understanding, Neithan handed his extra sword to Andomare and joined him. He lifted the princess easily in his great arms.

"Maybe," Neithan said softly, "she doesn't love you."

Kaleb looked as though his brother had run him through.

Neithan carried the sleeping princess to the door, and Andomare and Phillip followed him. Neithan stopped at the door and glanced back at Kaleb, who was sitting on the bed.

"Come," he said.

Kaleb raised his eyes but did not move. Neithan stared at him questioningly.

Kaleb's eyes dropped away. "There's nothing for me in Cordance now," he said.

Neithan stood there, looking at his brother. Andomare touched his arm gently. "Come," she said.

They all turned away and left the younger Prince of Cordance alone in the empty castle.

SEVENTH NIGHT

CHAPTER XXXI

LOVE'S KISS

They met the soldiers returning from the not-so-secret tunnel and left the same way as quietly as they could. The two who had been sent to escort the rescued women met them in the forest, reporting they had left the women to a happy reunion with Leonore's people at the farm. Not knowing how deep the conspiracy had run, they avoided both farms and the city on the way back to the ship. The soldiers had been told not to speak of what they had seen until the king decided what could and could not be repeated. The commander asked what had become of Kaleb, and they told him that he had been slain. It was the simplest story for them to agree upon.

The sailors had made good use of the days since they had left. The *Pride of Cordance* was repaired and restocked by the time the prince's party arrived, so they were able to depart as soon as everyone was aboard.

The ship was strangely quiet as they set sail for Cordance. They had found their princess, but she was not really with them. They had lost one man. Another would live but was badly burned and had lost the use of his arm from the guardian's attack.

Prince Neithan dealt with his pain by drawing inside himself. He stayed in his room as much as he could. The crew assumed he was worried about the princess. Only Phillip and Andomare knew the entire truth. Andomare did her best to console him, but Phillip had his own aches to nurse.

They had hoped the princess would wake up on her own, but after the third day they lost hope of that.

Seventh Night had been laid in the queen's

chamber. Phillip relinquished his spot in the guest chamber to the sorceress. He would have been content finding a place with the sailors in Kaleb's vacant cot, but Neithan insisted his friend should put a small cot in the king's chamber near him. Phillip believed Neithan did not wish to be alone.

It was in the queen's chamber, watching over the sleeping princess, he found himself late on the third day. The afternoon sun stole through the cracks in the shuttered windows. He had found himself here for most of the waking portion of the past three days. As apprentice to the royal family's personal physician, no one questioned his vigil, though there was little he could do. Unlike Kaleb, Seventh Night had no fever, and her sleep was not restless but unnaturally calm. That frightened Phillip. Except for the slow breathing, she looked dead.

Andomare assured them that, if it were indeed the same potion, the princess was in no danger from a few days or even a few years delay in waking her, but neither she nor Phillip put it past Sargon to use something else to mimic the same symptoms, another trap to keep Kaleb from betraying him. Andomare had no sample of the poison to test like before, so there was little they could do beyond watch and wait.

Phillip had talked to Seventh Night while she lay there, telling her about everything and nothing. He did not know if she heard but wished she would answer.

"I have a theory. I've been thinking about this a lot, because Kaleb was a liar. But I don't think he was lying about doing this for you. I think he was wrong, but I don't think he was lying.

"And I don't think you were lying either. You just... I know you think I was thinking about myself when I asked you to run away. Maybe I was, but it wasn't just about me. I watched you, and you turned into someone else when you were around him. It bothered me. You were playing the part of everyone's ideal princess, and he was pretending to be everyone's ideal prince, your ideal prince. So you fell in love with these characters that each other had created.

"I don't blame you. Most people wear masks at least part of the time. Might do the same thing myself with an arranged marriage, but it wasn't the sort of love that can break through a barrier... You were in love with a barrier."

SEVENTH NIGHT

Her face looked paler to him now. She looked smaller and fragile. He kneeled beside the bed and took her little hand in his.

"Andomare thinks your father might be able to break the spell," he said. "That kind of love can be very strong as well, and I know you love your father. Just hold on 'til we get home."

He stood and leaned over her. "Don't die, okay?" He gently kissed her lips. "I love you," he whispered, "and I won't get over it." He hovered there for a moment, hoping she would stir, but she made no movement. He kneeled back down and laid his forehead on her hand. "Don't die."

Seventh Night opened her eyes slowly and looked upon a strange ceiling. She felt something on her hand and looked down to see Phillip's dirty blond mop bent over it, forehead on her knuckles. He did not move, so she wondered if he had fallen asleep as well. She rolled up slowly, careful not to disturb him, and ran her other hand gently through his hair.

He looked up at her, a tear on his cheek. "Don't cry," she said, wiping it away with her thumb. He smiled and embraced her with a frightening speed.

"You're awake!" he said laughing. "I was so worried about you."

She returned his embrace. He pulled her off the bed and spun her around. She laughed and held to him for balance. "I knew you'd come for me," she said.

"I'd never leave you in danger," he promised, still laughing with relief. "But I did have some help."

Her face suddenly turned serious. "Oh, Magician, I have to tell you about Kaleb—"

"I know," he said, finally sobering. "He betrayed us."

"Where is he?" she asked.

"He wanted to stay in the Wizards Land," he told her.

"And Sargon?"

"He's dead. He can't hurt you anymore."

Seventh Night nodded and laid her head on Phillip's chest.

"Wait a minute," Phillip said. He took her by the shoulders and pushed her back a bit so that she would look up at him. "You love me."

"What?" she said, looking ready to protest.

"Andomare said the love had to be reciprocal," he said quickly and logically. "Kaleb kissed you, and you didn't wake up. But you woke up when I kissed you. That means you don't love Kaleb, you love me."

She tried to step back, but Phillip held her fast. "I—" she started indignantly. "Kaleb proved false, and you are my true friend. That doesn't mean—" Phillip's eyes bore earnestly into hers, and her tone softened. "I never said I didn't, but I can't, Phillip, I can't."

"Why not?" he asked her.

"I could. I do, but it doesn't change anything. I still have to marry Neithan." Her eyes began to tear. "The kingdoms have to be joined, or there'll be a war. Nothing's changed except now I don't want to get married. I don't want to," she sobbed.

"Shh, shh," he soothed. "We'll figure something out. We'll figure something out." He drew her to him and pressed his lips to hers.

And for the first time, she kissed him back.

SEVENTH NIGHT

CHAPTER XXXII

THE FORGOTTEN SOLDIER

"**I**s the floor moving?" Seventh Night asked after their lips parted.

Phillip caressed her jaw. "We are on a ship."

"Oh," she said and laid her head on his chest. "That makes sense."

He rested his cheek against her hair. "I've been wanting to ask you something," he said, hugging her to him. "Do you think love is logical?"

She shrugged inside his embrace. "Yes,

ultimately."

Phillip grinned. "Why?"

This was a subject she had rolled around in her mind enough to have a ready answer. "Love motivates people to be their best selves and do things for others, which demands a code of conduct that works to the benefit of society."

"You can't imagine how I've missed you." Phillip squeezed her tightly, then loosened his grip. "We should tell the others you're awake."

Seventh Night nodded her head against his shirt and slid out of his arms. The first step she took on her own was stiff and unsteady, so Phillip wrapped an arm around to steady her.

She placed one hand on the door and a finger over Phillip's mouth. "Don't tell anyone you kissed me."

Phillip's frown asked why, but she opened the door before he could voice it. They walked out into the narrow hallway, up the short steps, and met Neithan and Andomare coming the other way on the main deck.

"You're awake," the sorceress said, blinking back her surprise. "How—?" Her eyes slid over to Phillip.

SEVENTH NIGHT

"She just woke up," Phillip said, not quite meeting anyone's eyes, but Neithan was staring fixedly at Seventh Night. He seemed twice as tall as she remembered. "Sargon must have lied about what he used."

Neithan nodded and visibly relaxed. "Are you all right, princess?" he asked politely. He looked too much like Kaleb, but she could hardly blame him for that.

"I'm a little stiff and disoriented, but I should be fine," she replied. Neithan smiled with relief.

The sorceress smiled more broadly and embraced her. Seventh Night felt like a dwarf in a land of giants. "I'm so glad you're all right!" the redheaded woman exclaimed. "We were all very worried about you."

"I'll tell the captain," Neithan said, and he walked away, making quick strides with his long legs.

"Let's see if we can walk off some of that stiffness," the sorceress said, taking Phillip's place at her side. Phillip allowed himself to be pushed aside.

The crew that were nearby took their hats off and bowed their heads as the women began a slow walk across the main deck. The crewmen looked genuinely delighted to see her up and about, so she did her best to manage a smile for them.

She needed a bath and fresh clothes. Sargon's dress did not fit her well.

The sorceress caught her adjusting a sleeve. "Queen Loriga packed some dresses for you—" she began, but they were interrupted by a short man with white whiskers.

"Captain," the sorceress greeted him.

Captain Onnell made a deep if hasty bow to Seventh Night but spoke to the sorceress. "Lady Andomare, the lad told me how you tended his arm. I thought, maybe now the princess was better, you could take a look at that soldier who was burned in the attack."

The sorceress grimaced. "Oh dear, I forgot about him. I'll go now. Could you take the princess—?"

"Was he burned during my rescue?" Seventh Night interrupted.

They hesitated. "During the passing."

"I want to see him."

"Princess, it's not really a sight for—"

"I want to see him," she repeated firmly.

420

No one argued with her further. The sorceress led her through one side of a set of double doors and down a tight, narrow staircase.

"What did he call you?" Seventh Night asked her as they descended. She had the rails to grip now, so the sorceress walked before her.

"Andomare," the sorceress said. "I finally found a name that fits. Neithan's been insisting they call me *lady*, since we found out my father's a nobleman, but I'm not one for titles."

"Was anyone else hurt?"

"Minor wounds," Andomare said dismissively. "Phillip's healing nicely." She turned; the difference in the stair height brought their faces closer together. In the same quiet voice from before, she added, "We told them that Kaleb died, but he's fine. He just chose to stay behind."

"Phillip told me."

"I think you broke his heart," the sorceress said softly.

"What heart?"

The sorceress regarded her curiously. "Kaleb claims to have done what he did for love," she whispered. "To give you a greater kingdom and marry you openly. Neithan said it's your decision. If you'd rather marry Kaleb, he'll turn the ship around and take you back to him."

"He had me kidnapped on our wedding day," Seventh Night said indignantly.

Andomare patted her hand. "Just think about it."

The sick berth was only one flight down and not far from the stairs. It was a simple room with three cots, two stacked as a bunk, and a work station for the surgeon. There were three men inside already: one lying, one sitting, one standing.

The surgeon was a tall, dark-haired man with a thin frame and stooped shoulders. He might have been close to the sorceress's height if he straightened out, but even crooked he was still much taller than Seventh Night. He crossed to the women as soon as they entered. "I've done my best for him, but I think there's an infection setting into the leg. If we can't stop it, I'll have to cut it off."

The sorceress sighed. "I wish I'd brought more of my books now, but I'll see what I can do."

"I don't suppose this is the sort of thing that can be cured with a kiss," Seventh Night murmured.

"No, I wouldn't recommend that for burns," Andomare said with a touch of grim humor. "But I can make a salve, if you have the right herbs." The surgeon gestured to a closed door. "Why don't you have a seat and try to cheer him up. Maybe it'll make him feel better to know we were successful."

The surgeon nodded his assent and directed her to use the chair from his work station. The princess sat down and forced herself to look at the man lying on the bed. His eyes were closed, attempting sleep with a pained expression. The soldier's face was mostly intact, and she would guess him no older than twenty-five. His chest, however, was an ugly field of black and red. She realized some of the red was little bits of fabric from the red undershirt which was part of a soldier's uniform. This made her feel a little sick, but she swallowed back her unease.

"What's his name?" she asked.

"Tin, ma'am," said the soldier sitting on the bed opposite. He twitched his rusty red mustache and sniffed. "I was just telling him about our adventures in the castle, but I'm sure he'd much rather listen to you."

SEVENTH NIGHT

"I'm very sorry, Tin," she said.

The burned soldier cracked his eyes open. They were blue, but a different shade from hers or Phillip's. He gave her a tense but genuine smile. "At your service, Princess."

"And I thank you for it. You were very brave, but I'm rescued now, so I insist you recover."

He grinned. "Soldier's lot, ma'am. I'm not afraid of death."

"Then I'll pray for you," she said, and she did, though it only made her feel a little less useless.

The sorceress and the surgeon re-emerged from the storage room. "Can you help him?" she asked.

"I'll do my best," the sorceress said. Seventh Night sat while the sorceress mixed and encouraged the visiting soldier to continue with his story. The princess tried to keep her mind on Tin, for what was her heartache next to this man's pain, but she kept wondering about Phillip's wound and thinking *Kaleb did this*.

When the sorceress finished, she gave the salve to the surgeon with instructions about applying it and took the princess back upstairs. Being a royal ship, built with a queen in mind, there was a nicely carved tub and selection of soaps in the hold, and these had been delivered to her room and filled with water for her use. The sorceress said some magic words which heated the water. Seventh Night was very tired of people going to trouble over her, but it seemed wrong to be ungrateful so she thanked everyone, barred the door and windows, and took a bath. She wanted to burn the green dress but that seemed wasteful, so she resolved to give it to Andomare instead.

She soaked and thought for a very long time.

By dinnertime, she was clean and dressed, and they were all invited to the captain's table to dine with the officers. She asked them to tell her the story of her rescue, mainly because she wanted to hear Phillip's voice and avoid talking herself. Neithan kept his features arranged in a thoughtful expression and forced a pleasant smile whenever she glanced his way.

Some small part of her had hoped Neithan might be party to his brother's plan, which would give her grounds to walk away from the arrangement, but as the story unfolded she could find no room for this theory. Worse, Phillip and Neithan seemed to have formed some level of genuine friendship, which meant letting Phillip steal her away would strike as a personal insult as well as a political one. She doubted Phillip had ever thought of it that way but suspected Neithan, so steeped in traditional ideas of honor, would.

After dinner, they walked back to their cabins and stopped, crowded together in the short hall outside their doors. "Kaleb—" Neithan began softly.

"Kaleb betrayed us," Seventh Night said firmly.

"Still," Andomare said in a cautious voice as Phillip glanced back to see if anyone was close enough to overhear them. "If you could forgive him, don't you think having a country of wizards as allies might be nice?"

The little princess crossed her arms. "Assuming Kaleb can lie enough to get the crown and keep it. You said they had no ships or harbors. An ally across the sea is no good to Tivin without ships."

SEVENTH NIGHT

"She's right," Phillip murmured.

Neithan nodded, walked into his cabin, and shut the door.

"Phillip, why don't you go check on him?" Andomare suggested. "I'd like to chat with Seventh Night for a bit. I've been trapped with men for ever so long."

Phillip was not a master of social cues, but even he caught the dismissal. He touched their arms briefly as he passed in the close corridor. Seventh Night wanted to keep him for herself, but that was part of the problem too. She did not need Phillip. She wanted him like a spoiled child, but with potential threats on both sides, Cordance and Tivin needed this treaty. Neithan understood this as well as she did.

Andomare guided her into her room and shut the door. "You should stay with me in my room tonight. I know Sargon's dead, but you've been targeted too many times. We shouldn't relax our guard now."

Seventh Night nodded. She was too tired to argue, so she simply sat on the bed and slipped her shoes off.

"I can't imagine what you're going through," Andomare said, sitting down beside her and putting a comforting arm around her shoulders. "But you're getting the better brother. Neithan's unshakably good. I wish you could have seen how he carried you out of the castle, made a very romantic image. You both need a little healing time, but he'll make a great king and father, and you'll never need to doubt his loyalty as a husband."

"How's the soldier?" Seventh Night asked, her voice breaking a little.

"I think we saved his leg," Andomare said and smoothed her hair. "I may be able to treat him better when we get back to the rest of my books." She continued to stroke the princess's raven hair reassuringly. "He'll live. The world's not always so dark as it could be."

Seventh Night let her head fall against Andomare's shoulder, trying to accept the comfort that was offered.

"The things that happen to us shape who we are; there's no sense fretting about them," Andomare said, and kissed the top of her head. "Kaleb was probably wise to stay behind, wasn't he? I'm sure a prince can get away with a little more, but if a commoner did something like that to subvert this treaty, they'd probably put him to death, wouldn't they?"

The pain that shot through the princess's heart was physical, but she kept it inside like she kept most things and only said, "Yes."

SEVENTH NIGHT

Chapter XXXIII

Wedlock

The *Pride of Cordance* became visible on the horizon long before it reached shore, and the Seaside tower watchmen sent the word along. The escort that had followed them from Pinnacle to Seaside had lingered there, and any soldiers searching nearby were summoned back to the docks. So an even larger guard awaited the royal couple at the pier and rushed them home to the castle. Seventh Night's father wept openly with relief over her return. They sent messengers to call back the search parties

Tivin had sent out over land.

The wedding was set to take place the day after they arrived. The princess was given a new room deep within the walls of the castle. Both she and the prince had a constant guard and food tasters. The king did not want to take any chances even if Sargon was dead.

The entire castle was a blur of decorations, guards, and hurried feasts, but the princess had no appetite.

On the day of the wedding, Seventh Night insisted on dressing herself and ordered all the attendants out of her chamber. She was in no mood to be fussed over. Her first dress was lost forever, and she was glad. Partly because the symbolism was wrong, and partly because the new dress the seamstresses had found was far more comfortable. It was simpler, altered from an evening gown, but she thought it was far more elegant as well.

It was little consolation. They had been unable to think of anything.

She sat twisted in her chair, so that she could

rest her arms on its back. Phillip stood just inside the closed door. He had been allowed in to say goodbye.

"You look beautiful," he said lamely.

"Thank you," she said in kind.

He stood there awkwardly, playing with his travel sack.

"You think I'm a terrible person, to marry a man I'm not in love with," she said.

"No," Phillip said. "I think you're a wonderful person. A better person than I am. I'm sorry if I have made this unpleasant for you." He took a deep breath. "At least I don't have to worry about you. Neithan's a good man, and he'll take good care of you. If you let him, I'm sure he can make you very happy. And I do want you to be happy."

"Then you should stay," she said. "Stay as my friend. Best of my friends."

"I can't," Phillip said, shaking his head. "I'm not as strong as you are. It hurts too much."

"Where will you go?" she asked.

"I always thought it might be nice to travel," he said. "Most people never make it out of their village, and I want to do something different."

"I wish that I could go with you," she said

softly.

"I wish you could too," he said.

Seventh Night sniffed and looked away. "Will you stay for the wedding?"

"No," Phillip said. "I think I should leave as soon as I can."

"Goodbye, then," Seventh Night said.

"Goodbye," Phillip repeated and left the room.

He made it to the end of the hall before a gaunt elderly man came at him waving his finger.

"You, sir," Gadolin announced, "are the worst apprentice I have ever had!"

Phillip smiled dryly. "I am sorry about that."

"Bah," Gadolin said. "If you were sorry, you wouldn't leave."

Phillip sighed.

"Anyway, take this," Gadolin said, handing him a piece of parchment.

"What is it?" he asked.

"A list of ingredients I'd like to have," Gadolin said. "I don't have time to go after them, but I thought you might come across some while you wander around aimlessly. I'll pay you for the ones you bring back."

Phillip nodded, folded the list, and tucked it into his pack.

"Well, then," Gadolin said. "I'm very busy right now. On top of my regular concerns, I need to find a new apprentice. So go away. May your travels leave you wiser." With that he hurried off.

Most of the people in the castle ignored Phillip. He stopped by to see Neithan, and they exchanged some formal well wishes. As he walked away from the prince's chambers, a strong voice assaulted him.

"There you are," Andomare declared. "I'm furious with you."

He smiled and went to meet her.

"Making me like you, then running off like this," she huffed. "It's not nice."

"So what will you be doing now?" he asked.

"Oh," the sorceress shrugged exaggeratedly. "Swapping recipes with Gadolin and making a general nuisance of myself I suppose. He's an old bat, though, and as dear as Neithan is, he's a lousy conversationalist. Still beats the snake's skin out of the desert. I will miss you, Phillip.

You're a good friend."

"So are you," Phillip said. "I'm not going anywhere in particular. But if you would like to come along, I'd enjoy your company."

Andomare smiled brightly and leaned to give Phillip a tight hug. "Thank you," she whispered into his ear.

⚔

Seventh Night came to a decision. She burst out of her door, gathered her dress, and headed down the hall.

"Your Highness?" the surprised guard asked as he hurried to keep up with her.

"I'm going to see Prince Neithan," she said.

"Isn't that bad luck?" the guard said.

"Only if you're slave to your superstitions," Seventh Night said.

"I'm not," the guard pouted. "It's just...It just isn't done."

"Nonsense," Seventh Night said. "I'm doing it, aren't I?"

The guard did not know what to say to that, so he walked beside her silently.

They arrived at the door to the chamber where

SEVENTH NIGHT

Neithan was readying himself. It was not his normal room, but one deep inside the castle like Seventh Night's. Seventh Night stopped and stood impatiently until the guard remembered his duties.

"The Princess Seventh Night to see His Highness Prince Neithan," the guard announced.

The guards in front of Neithan's door looked surprised but dutifully knocked and announced her to the prince.

"Come in, please," Neithan said.

"I need to talk to you," they both said at once.

Seventh Night entered the anteroom of the prince's chamber. They both stared at the guards until the men understood they were not invited, and Neithan shut the door.

As it clicked solidly shut, they looked at each other.

"I don't want to marry you," Seventh Night said and realized Neithan's voice had again overlapped hers. "Okay, then, now that that's settled. What do we about it?"

"I don't know," Neithan said.

"I have an idea," Andomare said as she came from the other room. She looked shy. Which was so rare, Seventh Night was extremely curious.

Andomare stepped forward. As she did, she became smaller. Her skin lightened, her hair became black, and when she opened her eyes they were blue. Seventh Night stared openly, transfixed by the sight of herself.

"You would take my place?" she breathed.

"If it is all right with you," Andomare said in a fair imitation of the princess's voice.

Seventh Night nodded, overwhelmed by the sorceress's generosity.

Andomare glanced nervously at the door and changed back into her own form.

Neithan was staring at them in equal amazement.

"It's not that I don't like you, Neithan," Seventh Night said. "But—"

"It hurts to look at you," the prince supplied.

"Yes," Seventh Night said. "So you don't mind?" she asked, looking at both of them.

"Not at all," they assured her with such vigor that she realized she had missed something rather significant.

"How long do we have?" Andomare asked Neithan.

SEVENTH NIGHT

"The wedding is at sunset," Neithan said. "They'll want us before it touches the horizon."

Andomare grabbed Seventh Night's hand. "Come on," she said. "It's already low. You only have a little time to change clothes and teach me how to be you."

Phillip checked Thunder's saddle again to make sure it was not too tight. He had over tightened it before and learned quickly not to let it happen again. Trumpets erupted from the palace announcing the beginning of the wedding ceremony. The unicorn tapped Phillip's back with his wing.

"Yeah," Phillip said, giving him a pat. "I know."

He sighed and went to get his pack from its hanging place. Thunder snorted, tossed his mane, and stomped his hoof. Phillip looked at him curiously. The attacker jumped Phillip from behind and threw their arms around his neck. He pushed back at his assailant and pulled at their arms before they could choke him. His efforts paid off, and they let go. He whirled about and put his hand on the hilt of his sword. The attacker fell back a few steps, the motion knocking their hood back.

"Seven?" Phillip said.

"Were you trying to leave without me?" she said, sounding wounded.

"No," Phillip said, smiling. "Never."

He put her hood back up, and they both mounted Thunder.

The king had given Phillip a letter for the guards to let him out of the castle gate. Seventh Night hid her face against his back.

The guard looked at them curiously over his rusty red mustache, his eyes lingering for a moment on the unadorned hands clenched around Phillip's waist, but he shrugged it off and opened the gate for them. Thunder started the long trot down the mountain, and they rode into the setting sun.